NEVER ENOUGH FLAMINGOS

JANELLE DILLER

WORLDTREK PUBLISHING

Published by WorldTrek Publishing
Copyright © 2016 by Janelle Diller
Printed in the USA

This is a work of fiction. Names, characters, places, and incidents either are the product of the author's imagination or are used fictitiously. Any resemblance to actual events, locales, organizations, or persons, living or dead, is entirely coincidental and beyond the intent of either the author or the publisher.

ISBN: 978-1-936376-21-6
Cataloging-in-Publication Data available from the Library of Congress.

To Steve, my favorite flamingo.

Also By Janelle Diller

Adult Fiction:

The Virus

Children's Fiction:

For the Love of Gold

Pack-n-Go Girls Adventures:

Mystery of the Ballerina Ghost (Austria 1)
Mystery of the Secret Room (Austria 2)
Mystery at the Christmas Market (Austria 3)
Mystery of the Thief in the Night (Mexico 1)
Mystery of the Disappearing Dolphin (Mexico 2)

INTRODUCTION

ON THE SURFACE, THIS IS a story about Mennonites, that quirky, mostly misunderstood religion that many people—if they know anything about us—associate first with odd clothes and no guns.

Underneath, of course, it's about a whole lot more, but you'll see that in time.

If you already think you know everything about Mennonites (i.e., your last name is Miller or Hershberger or Schrag or you live in one of the Mennonite wombs scattered across the Midwest, Pennsylvania, or Virginia), you can skip this part. Otherwise, read on. The next few pages will be helpful.

Most people have funny ideas about Mennonites. They think all the women dress in that peculiar capedress style and wear those funny looking gauzy caps with strings. The men have beards and wear suspenders instead of belts. We all drive horses and buggies instead of cars, and we live without electricity and install telephones at the end of our farm lanes so that not only are we not corrupted by technology, we're very clever in how to follow the letter of our church law even if we're a bit crafty following the spirit of it.

Actually, those aren't Mennonites. Those are the Amish. In a manner of speaking, Mennonites and Amish are kissing cousins, but even that's a risky description since Amish tend not to kiss anyone but other Amish.

The Amish splintered off from the Mennonites in the late seventeenth century and proceeded to freeze in time. Mennonites, on the other hand, continued to change, although we, too, have had our moments when we've gotten stuck in time or fixed on an idea that had less to do with logical theology and more about just plain resisting anything new.

Mennonites were one of the early Anabaptists, a radical strand of the Protestant Reformation in the early fifteen hundreds. Martin Luther, who ignited the insurrection, would have been a hero to us, except he stopped short of a true theological *coup d'état*. He sold out, so he's more of a fallen hero. Of course, he lived a long and full life, even getting a religion named after him, so maybe he knew what he was doing all along. Mennonites, on the other hand, spent a lot of decades living secret religious lives, meeting in caves and out in the forest. Sometimes we didn't even sing hymns but just silently mouthed the words. Back then, we had a lot of motivation for keeping our religious lives shrouded. If we couldn't keep a good secret, we ended up without a tongue or without eyes or burned at the stake, courtesy of the ever-vigilant Catholic Church, who felt a little touchy about adults actually reading the Bible and making their own decisions regarding the destiny of their very own souls. Now *that* was a church that resisted new ideas.

But that's someone else's story.

You can imagine, though, how that sort of history gives birth to some, well, some theological oddities.

For the most part, Mennonites lived in Central Europe—the Netherlands, Belgium, France, Germany, Switzerland, and Prussia. Somewhere around the mid to late 1700s, Catherine the Great invited the German, Dutch, and Prussian Mennonites to come live in Russia. (Those Prussians were the folks who ended up not being from any country at all since Germany and Russia eventually muscled in on that part of the world and licked the entire country off the map without so much as a please and thank you.) Catherine the Great recognized the Mennonites as thrifty, industrious farmers, and she wanted them to do thrify, industrious things in her country.

It was a period in history when lots of people had the any-place-has-to-be-better-than-where-we're-living-now bug. So while some of our brethren moved west across the ocean to the new country of America and the fertile lands of Virginia, Pennsylvania, Ohio, and Indiana, a huge group of Mennonites who didn't know any better left the Netherlands, Germany, and Prussia and moved east. They settled in the Ukraine on the flat Russian Steppes where the soil deserved someone as gifted at farming as the Mennonites. For over a hundred years we lived there before some elder must have slapped his head one morning and said, "Ach! What are we doing *here*? We could be living in America!" And we migrated *en masse* to the United States. Literally. Entire villages packed up and lifted their roots and shipped off to places like Kansas and North Dakota and other places that made wiser people scratch their heads. Think about it. If you had a choice of living anywhere on the entire continent, would you choose North Dakota?

Of course, the decision didn't happen quite like that, but it does make you wonder why people would just pick up and leave a place where they'd lived for a century, doesn't it? We left because local politics had shifted against the Mennonites for a variety of reasons. For starters, Catherine the Great eventually died—as monarchs often do—and left a string of heirs who didn't have the same vision for making the land productive. They also began to renege on Catherine's promise that the Mennonite boys didn't have to be conscripted into the army. Mennonites have a couple peculiar theological twists that are a natural outcome of all that persecution and secrecy. The most distinctive is that we're pacifists. Since life has value, we're not to take someone else's life. We've really sunk our teeth into this concept over the years—some people would say at the expense of logic and reality, but in the late 1800s, when faced with a choice of stay and join the military or move, we moved.

The other reason the Mennonites left Russia was because, quite frankly, our neighbors had started to get a little irritated with us. True, we were excellent farmers. The land had never produced so much, nor had the Russian villages ever been so prosperous. Unfortunately, though, kind tends to kind. We certainly weren't the first group to think of this tenet, but during this period, we would have liked to have added it as an eleventh commandment. We bought from each other and sold to each other. We married only each other and hardly even learned how to cook the local food, borscht and verenika being about the only exception. Probably the greatest insult, though, was that we lived in the heart of Mother Russia for over one hundred years—more than four generations—and never trifled with learning the language, continuing to speak German instead. Of course, this saved us many heartaches. If Mennonite daughters couldn't talk the native language, they wouldn't go off and marry a foreign boy. This assumes, of course, that a boy can still be a foreigner when you've lived next door to his family for a hundred years. And you moved in a couple of centuries after they did. We could talk enough Russian for good commerce and to direct the hired help. But we didn't need to learn enough to discuss ideas. The Russians didn't have any ideas to speak of, and we Mennonites weren't about to give away any of ours.

When we Russian Mennonites first moved to the US in the 1870s, we saw ourselves as temporary residents here, too. We were planning to stay only a hundred years—two hundred at the outside. And what had worked for us the previous hundred years seemed to be quite workable for the next. In fact, when I was born in 1925, my family had been in America for forty to forty-five years and my parents still preferred to talk only German at home. It wasn't until my brother started to school in '28 that they made the painful switch to talking English. So somewhere amongst the folds of my brain, I have at least three years' worth of earthy umlauts and great, guttural syllables. To this day, German is like a comfort food to me, even though I don't understand it or speak it.

Everything I know about Russia comes from listening to my dad's parents, who had been old enough to miss it when they left. Gramma kept two old photographs on her dresser that spun lots of stories and made her sad. One of the photos was from when she was six or seven; the other was taken the summer before they abruptly left the Ukraine. The first photo was full of girls in white dresses with poofy white bows in their hair and stern-looking young men in stiff white collars, artfully arranged against the broad porch's massive white columns. Off to one side, Gramma's father sits in a satin-black surrey with two satin-black horses. Behind him in the distance is a castle-sized barn and a dozen working men, not working but standing stone-still as though they *could* be working if Gramma's father snapped his fingers. Gramma's mother is a rotund, bosomy woman who, even in a black-and-white photo, has rosy cheeks. She's planted on a white wicker settee in front of the porch with two more babies on her lap and my gramma leaning into her side, her skinny arm resting princess-like on her mother's chair. Even when Gramma got so senile she couldn't remember my name, she could still list off the various young people in the picture: siblings, cousins, a neighbor, a young aunt and her beau. Talk about what stays in the folds of a person's brain. What she didn't say but I could see for myself was that this photo wasn't meant to capture a moment in time. It was, pure and simple, a display of grand wealth. Maybe it was the financial statement Gramma's father took to the moneylenders.

The second photo was of Gramma and Granddad in their wedding clothes. Gramma has a comfortable, tiny smile, as though she knows she's destined to have her own porch full of pretty girls in white dresses and boys in stiff white collars and a satin-black surrey and two satin-black horses. Granddad looks like a thinner version of my dad, only more smug. He's thinking about the satin-black horses, too. Only things didn't turn out that way.

Actually, if I'd thought about it very much, those pictures would have made me even sadder than they made Gramma. The trend in the family's fortunes didn't bode well for me.

Heaven help my children.

— *Cat Peters*

How you get to where you don't know you're going
determines where you end up.

CHAPTER 1

I COME FROM A LONG line of storytellers, which isn't my fault.

The burden of this is that I can never just tell you something. I have to give you the context that frequently begins with *I was born in a small town in Kansas just before the Depression.* You'd be surprised how often that bit of information is important.

When we were children, you could have asked me and my brother, Ben, what we had for supper, and he, who somehow escaped the family curse, would have told you, "Potatoes and ham gravy."

Four words.

Of course, it lacks detail, substance, and nuance, even if it does actually answer your question.

I, on the other hand, would have felt driven to tell you about the drought, the price of pork, the relatives who gave up and moved to California, and the surprising ways you can stretch nothing into not much but enough to get full on. I'd eventually remember to circle around and tell you about the potatoes and ham gravy, but that'd be after I also told you about the piano lessons I always wanted but never got and the fact that my brother was a terrible speller and for his entire life spelled *women* "wemon." Ben used to say, *When you ask Cat [that's me] something, you better have your knitting along.*

I've speculated about why Ben doesn't talk much. Back in the '20s, we used to have bands of gypsies that would jangle along the back roads between here and nowhere worth going. I think they stole Ben from some dull Lutheran family up north in Pawnee County, and when they realized he was never going to be able to distract people with witty conversation, they dropped him off on our doorstep, thinking we Mennonites would never even notice he was boring. I showed up after he did, so although my mother always denied my version of things, I'm not convinced.

Of course, I'm only telling you this so you'll forgive me if I tell you more than Ben would offer about that awful day in the early '30s when the Sweethome bank closed, which was really the start of things. In fact, if you want Ben's version of those years, here it is: "The Depression nearly destroyed us. The war was worse."

My version? Well, I think you need to know a little more.

I was only six or seven at the time, but because it was such a rare treat to go into town, I might have remembered the day even if the Sweethome bank hadn't shut its doors.

We drove into town that day in our rackety old Ford truck, just Dad and me. The seats were so low I couldn't see out the window very well if I sat like a lady should, so I kneeled on a pillow and draped my arms over the bench back and watched the world dizzily speed by just ahead of our billowing dust. The wind whipped my braids around so much that Dad called me Piggly Wiggly.

We stopped at the bank first.

"Set your fanny there, Kittycat, while I take care of some business." He pointed to a stiff leather chair. "And don't go gettin' curious."

Cats and curiosity. He'd made that point before.

The chair gave me a good angle on some old maid who worked at the bank. If she wasn't an old maid, she must've been a widow lady with ten hungry mouths to feed since old maids and widows were the only kind of working ladies in the world. She kept a tidy desk. Two sharpened pencils sat ready to attack a stack of papers, but while I sat there, they didn't move. Her mouth did, though. She seemed right glad to talk to anything that had two legs, me included. But I didn't talk back because all my life I'd been told to mind my *p*'s and *q*'s and this seemed like a good place to practice. Besides, if I moved my mouth, I'd most likely end up moving my fanny, too, and I knew that would come to no good.

I felt right at home there, though, because the old maid had an itty-bitty framed picture that said *Jesus Saves* on it, just like the one at church where we children had our Sunday school openings every Sunday. We used to also have a picture that said *Jesus Lives* until one of the bigger boys—probably one of the toothy Fred Miller boys—wrote, "in Enid Oklahoma and he ain't none too happy about it" underneath the picture. The very next Sunday we had ourselves a new picture, this one with Jesus on the cross and with a glass cover. It didn't have any words on it. I guess they didn't want to spark anyone's imagination.

All in all, *Jesus Saves* made more sense since we kept putting our pennies and nickels in the offering basket for him. I didn't know what Jesus was saving up for, but Sunday after Sunday collecting all those pennies, I figured it was going to be something big. Yessir. Most of all, though, I hoped it was gonna be sweet and he'd share it with me. Store bought candy's what I had in mind.

Anyway, I wasn't all that surprised to find out Jesus was saving at the bank, too.

When Dad finally came out of the office, he was laughing and shaking hands with a short, bald-headed man. I know he was in high spirits because I hadn't seen him happy very often, and I thought it was odd a place like a bank would make him smile so much. I decided right then and there that when I grew up I'd never marry a farmer since they never laughed. I'd marry me a bankerman instead. That is, if a bankerman was in the "do" column of that long invisible list of dos and don'ts that Mennonites kept somewhere.

From the bank, we stopped at the feed mill, and Dad let me pick out the feedsack that the chicken feed that we were buying came in. I picked a pretty one with teeny tiny pink flowers. I always picked one with flowers because then maybe Mama would smile a little and sew the feedsack into a dress for me. In the '30s, some folks got to shop at J.C. Penney's, but not us.

We also stopped at the grocer and bought a loaf of bread. I know we must have bought some other things, too, but store-bought bread was as rare as a smiling farmer, so that sticks in my mind. Dad's last stop was at Brewster's drugstore, where he bought me a chocolate ice cream cone with two scoops of ice cream. He must've thought he'd get to finish one of the scoops, but I fooled him. I didn't aim to share anything that special with anyone. Dad had a whopping big piece of lemon meringue pie and then grumbled it wasn't nearly as sweet or tart or flaky as Mama's even though he ate every last crumb of it and looked like he would've liked to lick the plate, too.

After the ice cream and pie we headed back to the truck to go home. Just as Dad was cranking the engine, Elroy Perky came running down the sidewalk, his arms flailing. With his beak of a nose and long, skinny neck, Elroy was a twin to a goose. Today, he kind of tilted forward, too, which only added to the goose look. Running like he was with his arms flapping, he could have taken flight. He seemed to be calling out to the entire street and not to anyone in particular. "They closed the bank down! They just shut 'er down!"

Dad stopped cranking and got a funny look on his face. "What'd you say, Elroy?"

Elroy stopped a moment and wheezed in some more breath. He swiped his nose with his shirtsleeve and spit on the sidewalk. "They just closed the bank down. I stopped there to get some money out, and they locked the door in my face. Wouldn't even crack it open to talk to me. Talked through the glass."

Dad pulled out his pocket watch and studied it a minute. "They'll be opening it on Monday though, right? Usual time, right?"

Elroy's face crinkled up painfully tight. "That's what I'm tryin' to tell you. They just shut 'er down. For good. You got money in there, it ain't yours no more."

Dad's face slowly took on the same painful, crinkled look that Elroy's had. He dropped the crank and leaned through the window for his zippered canvas bank pouch. He opened it up and flipped through his papers once, twice, and then another time. His lip started twitching, so I knew I should be scared.

"Did we have money in the bank, Daddy?"

"No" was all he said. His voice sounded thick and hoarse.

I knew that voice. My tummy turned upside down. I didn't know what was wrong since we didn't have any money in the bank. All I knew was that whatever was worse than having money in the bank and then not having it anymore, we had it.

Dad pounded on the bank door's heavy glass, with each hit jangling the welcome bell that wasn't welcoming anyone. He pounded for a long time, and even though we could see people inside, no one would come to the door. The short, bald-headed man was in there, too, but he didn't look like he was smiling or laughing anymore. In fact, even through the window, it looked like he had the same painful, crinkled look on his face that Elroy had given Dad.

Now Dad started yelling while he pounded. "Bernard! Bernard, open the door." Bernard must have been the short, bald-headed man because he scurried into a back room. "Bernard!" Dad yelled again. "You didn't sign the papers. All I need is your signature. I already paid off the loan." He pounded some more but looked like it wouldn't make any difference. "Open the door and talk to me, Bernard!" he shouted.

By now, a few other cars came flying up to the bank. Dust swirled around us. A scattering of people came on foot.

Tight, edgy voices called out.

"Open up! Just give us our money!"

"We got a right to our own money!"

"What are we going to do without our money?"

Dad finally stopped beating on the door and wove his way through the gathering group back to the truck. Someone picked up a rock and heaved it at the door, barely missing the glass. The voices grew louder, meaner. A few more cars pulled up. Men hopped out, mad. Another rock flew. This one jangled the welcome bell and rattled the glass.

Dad cranked the engine a couple of turns and putt, putt, putted away. As we headed down Main Street, the sheriff flew past us, blowing his siren to tell people to get off the street. Since no one was on the street except for us, it was a pretty silly thing to do, but we might not have known how serious the sheriff was otherwise. My heart thumped in my ears, and I turned around in my seat to watch his dust cloud.

"Is he going to get his money out of the bank?"

"He's going to help the robbers." Dad's voice was raspy and tight.

I still didn't know what the sheriff was going to do. "Does that mean he's going to help the people inside the bank or outside the bank?"

But Dad didn't respond. He used words like he spent dollars—few and far between. He said little, but his body shouted. Even at my age I could read that language as well as I could read the words on a sign. Dad's muscles tensed, his mouth twitched, and he grew deaf. I figured the end of the world was near.

I held my breath so I wouldn't cry.

We didn't head home. Instead, Dad drove out past the grain elevator and miles out into the countryside where there were no trees, only endless fields where the wheat should've been a velvety green carpet but wasn't. I'd been this way before, but I didn't know where the road took us. It turned out the road took us to Simon Yoder's farm. When I grew up, I eventually realized that all roads would take you to Simon Yoder's if you followed them long enough.

I knew Simon from church. He was a big man with a handsome chin that had a line down the middle. Mama called it a cliff chin, but I couldn't ever see the cliff. I liked his face, though, and his happy, wide smile. When he let loose a laugh, you could see he had a shiny tooth outlined in gold. He was shiny on the outside, too. Simon wore suits he bought in Dodge City at Hartley Brothers Department store and had them tailored to fit. He had more than one suit, unlike every other man I knew, who got married and buried in their suits and wore them to church every Sunday morning and every Sunday evening in between. Sometimes to Wednesday prayer meetings, too. Maybe when it hadn't been the Depression they'd had more than one suit, but I'd only known life since the Depression, so I wouldn't have known those things then.

I didn't know why we'd gone here instead of home, but it was a good enough surprise. Ethel, Simon Yoder's wife, had been my Sunday school teacher once upon a time. Ethel was a soft, pillowy woman with pumpkin breasts that swayed reverently and frizzy hair sticks that wouldn't stay in a bun. She seemed like tapioca pudding to me: lots of lumps but no sparkle. She was all right with me, though, because when she taught Sunday school she purchased good behavior with sugar cookies. You could buy a lot with a good sugar cookie back then.

"Wait in the truck, Kittycat," Dad said, but I climbed out anyway, knowing that if he really cared, he would have used Catherine, my other name.

I s'pose I expected to walk into a cheery kitchen with racks and racks of steamy sugar cookies cooling and a smiling Ethel playing with flannel board Bible story cutouts. Instead, chaos reigned in the room. Dishes and unfinished plates of food cluttered the tabletop and sink drainboard. Ethel, looking ever so much like a fat bird on stick ankles, stood at the stove, soberly cooking up more chaos.

Helen, one of the Yoder girls, leaned against the sink, arms crossed, and lazily chatted with her mother.

My mama would have fallen through the floor if anyone had seen her kitchen look like that. So I knew that Helen was some kind of a no-good girl, even if she was a Mennonite.

Dad cleared off a kitchen chair and left me, wide-eyed and silent, at the table while he disappeared. Ethel put a couple of stale cookies in front of me and pinched her lips together to make a smile. Her eyes didn't get those sweet lines, though, so I don't think you could call it a real smile. I wondered for a little while whether it was better not to smile at all or pretend to smile but not mean it.

Helen's eyesight must have been bad because she didn't even nod her head my way but kept on chattering about her hair that she wanted to name "Bob." I didn't know girls named their hair. What I did know was that Mennonite girls didn't cut their hair. Eventually, they wrapped it up under gauzy white prayer coverings like their mothers and then had lots of babies. On Sundays, Helen's hair was always hidden under her covering, so I figured it was long like God wanted it to be and she was just a short time away from baby-making. But here she stood, talking about Bob and her hair, which was actually quite short, hardly to her shoulders. It was the first time I realized you could lie with your hair. Here everyone thought she was a virtuous girl and she wasn't.

I nibbled quietly, not understanding what I was doing at that moment in such a filthy spot on earth and being confused about why my old Sunday School teacher lived with dirty dishes stacked everywhere and feeling maybe a little sick. Three sugar cookies and no milk later, Dad returned with Simon Yoder. Simon's only son, Harold, slouched in behind them. Simon flashed a golden-edged smile at me and winked like we were long-lost secret buddies. I should have felt warm inside.

"Mama," Simon said to Ethel, "Ezra and I are going into town to have a little conversation with Bernard Hibble." He tilted his head toward Harold. "You drive little blondie home and explain to Rose why Ezra's going to be late."

Harold glanced in my direction but didn't move a muscle except to smile slyly. I knew this boy from church, but until this moment, I hadn't realized I didn't like him. I wanted to go home with my dad, not with this oily looking boy who wouldn't even stand up straight.

Helen must have stopped thinking about naming her hair because she perked up and noticed me finally. "I'll drive her." She said it fast.

I should have been relieved, but I wasn't.

"No!" I sounded more panicked than I meant to, but girls didn't know how to drive. I knew this was true because my gramma was a girl and I'd ridden with her lots of times and I knew for a fact she didn't know how to drive. I'd been in my share of ditches with that lady.

"It's okay," Dad said tiredly. "She can ride along with us. Rose will just have to sit with her worry. Won't be the first time."

So Simon, Dad, and I all climbed into the truck and headed back into town. I sat in the middle but scooched close to Dad. Simon talked while Dad drove. He said reassuring words. "Bernard will listen to me, Ezra. He owes his job to me, as well as a good share of the bank's business. I'll make him sign, or I'll see that the board votes him out." But Dad's mouth twitched anyway. Maybe he was already thinking about future debts.

Dusk fell around us, draping the fields and road in roses and ambers. The motor rumbled under my feet, steadily lulling me to sleep. I woke when Dad killed the engine. We hadn't stopped at the bank but in front of a broad brick house set back from the street. A low wrought-iron fence outlined the front of the yard and red brick front walk, nothing practical that would keep a cow in or out. A car sat on a brick driveway. It was so shiny we could see ourselves in it as we paraded past. The three of us looked like squat bugs, even tall, skin-and-bones Dad.

"Got your papers, Ezra?"

Dad nodded.

"Just let me do the talking."

A mouse of a woman with a halo of coppery brown hair opened the door. Her tummy was big and round, like she had a huge sack of feed under her dress. She rested her hands on the top of it while she talked. That seemed like a handy thing to be able to do. "Bernard's not here. He hasn't come home from the bank yet. I'll tell him you stopped by, though, Simon." She nodded at Dad and glanced at me without lowering the tip of her nose.

"Well, Alice, we'll just wait in the parlor for him then," Simon said as he opened the screen door. "I'm sure under the circumstances, he'll understand." He showed this Alice his gold tooth so it looked like he was smiling.

The mouse woman opened her mouth but only squeaked a protest before the three of us were standing in the entryway. I thought she might stamp her foot and huff at us since that's what I'd likely do if I had that look on my face, but she didn't. Instead, she shifted into the role of a fidgety hostess and ushered us into the parlor. She disappeared while we sat stiffly on a puffy davenport that was never intended to make a body feel welcome. Everything in the room that could be covered in fabric was, and none of it was the kind that had once been a feedsack. Flowers flowed everywhere: roses and peonies and dahlias twined down the heavy drapes, streamed over the furniture, and spilled onto the carpet. More than enough flowers to make me dizzy.

We waited, weed-like, in the room for a 'coon's age. The fidgety mouse woman Alice came in several times to tell us Bernard hadn't returned yet. We knew this already. She didn't offer us anything to eat or drink, so I knew she wanted us to give up and leave.

Once, the front screen door slammed. The three of us twisted our necks to see if this might be the bankerman, but it was only a long, lean boy with round brown eyes who took the steps three at a time.

Dad kept taking out his pocket watch to check the time, even though the grandfather clock ticked loudly enough to keep track of every single second that passed. Nobody talked. Simon tried to a couple of times, but Dad—who never was any good at small talk even in the '40s when wheat prices improved—certainly wasn't inclined to small talk in the flowery sitting room of the man who was cheating him out of his farm. So mostly we just listened to the clock tick-tock.

Long after the clock had gonged the hour at least twice, the short bald-headed man finally came in the door. He took off his hat and hung it on a hall tree. He was something to stare at because the top of his head was as pasty-white as his chin and cheeks. I didn't know many men who didn't make their living in the sun.

"Simon, Ezra," he said and nodded at each of them. He gave me a quick, nervous nod, too. "What can I do for you?"

Even at my age I knew this to be a stupid question. He had done business with my dad that morning. My dad had pounded on his window at the bank and shouted to him this afternoon. And now we'd been sitting in his silly looking parlor for close to eternity with a fistful of papers.

"He wants you to sign the papers." The words just popped out of my mouth. The clock stopped its tick, tick, ticking. Dad looked at me. I waited for the floor to open up and let me crawl in, but it didn't cooperate.

Miracles never happen when you need them the most.

"That's right, Bernard," Dad said, but he looked at me first, then the bankerman. "I came because you forgot to sign the deed. I made my last payment this morning. You gave me the paperwork, but you didn't sign it."

"Well, Ezra, why don't you stop by the bank on Monday—"

"You won't be open on Monday, Bernard." Dad's voice actually sounded like Dad instead of that tight-voiced stranger I'd heard all afternoon.

Mr. Hibble cleared his throat and shuffled a small dance-step backwards.

"Well, that's true. We won't be open on Monday. Tell you what, I'll take the papers with me, and I'll get someone to notarize them next week."

"No," Dad said and planted the papers in a fabric peony patch. He took out his fountain pen and offered it to the bankerman. "Simon and your wife can witness your signature."

Mr. Hibble didn't touch the pen but took out a wilted handkerchief and mopped up little beads of sweat on his upper lip. He wouldn't look my dad or Simon in the eye. "Ezra, I just can't sign these papers here. I'm sorry about all the confusion, but you'll just have to talk to someone next week about this."

Simon sighed grandly, "Bernard—"

But Dad touched Simon's arm. "Bernard," he said softly, "does the bank own my farm or do I?"

Mr. Hibble cleared his throat and mopped his upper lip again. He also took a swipe at his brow and the top of his head. He didn't look very bankerly. And he still wouldn't look at Dad.

"I paid off the last dime I owed on my farm, but you didn't sign the papers. I'm askin' you again. Do I own my farm or does the bank?"

Mr. Hibble's face wrinkled for a moment. Then he stuttered, "Well, you'll need the . . . uh, bank to sign off before . . . um, before the farm is really uh . . . really yours." He still didn't take the pen.

There Dad stood, roses and peonies and dahlias swirling overhead and underfoot. Finally, Dad gently poked Mr. Hibble's chest with the fountain pen. Twice. Dad, Simon, and I shuddered ever so slightly. We're Mennonites, which I don't expect you to understand, but this was his Mennonite equivalent of throwing a punch. "Then I know you'll do the right thing, Bernard. I know you to be an honorable man." This time, pacifist that he was, he didn't poke Mr. Hibble's chest again. I watched. But he still held out the pen.

The bankerman mopped his full face and head one more time. And then he mopped the back of his milk-white neck. The part of his white shirt that was showing looked like it was doing some mopping, too. He finally looked at Simon, who nodded. I think. Mr. Hibble sighed the kind of sigh I'd been hearing from my dad all my short life, and he called to his wife. "Alice. Come here please."

No one said a word as they scritch-scratched with a pen on the papers four times. Mrs. Hibble kept patting her tummy.

The entire afternoon and evening had pointed to these few minutes, and now we were done. Even with all the day's wrong turns, Mr. Hibble couldn't stop being a gentleman. So he ushered us out onto the front porch for some Kansas small talk before we left. For the few minutes the adults chatted about the weather and the wheat prices, the world wasn't teetering on the precipice of a cataclysm. But finally, Simon asked, "What's going to happen, Bernard?"

Mr. Hibble stood with his back to the corner street lamp, so I could only see the sad shake of his head and not what was on his face. "I don't know, Simon. I hadn't thought things could get any worse, but they just have."

And then he lit a cigarette and let feathery strands of smoke drift around us.

We sat on the street in the puttering truck a few minutes before Dad stopped shaking enough to drive. None of us said anything. Finally, I tugged at his sleeve, and he put the truck in gear. The papers signed, we drove down the dirt street into the soft charcoal evening. Behind us, back in the direction of the bankerman's house, it sounded like a car backfired once.

Pop!

 CHAPTER 2

DAD ALWAYS CARRIED THE GUILT of Mr. Hibble's death with him, even though he was no more responsible for that than for the wind. Over the years, we've made guilt out to be a bad thing. In reality it's good to carry a little guilt on your shoulders since it can also weigh down your impulses. But this didn't make Dad a better person, only a more burdened person.

"I shouldn't have made him sign the papers."

Mama looked at life more pragmatically. "You didn't ask him to do anything wrong. You'd paid your money, and he didn't sign the deed like he was supposed to."

"It wasn't worth having him take his life. I could've found enough money to make the last payment again."

Mama always sighed here. For some reason, they practiced this conversation as often as they could. "Ezra, that last payment was our wheat money and milk, cream, and egg money for the entire year. Where would you have gotten more money? They would've taken the farm from us before you could've scraped more together."

"I could have sold the cows."

"Ezra!" Mama always huffed when he said that. "And then we would have starved for sure."

"Simon Yoder could've loaned it to us."

"And Bernard Hibble would *still* have pulled that trigger. And then we'd still be obligated to Simon Yoder for something that didn't have to be."

Nothing helped lighten the weight of Mr. Hibble's death, though. If a person wants to feel bad about something, most of us are rarely short of events to choose from.

To my dad's way of thinking, back then a man's only value was providing for his family and subduing the earth. So for a farmer with a family in the ditch of the Depression, the only wealth he had was the gross number of things to feel guilty about as opposed to the net number of things he could feel good about. Consequently, in the grand scheme of things, my dad was depressingly wealthy.

It wasn't just farmers in Kansas who were burdened, either. The whole world felt helpless that decade. In Germany, folks lit their stoves with their worthless cash and banked on a strutting little rooster named Hitler to make their lives less miserable. The Irish seemed determined to forget their poverty by shooting each other. The Chinese kept nervously glancing over their shoulder at a whole nation that was just looking for places to stick a sharp Samurai sword. And the poor Russian peasant—which our group of Mennonites was thankful to no longer be—had all of it to worry about: finding food for the table, the bantam cock in Germany, *and* a knock on the door in the middle of the night. In fact, the only thing the Russians didn't have to worry about was worthless money since they didn't have any money at all.

It's a wonder anyone in the world slept at all during the '30s.

With the farm finally free and clear, Dad at least had one less worry, but just because the bank wasn't sending him notices didn't mean the rains came or the crops grew. In fact, if anything, money grew scarcer. Dad planted wheat that fall, the Turkey Red wheat that Granddad had brought from the Russian Steppes fifty years earlier. In good years, a fall soaker and a couple of light winter snows would hold the seed in the ground and germinate it. By February, the fields would look as lush green as the eye of a peacock feather. By May, the wheat would be high as a man's waist, with firm, stiff stalks and two dozen kernels on the head. The best June for wheat was hot and dry, which would ripen the grain to a sun yellow and ready it for the thresher.

In a normal year, an acre of wheat produced twenty to thirty bushels of plump wheat kernels. In 1934, the farm averaged five bushels to the acre. That was our *good* year.

Dad kept the seed to plant the next year, but in 1935, it didn't rain at all. Not a drop. The only clouds we ever saw were the pulsing gray grasshopper swarms that chewed up every green blade or the ferocious red dust clouds that gathered in the south and swept over us, insulting us for days at a time. We went to bed with wet kerchiefs over our noses and mouths and woke to damp, *o*-shaped dust cakes on the kerchiefs and an inch of fine, red silt inside the windowsills. Mamas worried about their babies suffocating in the night and even in the day. By the end of '36, we'd already gotten most of Oklahoma, but nobody in Kansas much wanted it. After all, everyone knew the only thing Oklahoma soil could grow was Indians.

Without rain, there was no wheat. Not in 1934, '35, or '36. If it hadn't been for Mama's chickens and pump-fed vegetable garden and the five or six milk cows that Dad had, we would have starved. The cows gave just enough extra milk that we could sell it and put gas in the truck. But it didn't replace tires or fix worn-out tractor parts. Mama made our dresses and Dad's and Ben's shirts out of cotton feedsacks from the mill. My shoes pinched my toes so badly that towards March, before it got warm enough to go to school barefoot, I started wearing an old pair of Ben's. I don't know what he wore since he was growing faster than a rooster. As it was, we bought nothing. And still we had no money.

Decades have passed, so we know now that '36 was the beginning of the end. By 1937, the rows of Osage orange trees the county extension office made all the farmers plant started to slow the wind from picking up the soil and carrying it to Nebraska. But in 1936, we didn't know this. For all we knew, this was the beginning of a long decade, or maybe even a century, without rain.

I remember one dusty red Sunday evening after church watching Leo Selzer rock back on his worn heels and listening to his loose talk about the drought. "Saw in *Capper's Weekly* that this here whole swath of central states been a desert before settlers started moving in and farmin' it." He chewed on a toothpick that might have been in his teeth since Sunday dinner. For all I knew, he was making paper with it. "It's the rains of the past twenty or so years that're the fluke. This drought here's the normal times. *Capper's Weekly* says we might not have rain again for years. This here part of the country could turn into the Mojave Desert." Only he pronounced it "Mo-jave."

Capper's Weekly didn't come with a pronunciation guide, so Leo used his best instincts and followed the silent *e* rule. He would have snorted in disbelief at a *j* that should sound like an *h*.

Leo always quoted *Capper's Weekly*, whether he'd read it or not. It gave him a certain amount of authority, if for no other reason than it meant he could afford the quarter subscription.

That summer I lived with a worry knot in my stomach. Even though I knew the farm was paid off, I still had this idea that some unnamed person could come and yank it away from us. Dad and Mama never talked about money, but the reality of our situation still seeped into my brain. I watched them talking about not going to town because they didn't have the fifty cents to put gas into the truck and praying thankfully for a bountiful garden and healthy cows. We were only a slippery half step away from the poorhouse, but we'd at least have a little cream money to put the gas in the tank to get there.

Jesus kept saving and so did we. We saved string, found new uses for baling wire, and recycled everything decades before someone in California invented the concept. We only ate what we could grow, and we ate every scrap of that since somewhere in China children were starving. Probably they were starving down the road in Sweethome, too, but most of the time we preferred praying for strangers rather than locals. Through it all, Dad's brow stayed perpetually furrowed. People say money can't make you happy. They're probably right, but not having any money sure can make you mean and tired. I know how much money we had because Mama kept all of it in a Mason jar in a cupboard. *All* of it. Even worse, there was plenty of room for more.

Long about the end of that summer, Dad and I walked out to the pasture one evening to round up the cows to milk. It must have been August because Mama was canning the last of the tomatoes, but we hadn't pulled the plants up yet. She'd let me take a break from the canning, which she knew I hated even more than she did. Dad and I walked but didn't talk. That was his style, not mine. He spent most of his days in solitude, staring at the back end of a horse. I suppose that sort of view gives you a perspective on life that you don't get from sitting at a desk and wearing a suit and tie. Dad, at least, had a daily reminder of humanity's niche in the universe. Anyway, all the quiet made him frugal with words.

I had a walking stick I'd found. I kept poking it into the giant cracks that crabbed anywhere the dirt showed through and knocking it against the weeds, never tiring of the poufs of dust I could shake loose. Off to the edge of the pasture, a murder of crows swam in a wide circle, dipping and rising and cawing nervously at the ground.

A couple of buzzards hunched on a low branch of the lone cottonwood.

I hated buzzards.

As I stretched to land in my dad's dusty footprints, I remember thinking that I was lucky that a thin, tall man had married such a thin, straight woman and had me and Ben. I just might be tall and straight, too, instead of round and soft like all the other mamas and grammas I knew. All four of us had been carved out of centuries of Germans that even a hundred-year sojourn in Russia hadn't changed. It gave us thick blond hair, dark eyebrows, and eyes the color of the blue noonday Kansas sky. I just hoped to the high heavens I wouldn't get the Peters nose, which was more suited to the kind of person who'd be digging potatoes all her life instead of playing a piano for important people. Of course, we didn't actually have a piano yet, but if you only dream about what you have, how can your world ever become something that it's not already? I often practiced playing my dresser so I wouldn't feel like I'd lost too many years when the day finally came and a piano arrived. I knew people would be amazed at my accomplishment.

Dad must have been deep in thought because we were almost to the slough before he realized something was wrong.

"Cat." He stopped walking and squinted at every corner of the pasture. "Where're the cows? Do you see the cows anywhere?"

"They musta broke through the fence." My stick had become a conductor's baton, like I'd seen in a picture of a symphony in one of Gramma's books. I was leading the orchestra in "Wonderful Grace of Jesus," after which I would begin the *William Tell Overture*. They both inspired a rollicking bass. I flung my head dramatically from side to side. My braids snapped through the air.

Dad shook his head. "They'd stay along the creek. Ain't nothing to draw them away from it."

He started walking again, marching faster towards the hedgerow and smudge of crows. I stopped my conducting and ran to keep up with him, but it hurt my feet because the weeds and grass were so dry and stiff. They poked like small sticks on my summer-toughened feet. The grasshoppers hated the commotion. They whirred and jumped in all directions, thudding against our legs and torsos in confusion.

Suddenly, Dad stopped. "No!" he whispered hoarsely. *"Es kann nicht sein."* It can't be. Weak with the moment, he covered his face with his hands and dropped to his haunches, sending a shower of grasshoppers on the dead cows in front of us. The cows, already beginning to puff up, lay lifeless as granite in the hot sun. Flies, mirroring the crows overhead, buzzed furiously in a black blanket around the bloated creatures, as though insisting they were going to haul this new find into safekeeping.

Ever so much like Lucifer's henchmen, two vultures picked at the flesh. They stopped long enough to glare at us and flap a menacing wing or two. Pink ribbons of meat—pretty and bright against the brown—dangled from their beaks.

Then Dad started to cry. His chest heaved with loud, anguished sobs that shook the earth.

I was terrified, and so I stood frozen onto the hot Kansas prairie, frantically searching for something comforting to say. But nothing came. Children cry all the time for no reason at all. I knew this because I'd done it myself. My brother Ben still cried from time to time, too, even though he was thirteen. I'd seen my mother cry too. Not lots, but enough not to be startled by it. But up until that moment, I'd never once seen my dad cry. He squatted there forever, just beyond the stench and the buzzards, his face in his hands. Those giant hands that I trusted.

I waited, all jittery about Dad and the buzzards so close. So I didn't move, maybe even to breathe.

When Dad finally stood again, he seemed like he'd shriveled a little somehow. He wiped his face with his shirtsleeve and took out a blue bandana to blow his nose.

But he still didn't say anything. He just stood there while the crows swirled in the sky and the two giants on the ground feasted. He couldn't wake the cows from the dead, but he couldn't leave either. He stumbled around the animals, keeping a little distance because the stink of them caught you deep in your throat where you wanted to puke. He poked at them with my stick, shooing the buzzards back to the cottonwood with their brothers. Several times, he stopped and took out his bandana and wiped his eyes. He didn't make any noise, but his shoulders shook from time to time, and his lips quivered.

I danced nervously just on the edge of the buzzing flies. Even though I was breathing through my skirt hem, the flies were so thick I was afraid they'd get confused and think my mouth was some fresh dead meat. With every breath, I took in a little puff of dust that left a fine layer of grit on my teeth. I had to watch the vultures, too. There were four of them, six dead cows, and two of us. If they could do the math, there was enough for all of us—actually more than enough since the meat was dead and putrid. It was paining me a lot because I wanted to ask Dad what we were going to do for milk and cream and butter and money to put fifty cents of gas in the tank, but he didn't look like he wanted any questions. That was the way it was most of the time, so I knew this look better than most of his other ones.

Finally, we walked back through the pasture to the house. Dad didn't look as straight or tall. He kept shaking his head like he was having a conversation with someone he didn't agree with. But as usual, he certainly wasn't talking to me.

I did my best to keep my mouth shut, even though all those questions—like how were we going to eat and did he have some money stashed somewhere to buy another cow and what in heaven's name were we going to do now—just kept swimming around in my stomach. But I didn't ask because I didn't need a swat on the be-hind for not minding my *p*'s and *q*'s. Once in a while I'd look back at the spot in the sky above the cows. Two chickenhawks had joined the circling crows, and I kept worrying they'd see me in my red-checkered feedsack dress and think I was some fresher dead meat and dive at me without warning. That would only enrage the buzzards for sure.

When we walked through the door, Mama was taking cherry red jars of tomatoes out of the blue granite canner. That was as close as we ever got to art.

"The cows are dead. They got into some locoweed. I thought I'd pulled it all but must've missed some," was all he could get out before emotion thickened his throat and he had to stop.

My mother wiped her hands on her apron and wiped the sweat off her forehead. German slipped out with a sigh. In some families, that would have been a moment for her to wrap her arms around Dad and give him some kind of comfort. Instead, she took a towel to the red jars that didn't need any wiping because in our good German household, affection seemed as frowned on as anger, although I still saw enough of the latter.

"We'll manage, Ezra. We've managed up to this point. We'll find a way." She didn't sound at all like she believed it. Even I could tell that.

"How will I provide for us?" He started crying again. His shoulders drooped with the weight of the question.

A little "Oh" escaped from my stomach. He didn't know any more than I did. That tangled knot in my stomach swelled to my throat and I started to cry, too, but I didn't cry out loud because I didn't want them to be even more unhappy than they already were, and they'd just tell me to shush myself.

Neither of them said anything for a long time, Dad's tears disabling both of them. Eventually, Dad went into their bedroom and shut the door. Mama just kept on wiping the canning jars with her back to me, and I just kept wiping tears and my dripping nose with my dusty dress hem. I kept smelling the pasture and the dead cows.

I was sure I saw the shadows of the buzzards in the trees. They'd followed us home after all.

Neither of us said anything.

About that time Ben came in from choring. The screen door squeaked before his footsteps and slammed behind him. It was an evening sound. He looked at me and started to laugh, "You paintin' your face with mud?"

"The cows got into some locoweed. They're dead," I said, and with some satisfaction because he'd just made fun of me.

Ben looked to Mama's back. She didn't turn, but her head and shoulders nodded that I was right.

"All of 'em?" Now he sounded like the rest of us felt. He knew what it meant.

Mama and I both nodded, but she still didn't turn around.

He slumped into a chair. "Holy smokes" was all he said. Mama didn't even cringe at the profanity. He leaned his face into his hands and rubbed his cheeks. "So now what are we going to do?" He asked, but I don't think he thought anyone would have an answer.

We didn't see Dad again until the next morning at breakfast. His eyes looked shrunken and red, and his jaw locked tight around his words.

"Cat, ride over to Granddad's and have him bring his team over to help bury the cows. Ride over to Henry

Schmidt's, too. See if he'll help." He paused while he mopped up some egg yolk with his zwieback. "Ben, hitch up the disc to the team. We'll break up some ground and dig a pit." He talked into his coffee cup instead of at us.

He'd said as much as he was going to say. It was an era where a parent never thought to say, "Don't worry. We'll be okay. I've figured out a way to keep us from having to live in a ditch and starve." I don't know if he even talked to Mama. If they had conversations about living or dying or selling the farm or even much beyond the lack of rain and the goings-on at church, I hardly ever heard them.

Ben helped me saddle Little Willy. With his red, tight eyes and furrowed brow, he looked just like Dad, only thirty years younger.

"What's gonna happen, Ben?" I wanted someone to tell me something. Anything. Even if it wasn't remotely possible. This would have been a moment to tell a whopper of a lie and Jesus would have forgiven it. There wasn't much for Jesus to save anymore.

Ben shrugged his shoulders in a jerky, rigid motion. "I guess I'll have to quit school and get a job." He held Little Willy while I stuck a foot in the stirrup and flung my leg over his back. "We gotta eat," he said, more matter-of-factly than his face showed, and he softly patted Little Willy's rump to get him going. Now we have this funny idea that thirteen-year olds shouldn't have to worry about helping the family put food on the table, but in the '30s, it was more common than not.

As I rode, I mulled over what I knew. I wondered if we were finally as poor as an Okie and if we'd pack up the truck and head for California. If we weren't poor enough yet, I didn't want to find out how poor we'd have to get before we'd give up and go.

I delivered my message at the Schmidt farm, spending five extra minutes in their chicken house with Suzanne while she gathered the eggs. What good is a best friend if you can't tell her the details firsthand, even if it might mean a swat on the be-hind for dallying? Then I rode on to my grandparents' farm.

Granddad was still choring when I rode into the yard. The screen door banged behind Gramma as she stepped out onto the summer porch. She wrung her wet hands on her apron as she squinted into the morning sun and shrugged away a couple of noisy black flies. Her white prayer covering flopped loosely on her back like an unneeded sunbonnet. She'd finally found a useful purpose for the decorative strings and had tied them in a bow in front.

"Can I help you get your covering on right, Gramma?" I asked her and dismounted.

She ignored the question.

"Agnes? *Bist du das?*"

None of us knew an Agnes, including Gramma, but that never stopped her from talking to her. More and more, Gramma was an attic full of treasures but no light string to pull.

"No, Gramma, it's me, Cat," I told her kindly. Most of the time she still knew me, but some days she didn't. Today, I didn't matter to her either way.

Gramma harrumphed a little and mumbled, "Well, if you see that Agnes girl, tell her to get her fanny in here and finish these dishes." Then she marched into the kitchen, probably to finish the dishes. The screen door slammed behind her, making the flies mad. You can never make summer flies happy: when they're inside, they want out; when they're outside, they want in. They're worse than a dog.

Granddad appeared in the barn door. He pushed his hat back and mopped his sweaty brow with a big bandana, the line on his forehead between sun-red and hat-shaded-white a banner for how he spent his life.

"Not a good day?"

"Not a good day." He shook his head. A sigh slipped out into the heat. "What brings you over this morning? Got an itch to help Agnes with the mending?"

"Nope. Dad needs some help burying his cows. They all got into some locoweed." It came out husky. I couldn't help the tightness in my throat.

"All of 'em?" Granddad's eyes widened and his forehead wrinkled up.

I nodded. "All of 'em."

"What's he going to do?" We all kept asking this useless question.

"I don't know." I felt like crying, but I said, "Maybe we'll all just have to go live with Agnes."

He gave a tired chuckle and tousled the top of my head. "You'll be okay, Kittycat. You got spunk."

I stayed with Gramma and finished her dishes while Granddad drove over to pick up Great-Aunt Hulda, who grannysat whenever Granddad had to be gone on bad days for a few hours. By the time I got back to our farm, Henry Schmidt was already there. By noon a half-dozen other men, mostly from church, showed up ready to dig the graves for the bloated cows. Even without telephones, word traveled.

By noon, too, we had gifts of three gallons of milk, several pounds of butter, a couple of fried chickens, a kettle of potato salad, and a gooey chocolate cake on our kitchen table. Funeral food. This was as close as you could get to a funeral time without a family member actually dying. While it was true that nobody had anything, for the moment we had even less, so they shared what they could with us.

Late afternoon, Simon and Ethel Yoder came riding up in his shiny green Oldsmobile with its deep, throaty engine and bug-eyed headlights. The cows were buried by this time and the other men had gone home, the smelly job only a sad story to tell their grandchildren in years to come.

Simon unfolded himself out of the car and shook hands with Dad. He winked at me, so a little tension melted. For him, at least. "Ezra, what can I do to help?" Everyone understood that moving some earth around to bury the dead cows wasn't the kind of help he meant. People like Simon didn't actually get dirt under their fingernails.

Simon was older than my dad, but he didn't have as many worry creases across his forehead or sun-squint lines around his eyes, and he didn't smell like homemade soap. He was one of those people whose touch, like his smile, was flecked with gold. In our corner of the state, where most land was too insolent to produce a good wheat crop, Simon had laid claim to over three thousand acres of land that was actually rich and fertile. He had an uncanny sense of when to plant corn before the price skyrocketed and when to sell his hogs before the price plummeted, and the prudence to rent his land to tenant farmers and avoid the game altogether. He'd had enough foresight to open an Oldsmobile dealership while there was still money in the county, and rumor had it he had enough faith in the country—and dollars—to invest in the stock market after the crash.

A visit from Simon could only mean one thing: hope. Well, two. It probably meant cash, too.

Actually, it meant more. It also meant obligations.

Dad and Simon stood under the rustling cottonwood while frizzy-looking Ethel, who put her skinny little ankles at greater risk with each passing year, visited with Mama in the kitchen and ate Dad's last piece of raisin cream pie. The women would find out later what the men decided. Probably. But no one expected women to have ideas of their own, even the women themselves.

Dad, who stood with his arms wrapped around his chest, and Simon, who had nothing to lose, talked till close to sunset. Several days later, Dad had two new cows, one fat with an unborn calf and one a skinny milk producer, which was the only kind of cow I'd ever seen. For payment, Ben dropped out of school for the fall to work for the Yoders.

Everyone got something more out of the arrangement than what they'd negotiated for. Dad got a start back from the edge and one more layer of guilt since he couldn't provide for the family by himself. Ben earned wages to pay off the family debt and got lots of new ideas. And Simon got repaid for the cows and gained a foothold in our lives.

So in the end, everyone lost.

CHAPTER 3

ACROSS THE OCEAN, THE BANTAM rooster continued to strut. A year earlier, Germany had shrugged a shoulder at the world and rolled into the Rhineland in defiance of the Treaty of Versailles. The world could have gathered a tiny bit of righteous indignation and told the strutting little dictator to obey the laws of common decency and go home. But no one did, probably because even though he sat on the back porch of half the countries in Europe, he hadn't yet invited himself into anyone's kitchen and eaten their dinner. Except for the Rhineland, of course. Everyone hoped if they just pretended nothing was happening then nothing actually was happening. This was a very good thing for everyone to pretend for the moment. Except, of course, for those people in the Rhineland.

Feeling cocky in his Rhineland success, the bantam rooster eyed Austria. He'd already flirted with controlling her once in 1934, but he backed down when Italy took offense and mobilized her troops. So the little rooster maneuvered his way into a treaty with the Italians, who were pretty cocky themselves now that they'd finally figured out how to run their trains on time. With an ally who was once an enemy, the rooster began preening for another cockfight once again. Austria was feeling nervous.

We Mennonites were still very German at heart, so we watched all of this out of the corner of our collective eye. A few Mennonites suffered from schizophrenia and were secretly pleased that Hitler was being a crafty steward and acquiring more land, as well as bringing order to the universe. But most of us only felt embarrassed horror at Hitler's disdain for Jews or, for that matter, for anyone who didn't carry only German blood.

"Simon says Hitler is going to take Germany to war. Simon says the US better not decide on an isolation policy, or the world will belong to Germany. Simon says it's a man's obligation to help where he can. Simon says a war would actually be good for the economy since it would put people back to work. Simon says it's scary to see what Hitler is doing. He's been maneuvering for Austria for years. Now that he's in cahoots with Mussolini, he'll get his way, Simon says."

Ben was thirteen-years old when he first started working for Simon Yoder, a perfect age to stop believing your parents and start believing anyone who casts a little different shadow. He was ripe for the plucking. Simon Yoder was good at many things, but he was especially good at plucking.

This was made all the easier because every week, Ben went home with Simon and Ethel after the Sunday evening church service. On Saturdays, Simon brought Ben back home. Simon was sowing, raising, and harvesting ideas in Ben's head faster than he could raise a crop of radishes.

Ben confided in me he was miserably homesick for the first couple of weeks, not just for Dad, Mama, and me, but also for his friends since most of them were in school. Distance made secrets safer, so he also told me that before the cows died, he'd been hoping to go out for the basketball team in high school. I didn't laugh out loud when he said it, but Mennonite boys in our town didn't play basketball—or any sports for that matter—not because it was wrong, but because they just never did it.

Of course, for Ben, that would have been part of the attraction.

We both knew playing any sport was a silly fantasy since Dad would have scoffed at anything so frivolous when he needed Ben home to do chores. But we both pretended it could have happened. And maybe it could have.

As much as Ben missed us those first weeks, I missed him more. And I kept on missing him long after he seemed to have shaken the rest of us off. Up to when Simon stole Ben away from us, we'd always been close, probably because we only had each other. This was an era of families the size of a small Kansas county. It was us against the world, and the world had at least eight more at home who looked just like them. I never knew why there were only two of us. That wasn't the sort of thing Mama and I would have ever talked about, even when I started having my own children.

Ben stood tall and lean; he would be a Peters for sure. He was big for his age and growing fast. Poor as we were, he'd never had a day without plenty of cream and butter, and instead of settling on his hips like it did for girls, all those calories found their way to his legs, which just kept getting longer and longer. He looked just like the pictures I'd seen of moose in the one *National Geographic* magazine we had at school.

Simon took a special liking to Ben. His own children were all grown and blown far away, like bad seed, including Harold, the slouching boy who had grown into a slouching man and who, except for a hopeful semester away at Bible school, didn't look like he was ever going to make his daddy proud. I guess too much money and not enough worrying can do that to a child. Ben said Simon never mentioned Harold without a little shake of his head. The girls, too.

From Saturday afternoon through Sunday supper, Simon stories filled our house.

"Simon says he's going to buy more cattle. He thinks with all the trouble in Europe, there's going to be a war and that'll drive prices right through the ceiling. Simon says he's not so sure Hitler is as bad as Chamberlain makes out. Look at what he's done to the German economy. Why, he's pulled it out of runaway inflation and started giving those people something to be proud of. Simon says he likes the way those new Oldsmobile coupes run. They've got a beast of an engine. Simon says he doesn't trust Hitler or Stalin. If we're lucky, they'll have at each other and save the rest of us the trouble."

And on and on. Each story came with Simon Yoder's authority stamped on it. "Simon says . . ."

If it bothered Dad and Mama that Simon had slipped up on the parental pedestal and elbowed them aside, they didn't fuss about it. In fact, at least in the beginning, we all took vicarious pleasure in Ben's stories. After all, Simon had predicted the rise in corn prices and the crash of hog prices. No doubt he knew more about the impending crisis in Europe, as well. It's only human nature to give a wealthy man credit for wisdom about all the world instead of just how to make money in his corner of it.

For all the acres he owned, Simon actually farmed very little of it. In the early '20s, he decided there were too many better ways to make money, so he leased his land out to tenant farmers. They paid rent for the use of the land plus a portion of the crop when it came in. In good years, everyone made money. In bad years, only Simon made money. True, he made less money, but he also didn't have any accounts to pay off at the mill or the grocery store or the bank. In the very lean years of '35 and '36 when it didn't rain, he forgave the rent portion of what his tenants owed, a generous stroke that won him even greater respect in the community and church.

Ben's job consisted of taking care of the small herd of cows, a couple of pigs, and some chickens the Yoders kept, as well as general upkeep on the fences and barn. The Yoders could have easily afforded to buy their meat, milk, and eggs in the grocery store, but that would have seemed like a frivolous waste when they could raise their own. Since thriftiness followed godliness and cleanliness in the Mennonite order in the universe, this frugality helped compensate for Ethel's trouble with that second mandate.

I asked Ben once if Ethel had ever figured out how to wash her supper dishes. Ben just rolled his eyes and said, "Thank goodness Dessie's there." Dess Schmidt was the fourth daughter in Henry Schmidt's gaggle of girls, the one just older than my friend Suzanne. The three girls older than Dess had also worked for the Yoders off and on in much the same arrangement as Dad had with Simon. Henry Schmidt was a very nice man, whose inability to farm was exceeded only by *his* father's inability to pick farmable land. Even before Kansas dried up and put the best farms on the auction block, Henry was borrowing money here and there from Simon to tide them over until the wheat came in or cattle prices rose. Henry gratefully hired his girls out to help with the mortgage. He was eternally thankful to the good Lord that Simon had married such a poor housekeeper that he was willing to throw good money away just to have clean sheets on the bed once a week.

I never heard Suzanne's sisters tell the world according to Simon Yoder, though. Apparently, Simon didn't talk much to them, and Ethel rarely said anything worth repeating.

By Thanksgiving, Ben had worked off the cows, but Simon let him keep working, the steady paycheck forever sealing his future in anything but farming.

Christmas brought a watershed decision. Ben could return home and commute daily to Sweethome to begin attending school again, or he could continue to live with the Yoders and make the much shorter three-mile commute from their place into town. Returning to live at home meant a half-hour drive, one way, with most of it on dirt roads that would turn to mud by April—if it ever rained again. The much shorter trip from the Yoder farm into town was entirely on oiled roads. Simon, ever the skillful negotiator, tipped an already weighted decision by giving Ben free room and board in exchange for Ben doing the chores and a couple dollars a week to Dad for Ben's wages for the extras he did around the farm.

It made Dad, Mama, and me sad, but none of us could come up with a good reason for him to live at home—other than the most important one: we all missed him. But common sense triumphed over the heart, as it often did in the '30s, and for all practical purposes, he was gone forever.

Ben continued to go home with the Yoders on Sunday night and return to our farm the following Saturday. So by the time any of us realized he'd gone out for basketball, he'd already suited up and played in his first high school game. I don't know which upset Dad more, that he'd once and for all lost his authority over Ben or that Ben was using his time so frivolously by joining the team. Or that Dad heard about it first from someone at church.

Pete Mueller, a squat man from the no-neck Mueller clan, spilled the beans. "That boy of yours can really grab the ball! Give him a chance to practice shooting some baskets, and he'll be someone to reckon with out on the court," Pete announced enthusiastically as we were climbing into the car after church.

Ben, who happened to be standing out of Dad's line of sight, winked at me conspiratorially. Just like Simon liked to do.

"Oh?" Dad said. He either didn't hear Pete, or the topic stood so far out of Dad's thought range that Pete might as well have said that it had snowed almost six inches on the moon last night.

"Yes, sir!" Pete gushed on. "It's nice to see a good strong Mennonite boy out there on the court. He's gonna make us all proud!"

"I see," Dad replied, clearly indicating that what he and Pete were talking about had whizzed right over his head.

My mother, who lived her life a flamingo in a sea of turkeys, understood not just what Pete was saying, but the significance of it as well. She nodded politely at Pete and said, "Ben's always thought it would be fun to play school sports. I'm glad he's finally having a chance." And she was, too, so that was the end of it for her, which surprised Simon the benefactor more than Ben or me.

Dad, who lived life more like a boulder in a pile of sand, had more to say. "When were you going to tell us, Ben?"

"When I thought I was really going to get a chance to play in a game. I never thought the coach would let me in the game so quickly." He sidestepped the entire issue since what Dad really meant was *Why didn't you ask me?*

My heart thumped. I couldn't believe *my* brother had managed to do something so exotic as play basketball.

"When can we watch you? Are you good?" I asked eagerly.

Ben only smiled. I grew a little lightheaded. I decided he must be very good.

"Ben, this seems like a waste of time. If you have so much time, you should be helping Simon more around the farm."

"Dad," Ben protested like he'd practiced the line, "Simon was the one who pushed me to go out for the team."

"Oh? Is Simon Yoder your father now?"

"Of course not!" Ben blurted back.

The question hung in the air for a long time after the answer had faded, though, leaving the rest of the ride home silent and thick with uneasiness.

Ben didn't tell any Simon stories at dinner, which was just as well since the Zeke Schrags and Granddad and Gramma—who seemed pretty clear that day—were there for Sunday dinner.

Like points in the web of a drunken spider, Mennonites are all connected to each other by some shirttail relative or other. This was true of even our mongrel Mennonite congregation that included German, Russian, and Swiss Mennonites. Bertha Schrag, Zeke's wife, was a first cousin once removed to Ethel's brother-in-law. I suppose that made Zeke think he was entitled to more than Simon's usual generosity. This had led to some undiscussed falling-out a decade earlier. Now Zeke could talk about Simon only in German since he didn't have anything fit to say about him in English. But since Zeke could talk about half the church and a good share of Kiowa County only in German, the language of parents, grandparents, gossip, and secrets, no one thought the less of Simon Yoder.

After dinner, Bertha, Mama, and I did the dishes while the men sat in the parlor and tried not to snooze. That was where they'd been before dinner, too. None of us, not Mama or me or certainly any of the men, thought anything about the division of labor. Even taking their dishes to the sink would have put their potency at risk. Of course, women could still slop hogs, so it didn't work in both directions.

The dishes done, Ben and I took advantage of the warm January afternoon and walked across the section to the Schmidt farm.

"Simon says basketball is a shooting man's game. He's going to buy a basketball and set up a hoop in the barn so I can practice after supper. He's even going to run an electric wire out to the barn so I can practice after dark." He danced a few basketball steps on the empty field.

I was both horrified at the expense and in awe of the generosity. "Don't ever tell Dad." As soon as the words fell out my mouth, I knew how ridiculous they were. And then I started to wonder what else Ben might not be telling us. The tiniest fissure appeared in our relationship. It had probably been there for several months without my knowing it, but it had been too small to see until this sunny winter day.

Ben only smiled and pretended to shoot a basket.

Dess, Suzanne, and Emily, the last of the Schmidt sisters, were still in the middle of the dinner dishes and were only too glad for the extra hands. Ben grabbed a towel and pretended he was going to pitch in, which was as close to dish drying as a boy ever got. All the giggling and teasing gave him an excuse to tug Dessie outside instead, which produced a new round of teasing. I should have figured out that was why he'd been willing to walk to the Schmidt farm with me.

"I think Ben's sweet on Dess," I said as soon as they were out of earshot. The new thought made me happy.

Suzanne rolled her eyes, "Ben's probably the *only* thing Dess doesn't hate about working for the Yoders."

"Really? Ben doesn't seem to mind much." I was in a mood to practice understatements.

"Well, it's different for boys," Suzanne said as she poured fresh hot rinse water into the tub. She left unsaid what an ogre Ethel must be to work for.

"What does Ethel do that makes it so awful?"

"That's just it. She doesn't do *anything!*" Suzanne huffed authoritatively and gave Emily a look that I couldn't decipher.

As soon as we finished the dinner dishes, Emily slipped off to read. Suzanne grabbed my hand and pulled me onto the back porch steps where the sun invited us to sit. "Promise you won't tell anyone?" she whispered nervously and glanced back at the empty kitchen. The Schmidts had so little else that they were more inclined than most to traffic in secrets because then they at least had something. And of all the Schmidt girls, Suzanne loved a good secret the most.

Suzanne's secrets fell loosely into three categories: The most common—and therefore useless—ones began with "Now don't say anything to anyone, but . . ." This was the clue that this was just gossip dressed up as a secret and everyone probably knew it already, but she didn't want word to get out she'd been the one to pass the story on. After all, a good gossip could go to hell just as easily as a murderer. Current crushes fell into this first category. So did crop yields and new feedsack dresses.

The second category upped the ante and began as this one did, "Promise you won't tell anyone?" Impending pregnancies and bankruptcies constituted the juiciest examples of the middle category. They were secrets to be held deliciously close but would soon be common knowledge.

The deepest, darkest secrets began with "Cross your heart and hope to die?" The don't-tell-do-or-die-poke-a-stick-in-your-eye moments were rare but ever memorable. They held the common characteristic that everyone would eventually discover the secret, but the pain associated with the news was always so great that people spent lifetimes pretending either that the secret wasn't true in the first place or that it didn't portend what everyone else knew it in fact did. Suzanne had three married sisters; two of the marriages had begun as a Cross-Your-Heart category secret, so horrified was the family. The third one should have been too, only no one realized it for the first few years.

"Of course I won't tell," I huffed lightly. "I never tell." And I didn't. Actually, the truth was, at my age, it wasn't so much that I was honorable as that I lacked a good secret-telling audience. That's what happens when you spend most of your working hours with vegetables and chickens.

"I know, I know, but this is really important," Suzanne began. She clutched my hand tighter and pulled me closer. "Dess says she's quitting school and going to live with Anna Joy in Wichita."

My heart stopped with the powerful richness of this secret. Anna Joy's marriage had been the darkest of all. The choicest morsels in the original secret included taxi drivers and movie theaters (pronounced in three full syllables by those of us who had never darkened the door to one).

"Live with Anna Joy? Is she going to choose your mother's casket before she leaves?" The thought just slid out of my mouth before I could catch it. That's another unfortunate outcome of working with vegetables and chickens. How do you practice keeping your mouth shut?

Suzanne didn't even notice though. She'd heard *all* the whispers about her sister. "She says she's not even going to finish out the school year. Instead of going to school some morning, she's going to Brewster's Drugstore and catch the early bus to Dodge City. Anna Joy says in Dodge they got a bus leaving for Wichita twice a day."

Her voice dropped even softer. "She'll be in Wichita before anyone even knows she's gone."

Speechless. That's what I was. This was an unknown state for me.

"If you tell a soul—even Ben—I'll never speak to you again. Ever. I'm trusting you, Cat!"

And now I was burdened, too.

"Why? Why is she running away?"

"Because she hates working for the Yoders. Hates it."

"So why doesn't she just quit?" I wondered distractedly if my dad would make me work some place I hated. Even as I thought it I realized how silly the idea was. Of course I'd have to keep working. For all practical purposes I was chattel. I never thought to be demeaned by it, though. That idea would take a decade more for me to form.

"Because Dad needs the money. We'd lose the farm without it." She glanced carefully over her shoulder, guiltily looking for eavesdroppers. She'd just given away a dangerous secret without eliciting any of the standard preliminary promises.

"But if your dad needs the money, wouldn't he just send you or Emily in her place?"

Suzanne picked at the peeling paint on the step. She didn't look at me. "Emily's too young. And I wouldn't go."

"Huh?" The whole conversation confused me, especially since working for the richest man in the county seemed pretty lucky to me. Surely some of that wealth and comfort could spill over, even to a cleaning girl. "What do you mean? Why wouldn't you go? Why would Dess leave?"

Suzanne stopped picking at the paint and looked at me like I'd said something stupid. Maybe I had, but I surely couldn't figure out what it was.

I tried another tack. "So why doesn't Dess go work for someone else?"

Suzanne snorted. "Anyone in particular?" she asked most politely, then affected a goofy rich-lady accent. "I hear Eleanor Roosevelt is looking for a good cleaning lady."

I flushed. "I still don't understand why she detests it so much. Ben never seems to mind."

"Of course he doesn't mind. I've already explained to you that he's a boy and it's different for boys."

What she'd explained to me was as clear as Willow Creek. Dess hated working for Ethel Yoder because Ethel didn't do anything. But wasn't that the whole point of hiring someone to work for you? I don't know if Suzanne would have made it clearer for me, but she didn't get a chance since Emily opened the screen door at that moment to invite us in for some popcorn.

I left the Schmidts wishing I'd never heard this secret. If only Ben and I had stayed home and listened to Dad and Granddad and Zeke Schrag complain about wheat prices. But you can't unscramble an egg.

I should have quizzed Ben on the way home to see what he could make of this secret, but I held to my vow of silence. I can't for the life of me now understand why I thought my word was more important than Dess running away, but that's how twelve-year olds think.

Unfortunately, come Monday morning, as long as Emily or anyone else was within earshot, Suzanne refused to talk about it. So our walk to school and back turned into misery, and the long school day grew longer. I lived all week with a knifepoint in my stomach, wondering if this would be the week Dess would run away and I would somehow be blamed for not telling anyone. I had two dreams about it that week, one of them during arithmetic. That one included an odd image with a bus leaving from Dodge at two o'clock and another one leaving from Wichita at four and wondering what time someone ate dinner on a train headed to Des Moines.

But it wasn't the week. When Dad, Mama, and I went to our first basketball game that Friday, Dess and the Yoders had already staked out seats behind the Sweethome team. We lined up, all of us like proud parents. Mama had let me bring Suzanne along, even though it would mean we'd be squished in the car on the way back since Dess and Ben would go home with us instead of having Simon bring them home on Saturday.

Ben only played a few minutes out of the whole game and he didn't score any points. It didn't matter, though. It also didn't matter that his dangling moose arms and legs seemed to belong to some other body, wild and loose flying like they were. And finally, it didn't matter that none of us but Ben and Simon had a clue what the rules of the game were. Truthfully, we would have been better equipped to debate—in Latin—the nuances of the Holy Trinity, neither of which (Latin or the Holy Trinity) Mennonites paid any attention to. We were all just tingly with excitement to have watched him play, even Dad, whose pedestal had just been chipped down yet one more notch. He'd be grumpy about the frivolousness of it all later with Ben, but for tonight he was shirt-button-popping proud.

After the game, Simon treated us all to pie at Dempsey's Cafe while we dissected what we thought happened in the game and what we thought should have happened. Ben laid out the basic rules and some strategy on a napkin. We were pleased to discover we'd had the gist of the game.

I watched Dess that night and finally stopped believing the secret. She looked ordinary. There were no furtive glances between the sisters or odd comments. She didn't seem jumpy, which is what I'd be if I planned on running away. She even chatted politely with Ethel, the woman Suzanne told me her sister wanted to run away from. I didn't know exactly what I thought she'd say or do, but she didn't look like a girl who intended to slip away. I decided I'd made the right decision not to tell Mama about Suzanne's secret.

The game hooked us into basketball. Even though Dad snipped at Ben from time to time about all the time and money basketball took, I don't think he missed another game in Ben's years of play. Neither did Mama or I. We even managed to convince Gramma (sometimes with imaginary Agnes, sometimes not) and Granddad to join us that first winter. The rules of the game must have been in the same foreign language as the rules of driving because Gramma never, ever understood what she watched. All she ever knew was that when the blue and gold boys made a basket, we cheered. When the other colors made a basket, we didn't. Before the war made German a taboo language, in her own polite Mennonite-lady sort of way, Gramma often resorted to German to express her own dynamic interpretation of the rules.

Lucky for us, none of the refs understood German.

CHAPTER 4

THE GAME MUST HAVE HOOKED Dess as well because she waited until the end of the season before taking flight. I'd stopped worrying about the possibility of her leaving, so of course I felt all the more responsible when she actually did.

Though both our families had given in to the extravagance of telephones by then, Suzanne didn't call to tell me but waited until I stopped by her farm on the way to school. It was the safest thing to do since the folks on our party line thought even a dinner menu was worth listening to and repeating, especially the Wenger twins. The old maid sisters perched on our party line, so whatever we knew, they knew too. And once they knew it, everyone else knew it, or some cobbled version of it. It was odd sometimes to pick up the receiver and hear your own stories being repeated, complete with whatever delicious nuggets Flora and Fannie Wenger created to fill in the missing gaps. I learned within weeks of getting our first phone to be cryptic even though Mama rarely let me call anyone.

As soon as I stepped in the door, Suzanne grabbed my arm. "Dess ran away yesterday!"

"Suzanne!" Marie Schmidt gave her daughter a cross look, I guess for telling me Dess had run away.

Suzanne ignored her mother and tumbled the words out fast before she could be stopped. "She went to school with Ben but wasn't there at the end of the day. Ethel found a note on Dess's dresser saying she'd gone to live with Anna Joy."

"Please don't say anything at school, Cat. We'd just as soon that not everyone knew about this." Marie wrapped her pleading in the words of the lightest category. If she'd been twelve-years old, she would have insisted on the do-or-die oath. But she was an adult.

I could affirm—Mennonites didn't swear—on a stack of Bibles that I'd never tell, but that single telephone call from Marie to her brother to ask him to chore while she and Henry went to Wichita to pick up Dess would have spread the word like melted butter anyway. "Simon himself drove over late last evening to tell us. Mama wanted to go straight to Wichita last night to go get her, but Pops didn't know where he could get gas on the way, so they had to wait till this morning. Mama cried all night. All night!"

True to her night, Marie's face looked puffy and red. Every few minutes, she blew into a bandana, apparently having forsaken her daintier hankie for a kerchief that could handle her grief. Chaos consumed the Schmidt household. Suzanne and Emily intended to take full advantage of it and not go to school, but Marie discovered her backbone for once and pushed the girls out the door. "Go home with your Mueller cousins. Uncle Albert will come over and chore for us tonight."

Reluctantly, Emily, Suzanne, and I left for school. We might as well have spent the day fishing, though, for all the attention any of us paid the teacher.

Marie and Henry returned the next day with a sullen Dess safely tucked between them on the front seat of their car. I didn't know why Dess had thought it wouldn't turn out this way since she'd deliberately left the trail of breadcrumbs behind her. Of course, later, Marie and Henry deeply regretted that they hadn't just let Dess stay in Wichita. But no one needed to see into the future because all the pieces for the jigsaw puzzle had been there for years, jumbled together in the box of our lives. If anyone had thought to sort the pieces and put them together, they wouldn't have been surprised at all at what followed.

Ben was as bewildered as Henry and Marie about why Dess ran away. He couldn't openly admit it, but on one of our walks home across the section from the Schmidts, he confided that working for Simon Yoder was the best piece of bad luck he could ever hope for. Simon had turned into a mentor, generously doling out wisdom on everything from how to build a stronger fence to why Ford was losing its edge to General Motors.

"It's not that I love Mama and Dad less," he began cautiously, "but there are times when I wish Simon were my dad."

The heresy annoyed me. Maybe I was jealous. "But then you'd have Ethel for your mama."

Ben shuddered, probably in revulsion. "I don't know what that woman does all day. She just sits in her bedroom with the shades pulled down." He kicked at a rock-hard clod. "She comes out for meals but never says please or thank you. I don't blame Dess for not liking to work for her."

"Is Dess going back to the Yoders?" It had been over a week since the prodigal daughter's return. She hadn't gone anywhere. Not to school, not to church, and definitely not to Simon and Ethel's to cook and clean and do whatever it was that cleaning girls did.

Ben shrugged. "Dunno. She says she ain't, but she also says if she doesn't, her dad'll lose the farm."

In the end, Dess managed to hold on to only another two weeks at home before she was sent back to the Yoders And this time, she didn't risk her secret with anyone. Like Moses and the children of Israel, she just up and left. Took the bus to Dodge City and disappeared. No one knew where she'd gotten bus fare, but that was the least of the questions people asked.

At Wednesday prayer meeting, Fannie Wenger, the chattier half of the eavesdropping duo, explained, "The family thinks she's in the Promised Land with Henry's cousin Amos Pete Schmidt." Flora and Fannie had themselves escaped Oklahoma in the early '30s. But by this time, the Okie moniker for California had latched so firmly into their brains that they could never remember to call California by its given name, even in the '60s, when decadence grew more prolifically than oranges. And, of course, the Schmidt family had no such thought about Dess's whereabouts since Cousin Amos Pete Schmidt hadn't written for years.

The whole church sang funeral dirges and just prayed she was anywhere but dead.

Mama let me go home with Suzanne after church for what seemed like a funeral dinner. Ladies from the church had fried a small flock of chickens and baked enough pies for a Schmidt family reunion, which this had become. Suzanne's sisters, Inez, Betsy, and Anna

Joy from Wichita, were all there. Both sets of Suzanne's grandparents were there, too, along with all of Marie's siblings and their families. Even Henry's brother and his family from Hutch came over, making this an occasion as significant as Christmas since that was the only other time he made the sixty-mile trip.

For all the food and people, though, this wasn't a party, but an ushering in of a season of grief. This household, which had already had nearly a decade of tired living, faced more. It wasn't just the empty bank account that had worn them down, either. It was also the progression of bright, spirited daughters who seemed destined to choose doom.

Barren Inez, the oldest daughter (and my favorite of Suzanne's married sisters) had fallen out of the nest at seventeen when she got married. This devastated the good Mennonite boys, who never tired of watching her while they chewed on toothpicks and talked to each other on hot summer Sunday nights. She had a careless sway to her walk and a lazy smile that meant one thing, but was interpreted by the boys as another. And although she could have had her pick of any of a dozen Mennonite boys, she chose to marry Tim Smallbrook, one of the few forgotten Kiowa Indians in Kiowa County. In later generations, this would be interpreted as giving her Mennonite upbringing a rude hand gesture. In the current generation, it only meant scandal and shame.

To everyone's surprise, shortly after Inez and Tim got married, they started showing up in church. And not just Sunday morning, but Sunday evening and sometimes Wednesday prayer meeting too. Not only that, Tim volunteered to mow the cemetery in the summer and light the church furnace in the winter. He also asked to be baptized, which was the ultimate befuddlement. Even though Mennonites firmly believed people should be baptized as adults and not infants—such a decision belonged to adults—it surprised the socks off of them when an adult came to Jesus who hadn't already met him as a child. Furthermore, "What kind of name is 'Smallbrook'?" everyone whispered to each other.

Even more shocking, years later, when Tim was called before the draft board, he could have pleaded for a farm deferment. Instead he said he was a pacifist and couldn't in good conscience go to war and kill anyone.

Ike Bonner, who was chairman of the draft board at the time, was so stunned he forgot to even question him. Ike Bonner was the sort of man who never let the facts distort his convictions. Having been born and raised in Kiowa County, he naturally assumed every good injun in the county would be just itching to go fight, like they might show up for the bus ride to Kansas City to get military physicals wearing war paint and carrying tomahawks. Ike Bonner was like most Kiowa County natives. They knew about as much about their county's namesake as they did about Jews in New York City. They held only slightly more prejudice against the natives.

Of course, the biggest irony was that Tim Smallbrook could attend church every Sunday of his life, volunteer enough hours to put the minister to shame, and yes, even be baptized, but he'd never really *be* a Mennonite. On the other hand, Betsy's husband, Pete Bontrager, who was bred from good Mennonite seed, raised in the church, and could sing "Gott ist die Liebe" in a tear-rendering tenor but never, ever darkened the church door except for weddings and funerals, would be considered a Mennonite until the day they laid him out in a pine box dressed in his not-very-worn Sunday suit.

In contrast to Inez, Betsy had followed the party line when she married Pete, a likeable Mennonite boy from over by Harper. He came from a good, if somewhat disorganized, family whose patriarch had been a bishop in the church before his untimely death a decade earlier. Pete had even gone to a semester of Bible school, so there was a lot of not-so-quiet talk about him becoming a preacher one day. His pedigree certainly looked safe. He might have been, too, if the demon rum hadn't discovered him. Or maybe it was the other way around. By the time anyone thought to ask Pete, life was pretty much one big fuzzy slur. He had a difficult time thinking much about anything. At least he certainly didn't think much about planting wheat or harvesting crops or any of that other good stuff that would have kept Betsy, their passel of motley children, and him in shoes and an occasional loaf of store-bought bread even in the bad wheat years.

In the early days, when Pete was just learning to be a drunkard, he wasn't very good at it. It took him only a quarter of a bottle of whiskey to start weaving and saying stupid things very loudly. People could spot right off that he'd been sneaking out to the barn to do more than milk the cows. After he'd practiced drinking for a few years, though, he got quite competent. It took him almost a whole bottle to be as fuzzy on the outside as he felt on the inside.

By now, Betsy and the rest of the family had long given up the idea she'd married a preacher in the making. And while it's true Betsy would have at least wanted Pete to be a farmer in the making, it probably didn't matter much that he wasn't that either. For Betsy was sneaking out to the barn for more than a little milking herself. By midafternoon, both of them could pretty easily forget they even lived on a farm.

Although scandal and wagging tongues accompanied Inez's marriage, and disappointment followed Betsy's, neither daughter could match the horror of Anna Joy's marriage. Poor Anna Joy. Of all the girls, she was the one who ended up with the no-neck, wide-body peasant genes that distinguished the Mueller clan, which was her mother's side. Since she was short, big-boned, and thick, not even a leftover Indian or a poor, Mennonite drunkard would have seen her as a catch. It didn't matter how well she sewed or cooked, a good roast beef just wasn't going to be enough for a Willems or a Miller or an Unruh boy to say, "That's the girl for me."

To Anna Joy's credit, she *was* at least smart. And so after her sophomore year in high school—which was at least two years more than any good Mennonite girl needed that particular year—she trekked off to Wichita to become a maid for a family made fat, happy, and wealthy by the discovery of oil on their wheat farm.

Anna Joy cleaned and cooked—she made a decadent pot roast. She also watched the two children in the family, one of whom had a personal best of sitting still for almost three minutes. Through it all, Anna Joy lost some of her farm-girl heftiness, gathered a few boy-catching makeup tricks (which in the early years always got wiped off before she set foot on the bus back to Kiowa County), and developed a little city charm. Although one would *never* call her pretty, one might say that she developed a . . . well, she developed a look. And because her smile—in contrast to her sister Inez's smile—meant exactly what boys took it to mean, she found it much easier to be the honey that attracts city boy flies than it could ever be in Kiowa County.

So Anna Joy found herself being a joy to many boys in many ways. The one she snagged happened to be the taxi driver who picked her up outside the Crown Movie Theater. Later, when she wrote home about it, she decided a taxi driver sounded even more shameful than a movie theater, so she conveniently left out this detail—in addition to leaving out the detail about the movie theater.

Sometimes Mennonites confused what was foreign and exotic with what was right or wrong. So while most people would never have thought a taxi driver to be a sinful occupation, it didn't take much for the ladies' sewing circle to decide that driving a taxi represented all that was bad in the world. Taxi drivers spent hours, often nighttime ones, driving around aimlessly, picking up total strangers, and taking them to bars and dance halls—all for money. If this wasn't living in sin, it was at least living close enough to the edge that a good rainstorm would send a body slip sliding down its muddy chute straight into the gates of Hell. Their conclusions were made all the easier because none of the ladies at the Sweethome

Mennonite Church sewing circle had ever actually seen a taxi, let alone had a reason to ride in one.

Anna Joy was as smitten with Tom Badzinski as Tom Badzinski was with Anna Joy. At least for the first two years they were married. By the third year, Tom's taxi-driving ways intruded on their bliss. At least that's what Henry and Marie explained at Wednesday night prayer meeting. Their deep humiliation was only slightly less than their fear of being ostracized and treated as total outcasts by their church family for having given birth to such a wayward daughter. What they didn't explain but Suzanne whispered to me was that their taxi-driving son-in-law had given up his nighttime cruising and agreed to a constricting daytime job so he could keep track of his wife at night. Although Anna Joy didn't actually even know how to drive, she herself had developed some bad taxi-driving habits. Anna Joy had begun to stay out till two or three in the morning picking up strangers for a little pin money, and it sounded like she might have been spending as much time in the back seat of the car as the front.

Unfortunately for Anna Joy, Tom was actually a pretty straight arrow, even if he *had* driven a taxi at one time. He had no patience with her behavior. Eventually, he set all of her worldly possessions on the front lawn and filed for divorce. Her parents would have rather received a telegram announcing her death. At least then the church family would have been able to offer cakes, casseroles, and condolences. Now they could only whisper about the Schmidts and pretend they didn't know what everybody knew about this disgraceful calamity that Anna Joy's parents would have to silently bear.

If Anna Joy had only had a shred of dignity, she would have come home and turned into a barren recluse who only showed up at church functions but never actually talked. Instead, she saw the divorce as a ticket for more fun. Although for the precious moment she was without a man, she eventually found herself a second husband, this one even more inglorious than the first because he was in the military. And because Anna Joy collected husbands like quilts, she plucked herself a third one, too, after the delicious thrill of the uniform wore off, but that was lots of years later.

The Schmidt girls had gone from bad to worse to apocalyptic. It was too early to tell where Dess's departure would fall in the lineup, but the trend didn't bode well.

"It's worse than death," Marie kept mumbling through her tears. She sat at the kitchen table and sobbed while the Schmidt girls and I did the dishes.

"Mama, it's not worse than death," Inez insisted softly. "As long as we haven't heard otherwise, we have to assume she's alive."

"I'm sure she's on a bus to somewhere right now, probably to that Hollywood California place we keep hearing about," Betsy added, trying to smile through her tears.

"One of these days we'll probably get a postcard from her," Anna Joy said, almost cheerfully. "Dear Mama, I've become a famous movie star. Clark Gable sends his best. Wish you were here. Love, Dess."

Even Marie laughed, although if they ever did get such a postcard, it would put Dess right after apocalyptic in the daughterly lineup. Hollywood and Hell didn't start with the same letter for nothing.

"I'm sure we'll hear from her. It might take her a while to land someplace and write us," Inez said confidently. "You know how hard it is for us Schmidt girls to find stamps."

"But she will."

"She loves you too much, Mama."

"Then why did she run away?" Marie asked and began crying all over again.

Henry and Marie remained inconsolable.

"He paces. Every night I hear him walking around the house, down the stairs, in the kitchen, out on the porch, then back upstairs, and then the bed creaks. Then he starts all over again," Suzanne said. "Mama just cries all the time." Suzanne's own eyes looked puffy and bloodshot. "I keep telling them it's not their fault, but we all know I'm wrong."

Not so surprisingly, Ben came home from the Yoders saying much the same thing. "They're heartsick. They keep saying they feel so responsible. I keep telling them it wasn't their fault." But, of course, they knew he was wrong.

As a show of remorse, Simon offered to erase Henry's considerable debt. At first, Henry and Marie refused, but eventually, they got practical and loudly accepted.

Still, there was no word from Dess. Week one turned into week two, week two into week three. Week three stretched into summer. Letters came back from all the possible hiding places saying, "She's not here. We'll be praying for you."

"If she'd just write and tell us she's okay, we wouldn't make her come home," Suzanne said long about June. "We just want to know she's safe."

I was spending the night at the Schmidts, their house of two girls now almost as quiet as ours of just me. We'd dragged a mattress out to sleep out on the cooler screened-in summer porch where the mosquitoes couldn't feast on us. Out in the dark, the cicadas sang a chorus of woe to each other, vibrating louder then softer, then louder again, with some unseen cicada choir director. It was a starry, starry night without so much as a splinter of moon.

"She's made her point. Now she should just come home." Suzanne burst into tears. I reached over and squeezed her hand. I missed Dess, too. Sweet, pretty Dess. Even if I'd known she was safely tucked in bed somewhere tonight, I would miss her because she was the sister of my best friend.

"I just hope she's not dead," Suzanne said between sobs.

"I don't think she is," I comforted her. My words weren't empty ones since in my heart I knew Dess was alive somewhere.

"I just hope she's not worse than dead."

That I didn't know, so I didn't have any more words of comfort.

CHAPTER 5

SUZANNE'S SPARKLE BEGAN TO TARNISH. Great loss does that to a person. But she was my best friend for the good times and the bad, so I tried to stay her friend. Now that school was out, we began our summer ritual of weekly sleepovers. At one point, the sleepovers would have been a study in contrasts: Suzanne's household noisy and chaotic, ours subdued and orderly. Now we didn't see much difference. Our parents made polite small talk with us, but Suzanne's parents seemed lost in their losses and mine seemed unable to talk about ordinary things when something so extraordinary had happened. I know Dad and Mama also felt awkward since Ben continued to work for Simon and Ethel and continued to enjoy it. Suzanne and I never talked about it, but I felt slightly traitorous—unfairly so—that Ben didn't abandon the job to show his respect for Dess, wherever she was.

With summer started, Ben could work full-time again for Simon. Dad could really have used the help at home with his own fields and chores, but he let him go to the Yoders, which only says how much we still needed the money.

One blazing Saturday morning, Mama and I were weeding and carrying water to the tomatoes, which didn't like the heat any more than we did. I could see Simon's dust cloud rising plume-like behind his fat green Oldsmobile a mile or more away. Even if I hadn't recognized his car, I would have known by the time of the week it was Simon bringing Ben home. So few cars passed our farm that the rare passerby would be suppertime talk.

Did you see Ray Huske drive past today?

Wonder what he was doing out here.

As was his usual pattern, Simon stepped out of the car to visit a few minutes with Dad and to hand some dollar bills to him for Ben's week. They stood in the shade of the big cottonwood and unconsciously mirrored each other as they pushed back their hats and scratched their sweaty scalps. A couple of cats patrolling for rats found the men and rubbed up against their legs and whined until Simon scooted his away.

At dinner, Dad relayed his conversation with Simon. "Ethel could really use some help around the house.

Simon admits she's never been much of a housekeeper and now she's gotten even worse these last few years." He paused and helped himself to more potatoes. He couldn't look me in the eye, and I had an eerie sense of what he would say next.

"He was wondering if Cat would want to come help out this summer."

"That would be perfect!" Ben blurted.

My stomach swam. The richest man in the county wanted *me* to work for him. If Ben ended up playing basketball, what could I hope for? Piano lessons?

But then there was Dess.

Mama just frowned at her plate.

"He knows Cat wouldn't be the same kind of help as an older girl, but she'd learn fast," Dad continued. He walked a delicate line. "Simon's been real impressed with how hard and how smart you've worked, Ben." He tilted his head toward Ben. "He thinks even at twelve you'd be good help, too, Cat." He puffed a little with Simon's compliments about his children.

"She's too young," Mama said firmly.

Dad snorted softly. "Lots of girls go to work at twelve. All of Pete Drescher's girls worked full-time in the summers by now. Shoot, they quit school and worked all year long."

Mama shook her head. "They were out of eighth grade, so they were older by a year." Then she repeated, "Cat's too young."

While two flies buzzed over the sugar bowl, I stood on a tightrope line. I could fall whichever way I leaned.

"She's not too young," Dad said firmly. They never disagreed in front of Ben and me, mostly because Mama never talked back. "We could try it for a week or two and see what happens."

I churned inside, caught at the awkward point of not wanting either outcome and desperately wanting both.

"No," Mama said simply.

Dad looked confused. None of us ever openly challenged him, the head of the household. "Look at how much it's helped to have Ben work. Look at how much he's grown up in just the past year."

Ben blushed at the unusual compliment, even if it was given more to bolster Dad's point than to make Ben feel good. In our house, compliments appeared about as often as rain because getting a big head was deemed a dangerous sin. Since pride went before a fall, compliments were as good as anything to trip on.

"What happened to Dess Schmidt?" Mama finally asked. She looked Dad straight in the eye.

Dad scoffed, waving his zwieback in the air. "Look at any of Henry Schmidt's older girls. They're a rebellious lot. Ben's had nothing but good to say about Simon Yoder. Whatever chased Dess off had nothing to do with him and Ethel. It was just an unfortunate coincidence that she was working for them when she got that fool notion in her head to run off."

Life was simpler in those days. If Dad said something, it was the truth, whether it was true or not. "We're not going to turn down Simon Yoder's generosity."

It was done. At least the words were finished. Mama sighed over the decision for the rest of the day, hardly talking. Dad took more time than usual out in the barn choring before supper and had to fiddle with some unnamed task after supper. For them, a fight usually consisted of no eye contact and choppy movements, so this was a doozy.

On Sunday afternoon, I packed my cardboard suitcase and readied myself to leave for a week. I honestly couldn't tell if the knots in my stomach were from pleasure or fear or what.

It had tried to rain all spring. It would lightning and thunder, but mostly they were the dry heaves of a sky that had forgotten how to let loose its clouds. Large, dirty drops spit from dark, fat clouds, but rarely did the ground even get damp. Mostly, the raindrops just pocked the layer of dust that covered everything.

That Sunday afternoon, though, the skies opened up and pounded wickedly at the ground like an angry fist. The elms folded their leaves down, as if to shield themselves from the needle sting of the driving rain, turning dusty summer green into sea-foam gray in moments. The wind shook the cottonwoods and weeping willows, bending them eastward in the wind as the storm hurtled through.

The gullywasher bled the dust off the road and into the ditches, creating skinny cinnamon rivers on both sides of the road and making the fields too muddy to walk across to the Schmidt farm. Even though we'd both been at church that morning, I hadn't been able to tell Suzanne that I was going to the Yoders for the week. The sensible part of me didn't know how to tell her I was, of my own free will, going to live in the lion's den for a week. The foolish side of me didn't want her to talk me out of the chance to spend the week with Ben and to work for the richest man in the county. So when Dad said he didn't trust his tires on the muddy road and we'd just stay home from church rather than risk landing in a ditch, I felt secretly relieved since I wouldn't have to choose whether to tell Suzanne or not.

Dad called Simon, who came on Monday morning to pick up Ben and me. Mama cried when I climbed into Simon's car. My own throat felt thick, so I didn't dare look at her as we pulled out of the drive.

The trip to the other side of the world took less than half an hour. We slid around a bit on the slippery mud roads, but enough rain had soaked in by then that the road was already becoming crusty and rutted in spots.

The Yoder house nested on a hill in a Kansas oasis of cottonwoods and elms, but mostly cottonwoods. It would sound the same as home, where the cottonwood leaves chattered in the smallest breeze. The farm looked crisp and lovingly maintained with a freshly painted barn and fences that ran unbroken. The whole farm was as shiny as Simon's Oldsmobile. I don't think I'd been to Simon and Ethel's since the bank holiday, but surprisingly, the house looked every bit as broad and high as my memory of it. A wide porch wrapped the north and east sides—the cool sides—of the house. Back then, houses had front doors, so this one did too, but no sidewalk led to it. Even total strangers wouldn't be so audacious as to think *they* were special enough to be greeted at the front door. Instead, everyone would have entered through the kitchen door, the house's heart.

Ethel put me in one of the four upstairs bedrooms, the one next to Ben's and cattycorner from her and Simon's room. Each room took a full corner of the upstairs and had two massive floor-to-ceiling windows, so you could see forever in not just one but two directions. My room looked palatial, like something out of a ladies' magazine, with a padded rocking chair that even matched the curtains and bedspread, a true closet, and space enough to feed the relatives at Christmas. No wonder Ben liked working for Simon. I thought I'd died and become an Arabian princess. I wondered if it had been this pretty when a Yoder daughter lived in this room. How lucky that girl would have been. How lucky I was to be living here now.

After I unpacked, Ethel put me to work on their laundry from the past two weeks. I hated laundry day at home. I hated carrying the water and running the wringer. I hated feeling the caustic homemade lye soap on my hands and watching for buttons that were bound to break if they went through the wringer at the wrong angle. In winter winds, I hated the icy wet clothes slapping me as I hung them on the line. In summer winds, I hated hanging them and watching the fine coat of inevitable dust settle on them, making them dirty before I was finished making them clean.

So my first lesson at Simon Yoder's was that washing a rich man's clothes is no more fun than washing a poor man's clothes.

While I skirmished with the laundry, Ethel put together an unsatisfying dinner of scrambled eggs, unseasoned boiled potatoes, stale zwieback, and nothing from the garden. A white meal.

After dinner, Ethel told me to do the dishes while she rested. At home, Mama and I would have had a division of labor—one of us would have done the dishes while the other one continued the laundry.

So my second lesson at Simon Yoder's was that since I was getting paid to cook and clean and do the laundry, I would be cooking and cleaning and doing the laundry by myself until I fell into bed each night, exhausted.

Midafternoon, Ethel came out of the house long enough to tell me I'd better get some beans picked so I could cook them with some of the leftover ham for soup for supper that night.

My third lesson at Simon Yoder's—they were coming fast and furiously—is that if you're paying someone to cook and clean and do the laundry, you no longer have to say please or thank you. Your dollars will say it for you at the end of the week.

I finished hanging my washer load and started the last load soaking. I found a good-sized pot in the kitchen and then went out to look for the garden. It hadn't struck me as odd until that moment that I didn't have a clue where the garden was, which was akin to being on a farm but not seeing a barn. I finally found it behind the chicken coop. Like the broken china plate a child hides from his mother, Ethel had hidden her garden for good reason. It looked like she was raising a bumper crop of pigweed and sticker patches that year. I felt teary—a ridiculous emotion for vegetable picking—as I searched the scrawny plants for beans. My own mother's garden spilled color and flavor in every direction. All spring, summer, and fall, Mama spent her extra minutes planting, weeding, watering, and harvesting. In the winter, I occasionally saw her standing on the edge of the empty plot. Dreaming? Planning? Picturing? I didn't know. But that was where her heart lay.

Every spring we planted corn, beans, lettuce, peas, gladiola bulbs, radishes, potatoes, onions, more glad bulbs, tomatoes, turnips, squash, beets, dill, cucumbers, and another row of glads. I was in early grade school before I realized no one else planted glads in their vegetable gardens. Until that point, I had this vague idea they were just gorgeous vegetable plants that Mama had trouble coaxing to bear fruit. Throughout my life, I've carried a soft spot in my heart for glads, probably because it was the one thing out of the vegetable garden we never had to can.

The flower beds around our house gushed color, too: blue cornflowers, purple lilacs, yellow forsythia, black-eyed Susans, lilies, daisies, and roses everywhere. I'd seen real florist roses in a window once at Dodge City. Ruby red and perfect. But they weren't pretty. The stems weren't stems at all, but trunks, stiff, straight, and unbending.

My mother's roses clustered loose, full and rich, with stems that bent gracefully under the colorful weight and dropped scented petal bouquets on the ground.

Sitting in the middle of Ethel's desert, I learned my fourth lesson at Simon Yoder's: I wasn't home anymore.

I dug up an onion and snipped some summer savory, cut up the couple of handfuls of wilted beans and put it all with the ham bone. I made biscuits. Twice. The first batch I charred in Ethel's gas oven—I'd only ever cooked on a wood stove up to that point. I was lucky I didn't char the house, too, when I lit the gas oven for the first time in my life. Ka-PHOOM. I also salvaged enough leaf lettuce out of the garden to make a wilted lettuce salad. It wasn't a meal Mama would have been proud of, but no one starved.

Ben must have understood the challenge well enough to compliment me in front of Ethel and Simon. The tender gesture brought me to the edge of tears, exhausted like I was. Simon must have realized what a tough day it had been for me as well because when he got up from the table, he gave my neck a playful squeeze, a gesture so foreign to me that it made me feel a little sick inside instead of happy.

My fifth lesson at Simon Yoder's would have run across my toes if it had been a rat. But I missed it.

Just as Ben had predicted, Ethel evaporated after supper, leaving me with the dishes and the laundry I'd forgotten in the washer. Even with Ben helping me—he was about as adept with clothespins and wet clothes as I was with a gas stove and match—it wasn't until well after ten o'clock that I finished my work and fell into my new princess bed in my new princess room, where I finally understood the story of Cinderella in a whole new way.

Just as I arrived at the edge of sleep, I realized in exhausted horror that Ethel slept in baby bliss because she'd hired *me* to get up early and fix breakfast.

And thus ended the first day.

 CHAPTER 6

BEN HAD A SIXTH SENSE. That or he desperately wanted to make sure I didn't fail and taint him in my fall because he woke me the next morning before he went out to chore.

"Dess always had breakfast on when we came in after choring. Eggs and bacon. Fried potatoes. Coffee. That sort of thing."

I staggered up on one elbow and nodded. As soon as Ben closed the door, I flopped back on my princess pillow and shut my eyes to wake them up.

"Cat!" Ben shook my shoulder. "Cat! Breakfast!" He whispered loudly and urgently.

"I'll have it ready when you come in from choring," I responded, while resting my eyes a moment longer.

Ben tried to drag me into a sitting position. "Cat, we're *in* from choring. Simon's wondering why we don't have breakfast on the table."

The adrenaline tumbled me out of bed, into my dress, and down the stairs.

Simon sat looking patient and relaxed. He was reading the *Mennonite Weekly Review* and glanced up only long enough to wink and smile. I flushed in relief.

"How about some coffee, Kitten?" Simon said playfully.

"I'm sorry I don't have breakfast ready," I mumbled and scrambled to look for the coffee. Neither Simon nor Ben had a clue where Ethel kept the coffee, even though they drank it for breakfast, dinner, and supper. Men were like that in the 1930s.

Simon laughed. "It's only the second day. You'll get it figured out."

I found the coffee in a canister and put the coffee pot together only to realize I needed a recipe to make it. Mama always made the coffee at home. Just last week I'd thought I had at least another five or six years to learn how. I wondered what else I'd learn I didn't know before the end of the first week.

I looked at the phone out of the corner of my eye. Just a quick call to Mama would solve so much, but it seemed too audacious to ask Simon for permission to ring Mama up. So instead, I dumped enough coffee and water into the pot to float the coffee in the perforated basket, which seemed like a logical amount, then tried to coordinate the match, the gas knob, and the angle of my tongue without singeing my eyebrows or knuckles or giving a surprised yelp like I had with each match and flame the day before. Just to be safe, I tossed both braids behind my back. The quiet *kaphoom* of the burner only startled my insides. My outsides appeared calm, like I was an old hand at lighting gas stoves.

Progress.

I knew fried potatoes would take too long, so I attempted pancakes instead. In my discombobulated state, I accidentally used baking soda instead of baking powder and added too much salt and not enough sugar. Meanwhile, the coffee didn't perk, but sputtered peppery water all over the stovetop.

I forgot to start the bacon until the pancakes were ready to fry, which was actually okay since it hadn't occurred to me that I couldn't just pour the batter onto the hot griddle surface like I did on our wood stove at home. I would need a pan of all things. I snorted softly in disbelief. I would *never* buy a gas range when I had my own kitchen.

My first breakfast at Simon Yoder's: pale coffee full of coffee grit, inedible pancakes and no syrup, hot but limp bacon, and ten scrambled eggs for the two men. If I'd only known the word "mortified," I would have been it.

The second day went downhill from this point.

Ethel roused about nine o'clock, as I was finishing the last scouring of the kitchen. In my mind, I'd been planning to perform some triage in the garden. I wanted to water, weed, and prune, but Ethel, of course, had other ideas.

She opened up an ironing board and stacked a month of shirts, overalls, and dresses on the kitchen table. I was curious to see how we were going to heat the iron. It didn't seem logical to put it on the stove like we did at home. I was quite pleased to see that we could plug it into an electrical outlet and it stayed hot the whole long, long day of ironing and scorching and finger blistering.

Fixing dinner and supper provided my only break that day, dinner being only slightly less of a disaster than breakfast, and supper being only slightly worse. I created meals of contrast: what wasn't burned was doughy or raw; what wasn't too salty was too sweet; what should have been smooth was lumpy. Even the mint tea failed to meet my intentions since I started it too late and didn't have any ice to cool it.

And so the week went. The only saving grace came as I listened to Simon and Ben banter comfortably about the farm, the weather, and the world. Even as I fumbled around the kitchen, I picked up the significant difference in the way Simon and Ben talked and the way Dad and Ben talked. Simon treated Ben like a grown man, as much of a peer as Simon ever had. No wonder Ben liked being here. I even felt flattered that I was the sister of someone Simon Yoder listened to. He had that kind of effect on a person.

Up until this point, Ethel hadn't had much to do with me. It wasn't that she was rude or demanding as much as that, apparently, one of us was invisible. At the beginning of the week, this created an ocean of frustration for me since a little help—like how to light the gas oven or how much water and how much coffee to use—could have prevented numerous small disasters. If nothing else, I might not have felt so sickeningly homesick. In fact, if it hadn't been for Ben and a letter from Mama on Wednesday, I would have run away myself. I at least thought I understood Dess's unhappiness better.

By Wednesday, when Ethel finally started talking more, she still didn't say anything warm. Instead, she picked at me in little ways.

"Catherine"—she wouldn't call me Cat, which suited me just fine since I didn't count her as one of my friends either—"certainly I think the tea could use a little more sugar, don't you think?" Or "Next week, let's try to fold the towels a little neater." Or "I like to put a little whitening in with the whites, so the undershirts don't look as dingy as these do."

Heaven knew I had plenty of failures for her to glory in, but for some odd reason, she chose to needle at what had come closer to a success, as if she wanted to snip off any buds of hope that might start forming.

I hadn't folded the towels neatly enough?

She needn't have worried. Unfortunately—and fortunately—I wasn't the least bit confused about what a dismal week I'd made for all of us. Even though my cooking gradually improved to the cusp of edibility, it didn't come close in taste or organization to how I cooked with Mama within shouting distance. I made a tiny bit of headway in the garden and only a little more progress in Ethel's previously abandoned housework, and I don't think I ever did make the coffee right. But I had arrived in chaos and chaos remained. I didn't know yet whether I'd shamed the whole family or just myself. I did know, however, the Yoders wouldn't be risking a second week with Ben's sister. All week long, when Ben wasn't giving me syrupy sympathy, he looked like he had a wasp down his overalls. Simon's patronizing pats on the back or casual shoulder squeezes only made me feel like a bigger failure.

I managed to keep from crying in the car ride home, even when Simon chatted with me over his shoulder about letting me go with him and Ben into Dodge to the stockyards the following week. "Kitten, you won't believe how many cattle they run through there in a day. It's a sight to behold!" And then he and Ben veered off onto cattle prices, pasture grasses and alfalfa, and what the tensions in Europe were doing for the farmers in Kansas.

"I don't wish a war on anyone," Simon said as he turned into our lane, "but those boys over there are going to be too busy working for old Herr Hitler to be at home feeding the cows. I don't know how a fella could go wrong."

Unfortunately, before I could stumble out of the car with my suitcase, I saw Mama picking beans and my tears welled up. I hated for Simon to see I was such a baby, but it couldn't be helped. By the time I reached Mama, I was sobbing.

Mama stood up, panic across her face, and wrapped her arms around me. I think she was crying, too.

"Oh, Mama," I whispered. "It was horrible! I was horrible! Ethel was horrible! I missed you so much!"

"I missed you, too!" She turned our backs to Simon and Dad, and we strolled farther into the garden where the colorfully unfolding gladiolas spiked upwards. "So start at the beginning and tell me everything."

I couldn't for the life of me figure out where the beginning was, so instead I asked her how to make coffee.

She laughed a little, maybe in relief. "That was the worst of your week? Making coffee?"

"Making everything!" I blurted. The bits and pieces of the week bubbled out of me like an underground spring. I couldn't stop the rush of details.

At dinner, Ben added his own spin, but somehow he managed to make the week lighter, almost funny. "Cat made tea with a little sugar, but Ethel wanted a little tea with her sugar instead."

Dad smiled, which was all the encouragement Ben needed. He slipped into Ethel's syrupy sweet voice. "Catherine, next week I'd like you to iron the towels before you put them away. Oh, and Simon, don't you think Catherine should do something about that awful smell in the pig shed? Surely, if she just used a little more bleach, it would smell just as fresh as we like it."

I giggled in spite of myself. Dad and Mama snickered, too.

Enjoying his captive audience, Ben pushed his chair back from the table and shuffled, old-lady-like, over to the window and peered out. "Well, Catherine, it looks like over dinner you let some of Oklahoma land on the south forty. I'm sure you can have that sifted out by supper time." He shuffled toward the parlor, turning before leaving the room like he'd just remembered something. "Oh, I have to go read my Bible for a while because I've forgotten everything I read in it this morning. You won't mind butchering a hog for supper tonight, would you, Catherine?"

After having felt like crying for an entire week, laughing hard like this loosened the lump in my throat and untwisted the knot in my stomach. Unfortunately, though Ben only meant to cheer me up and put Ethel in perspective; ultimately, he sealed my fate for the next week since he had made the Yoder household sound a little crazy but harmless. When Dad said Simon thought the week had gone well and would be tickled pink to have me come back, I thought he was teasing me.

I shook my head, more annoyed than confused. "The only thing that went well this week was that I managed to bring the mail inside without losing it or burning it." I looked at Ben for help, but he was laughing at my joke that wasn't a joke at all.

I tried again: "It was an awful week. I don't know why Simon Yoder would tell you otherwise, let alone say he wanted me to come back," I said, drunk with disbelief.

Still, no one responded.

"And I'm not going back." I looked to Mama for help, but she was staring at her plate, which was useless since it looked the same as it had at every other meal she'd eaten in the last fifteen years.

"Next week will go better, I'm sure," Dad said simply. He was finished. He stood up from the table and took his hat off its peg. "Ben, I need your help in the barn," he said and left, closing the subject and the door behind him.

I should have spent the day picking mama's brain while I helped her bake the coming week's bread. Instead, she felt so bad for me that she let me sit on the kitchen step stool and talk while she measured and sifted and kneaded and shaped.

Looking back, I realize she must have missed me as much as I her. And not just for the housework or the cooking. Since Dad might have said all of ten words that week, she must have been as starved for conversation as I was for comfort.

By suppertime, my heart had mended a bit, and I was able to make it through the whole meal without tearing up, but I couldn't look Dad in the eye. I guess we were fighting.

I fell asleep that night and dreamed about locust plagues and the Red Sea crashing in on me. I didn't know what I'd say to Suzanne in church.

CHAPTER 7

BACK THEN, MENNONITES UNDERSTOOD HOW wily temptation could be. So the men sat on one side of the church and the women on the other on Sunday mornings and evenings, impure thoughts being a distracting nuisance like they were. At prayer meeting on Wednesday evening, husbands and wives sometimes sat together, probably because after a long day of farming, everyone was too exhausted to think anything unchaste even if a fine young thing's elbow happened to be exposed.

We were all creatures of habit. Sunday after Sunday, we were drawn to our same spots like iron filament to a magnet. Middle of the week, I could close my eyes and draw a seating chart as accurately as I could draw a map of our kitchen. As eyesight and hearing dwindled, the congregates moved a bench up. Not en masse, of course, but individually, a little like checker pieces. This meant that the right side of the sanctuary—the women's side—grew younger, leaner, and prettier the farther back you went. By the second or third row to the back, there were just teenage girls who mostly giggled and sent furtive smiles at the teenage boys across the aisle. The very back row or two were reserved for mothers—and an occasional father—with babies or young children, both boys and girls. When the boys could sit still enough, they would graduate to the men's side of the church and sit with their fathers. Fathers didn't mess with keeping toddlers quiet in church since it would prevent them from listening to the sermon or noisily meditating with their eyes shut, however the spirit descended on them. Apparently, women were too busy wondering if they'd fried enough chicken for the potluck to listen to sermons, so what was one more distraction of a fussy toddler for them?

Sitting near the back row on Sunday mornings, I used to think the gauzy coverings on the women's side looked like a covey of doves had landed. They'd bob slightly and occasionally droop forward, but not as often as a shiny head would slump on the men's side. The men had better sound effects, too, with an occasional soft snort. Nowadays, men don't snore as much in church because they sit by their wives, who firmly plant elbows in the offender's rib cage. Nothing like a sharp and sudden pain in the side to wake you up to Jesus.

Anymore, Suzanne and I always sat together, having finally graduated to the back rows.

That morning, Suzanne brimmed with whispers. "Why didn't you tell me you were going to work for the Yoders?" She looked cross.

"I didn't have a chance since we didn't go to church last Sunday evening, and Simon didn't make us go to prayer meeting on Wednesday."

"Was it awful?"

I nodded. Across the aisle and up a few pews, Simon Yoder cocked his head at us and winked. He couldn't possibly have heard. Still, I glanced around to make sure Ethel had planted herself in her usual pew towards the front.

"It'll get a little worse each week, but you'll make it to September." It was an odd thing for her to say. She grimaced slightly. "Of course, you're a Peters, not a Schmidt. You just might make it forever."

She was talking Latin to me. "What are you saying?"

She sighed and shook her head. "Just don't let them pressure you to go to school in Sweethome and stay with them."

Actually, Suzanne was wrong. My second week was considerably better than my first. I started to get the hang of the gas stove and cooked fewer disasters. Since I'd cleaned the week before, the dust wasn't quite so deep and the piles of mending and laundry quite so high. True, Ethel still only talked to me instead of with me, and she continued to deliver advice I didn't need or appreciate, but Ben helped me keep my perspective with second-long pantomimes behind her back. It wasn't nice, I know, but in the order of the universe, survival comes first, nice a distant second. It helped, too, that the week held little surprises.

Monday night, after I finished the dishes, Ben and Simon led me out to the barn. "Promise you won't tell Mama and Dad?"

I nodded, curious but silent. I expected to see some worldly 4-H project. Instead, Ben flipped on a light, picked up a basketball, and started to bounce it on the cleanly swept concrete barn floor. A silly grin spread across his face. On the far side of the barn, an orange basketball hoop and net attached to a beam, as incongruous as a Negro on a Mennonite church pew.

"Watch this," he said, as if my attention might wander to the haymow. He paused and shot. The ball kissed the backboard and slipped through the net.

Before I could say anything, he sped under the basket, picked up the bouncing ball, and said again, "Watch this!" Again, he shot and sunk it.

And again.

And another time.

"Ben! Where did you learn to shoot baskets like that? Mama and Dad won't believe this!" I could hardly breathe. I honestly didn't know a single person who owned a basketball, and now my very own brother could actually bounce one *and* slip it through a net time after time.

"Now, Kitten," Simon said. He grinned proudly and chewed on his toothpick. Mennonite men didn't smoke or chew tobacco, so they had to pacify themselves with toothpicks. "You promised not to tell. This is going to be our little secret until basketball season starts."

Our little secret. Just Simon and Ben and me. Who doesn't love to be included in such a good secret?

"You'll be the best on the team. No one can shoot like that, not even the seniors." I felt dizzy. Famous.

Ben just grinned and kept on shooting. He shot ten times in a row before missing once, and then made another half-dozen perfect baskets.

"It'll be different in a game," he said modestly after he made another ten in a row. "More pressure. More noise. I won't have time to aim."

"He's a natural," Simon said. "He's already hitting more baskets than the other boys can hit at practice." He nodded confidently as he waved a fly away. "He'll be the star, all right."

"Thanks to Simon," Ben told me later, after Simon had gone back in the house. "I started out every morning before chores shooting a hundred baskets. In the evening I did the same thing after chores. But I didn't quit until I'd made three in a row. After the first week, I upped it to five, then ten. Now I've upped it to twenty." He paused to let the number soak in. It did. "Can you believe that? A year ago I had hardly touched a basketball and now I can make almost twenty-five baskets in a row. It's all Simon's doing. He says you just nibble at what you want little by little. Before you know it, you're there."

He was right about that.

On Thursday, true to his promise and in spite of Ethel walking around all morning with her lips pinched together, Simon took Ben and me to Dodge City to the stockyards. Mostly all I remember about that day was there were cattle—and cattle odors—as far as the eye could see and my nose could smell. Simon bought us hot dogs and grape Nehi pop. Everywhere we went, people seemed to not just know Simon, but defer to him, which seemed odd to me since he wasn't buying or selling any cattle and didn't even own more than a modest herd as far as I knew. But I knew he was a wealthy man, and people sometimes confuse net worth and personal worth. I know I did.

For supper that night we stopped at Betty's Steak House in Dodge. I think that was the first restaurant meal I'd ever had. I wanted to stare at everything and take home the smells since Betty had thought of everything to bedazzle the likes of a hick like me. Ben dug his elbow into my rib cage. "Close your mouth, Kittycat. The flies are counting your molars." He winked at me and pushed his chin up to close his mouth.

I blushed for being such a country bumpkin, but I shut my mouth. Still, I wanted to breathe in the moment through all of my senses.

"Order anything you like," Simon said.

When I said I'd like fried chicken, though, he wouldn't let me order it, so apparently I couldn't *really* order anything I liked. "You can eat fried chicken any day of the week at home." Which certainly wasn't true. "This is cow country, Kitten. Order a big juicy steak!"

Even though we occasionally butchered a cow at home, steak was still only a fancy name for a better roast, and it didn't sound like anything special. But Simon wouldn't hear otherwise, so I finally handed my menu to him to order the rest of my meal. I figured I'd bungle the drink and dessert choices, too.

When my steak came, I had a whole new appreciation for those lazy beasts we raised. I hadn't realized they had been just ambling around in the pasture, building up those fine thighs and shoulders for someone like Betty to take advantage of. It was melt-in-my-mouth tender, salty and slightly sweet, crisp on the edges but juicy on the inside. For the rest of my life, I'd compare every steak I ate to this one. From that moment on, cows took on a different meaning and I loved them.

Simon and Ben both had plate-sized steaks, and they ate every scrap, including the fat because the government wouldn't think to tell them not to for another forty years.

"Ben, you gonna have a slice of that cherry pie again for dessert?" Simon winked at me and then added, "even though it's not as good as your Mama's?"

Ben leaned back and stretched. "I surely don't want to insult Betty. I can probably choke down a slice or two."

"Best meal I've had in a month," Ben said as he pushed in the last bit of pie, "with the exception of that breakfast you fixed the first morning at Simon's." At this particular moment—stomach full, eyes and head overwhelmed with the day—I could take the teasing, and we all laughed.

While Simon paid, Ben and I stood outside on the porch. Ben chewed on a toothpick. I would have liked one, too, but it wasn't ladylike. "Not bad, huh, Cat?"

"I could eat here again." I was at an age when I thought understatements were clever, but only because I couldn't actually think of something clever.

"Simon comes up to Dodge about once a week. He's brought me up with him five or six times already." He stood silent and squinted at the sunset, a burst fireball on the western horizon. "He's a good boss," he said thoughtfully. As an afterthought, he pointed his head back at the restaurant. "You figured out that Simon is part owner of the stockyard, didn't you?

I hadn't. But that explained a lot.

"Everyone at church thinks Simon is rich, but they don't know the half of it 'cause he's so modest about it."

The days dragged a little faster because of our Thursday field trip, but it still seemed like the week lasted a month. On Friday evening, Ben went back out to the barn to practice shooting baskets while I packed his things and then my things. Ethel was tucked away in her room, again with the door closed. No doubt her lips were still pinched, too.

I heard Simon come up the stairs. He knocked on my door and then poked his head in.

"Packing?"

I nodded.

"Well, Kitten, I hope this week went a little better for you than last week." He flashed his golden smile and let himself into my room.

I nodded again. It felt slightly awkward to have him inside my room, even though this was his room.

"Did you enjoy the stockyards?"

I nodded again and smiled shyly.

"Betty's too?"

"It was the best meal I ever ate."

Simon laughed comfortably. He was in his own house, after all. "Better than a church potluck?"

"Better than a church potluck." I smiled at the contrast. No matter how many bowls of Jell-O the ladies brought, it could never compete.

"Well, we'll have to go again in another week or so," he said and sat down in my rocking chair, which was really his rocking chair. I felt fidgety to have him sit there, but I still didn't understand why since this *was* his rocking chair in his room in his house.

"It's nice to get off the farm every now and then. Opens a whole new world when you see something different. Don't you think?"

I nodded again and kept on folding my clothes, which was the one thing in Simon's house that was actually mine. It occurred to me that I was conversing as eloquently as my dad.

"We'll probably wait till after harvest, now." He rocked for a moment and didn't talk. I didn't like how the quiet made the room feel small, but I couldn't think of anything to say. Simon must have thought the same thing because he said, "What's the wheat looking like over at your place?" And then he laughed like he'd told a little joke. "That's a question to ask Ben. You probably don't pay much attention to the wheat. You probably take more notice of your mama's roses."

"I miss her garden," I said too fast. I must have sounded rude, but if I'd offended Simon, he didn't show it.

"Your mama has the prettiest garden in three counties." He smiled at me again. "Maybe four." He leaned forward on the rocking chair and stared absently out the open window. Out in the dark, the basketball *thump, thump, thumped* on the barn floor, then rattled the hoop. "There's lots of things I wish Ethel were better at."

Even though I could have named over a hundred and fifty things myself, I kept my mouth shut. This wasn't a conversation I should have been having. I wanted it to be over.

"She's not easy to live with. But things are as they are." He shrugged, as if to break his mood.

Thump, thump, thump, rattle. Thump, thump, thump, rattle. Ben "wheehawed" a triumph and Simon laughed.

"He surely is having fun with that basketball. I can't wait to see the look on your dad's face this winter."

"He'll surely be surprised."

"I think he was pretty unhappy with me at first. But it worked out. Ben's going to be the star." What he didn't say but I understood was *look at what Ben would be missing at home.*

Simon stood up and leaned against the window frame for a long time, staring out at the night, listening to Ben dribble and shoot, dribble and shoot. I finished my packing and wanted him to leave. But it was his room in his house.

Finally, he said, "I'm glad you're here, Kitten. Ben was devastated when Dess left. I was afraid he was going to quit working here."

"I think he likes working here too much to ever quit."

"I hope so. These days, he feels more like a son than Harold." The sloucher. I'd forgotten about him the last two weeks. The three girls, too. "I shouldn't say that. Harold's a good boy. He just had life too easy, which is no one's fault but my own."

A father could commit worse sins.

"I'm glad you're here, Kitten," he repeated and turned to look at me. "I hope you keep coming back. I have a feeling you're going to grow to feel like a daughter."

My heart raced at the thought and the all-too-generous implications. I smiled shyly at him, but I was afraid it looked like a greedy smile instead of a pleased one, so I tried to end the smile.

"I know Ethel's hard on the hired girls, but I promised myself I wouldn't let it happen again. I can't sleep some nights thinking about how we had a part in running Dess off. I keep thinking that if I'd paid more

121

attention, I could have seen what Ethel was doing and stopped her. I promise you, Kitten, I'll protect you from her." He looked so sad, so remorseful. I believed him and felt safe in this rich and powerful man's house. What happened to Dess would never happen to me.

And then he walked over, brushed his hand against my neck, and kissed me on the cheek. Sweetly. Romantically.

"Goodnight, Kitten."

He twisted my insides and left the room, closing the door behind him.

Goodnight, Kitten.

CHAPTER 8

I DIDN'T KNOW THE WORD "inappropriate" but I knew the meaning, and that was how Simon's kiss felt. I lay in bed for a long time, feeling slightly nauseous and wondering why he did it, and what I'd done to provoke it. I could still feel the kiss, steamy on my cheek even though I'd scrubbed my face hard with soap and water. My own father hadn't kissed me for probably two, three, maybe four years, not even goodnight, good Deutscher that he was. Mentally, I sorted through the day, event by event and conversation by conversation. I couldn't get the Miller or Willems boys to look at me at church even during an eyelid-dropping sermon, so what must have I done to make this happen?

The next morning, as I got breakfast together, I didn't know how I was supposed to act around him—if I was supposed to be embarrassed for him or for me or for both of us. But Simon didn't act any different. He was the same man he'd been on Friday morning and Thursday morning and Wednesday morning. He and Ben talked their usual breakfast talk about the weather and harvest. Ben proudly announced he'd sunk twenty-six baskets in a row the night before, and Simon proudly proclaimed him the best basketball player this side of Dodge City.

They laughed and joshed, father-and-son-like, or how most fathers and sons wished they could but not like any fathers and sons I knew.

By the time we reached our farm, Simon's nonchalance confused me into deciding that it must have been a goofy misunderstanding, that the kiss wasn't a kiss at all. Or at least not the kind of kiss I'd thought it was the night before. Grown men didn't kiss young girls romantically. They kissed them like a father kisses a daughter. My problem was that since my own father had kissed me so little, I wasn't totally clear on what a fatherly kiss should feel like. It kind of surprised me that it would feel like Simon's, but I finally figured it could happen that way.

Still, whatever *had* happened subdued me, so while at least I didn't hover on the verge of tears, neither could I gush as enthusiastically about the visit to the stockyards. Ben didn't notice but gushed sufficiently for both of us. Dad harrumphed at the very un-Mennonite extravagance, but Mama was in awe of everything, from the gasoline to get us to Dodge to the cost of three steak dinners at a place called Betty's.

I wandered through a moody and contrary weekend as I sorted through how I would feel come Monday morning, needlessly snipping at Dad several times along the way. As confusion knots sometimes do, this one had gotten more tangled as I'd tried to untangle it. So somehow all of this ended up seeming to be Dad's fault since if he'd showed more affection over the years I wouldn't be so befuddled now.

By the time the Sunday evening ride home with Simon and Ethel whirled around, I had relived the kiss somewhere around three hundred and fifty to four hundred times, or roughly once every five minutes of my waking hours. Of course, I'd sat through two of Brother Bender's messages, so that raised the average. Fortunately, the games of Sunday afternoon checkers with Granddad lowered it. I at least had the common sense to know that anything I spent so much time sorting through probably wasn't the same when I finished with it as when I started, so I tried not to put too much stock into either end of the weekend and just continued to unconsciously clench my teeth and fret.

Simon and Ben bantered the whole way home, mostly about the impending wheat harvest, but also about some roadster Simon was planning to get. I didn't say anything and Ethel only huffed just loudly enough that it could have been mistaken for a sigh. As soon as we stepped in the Yoder kitchen door, Ethel waddled upstairs, fiddling with the pins holding her prayer covering with one hand and holding on to her Bible with the other.

"Mama," Simon called after her, "this feels like a popcorn night."

She didn't respond, but softly huffed again.

Simon just smiled like she'd given the punch line to a private joke the two shared. He fumbled through the pots and pans in the pantry, pulled out a heavy roaster, and scooped some lard into it. Ben turned a kitchen chair around, draped his legs around the seat, and rested his arms on the chair back. While the lard melted and started sizzling, Simon banged through the pantry some more until he found the popcorn jar. Then he dumped some kernels in, dropped the lid on the pan, and started to shake it. I figured popcorn must be Simon's specialty. For some reason, a number of men I knew couldn't fry an egg even if the hen dropped it into the skillet herself, but they'd found out how to cook one thing and do it well. My dad made peanut brittle. Granddad could make apple butter of all things. Both required great culinary finesse that should have lent itself to other things but didn't. It must have given them a sense of security: no matter how early Mama or Gramma might pass over to the gloryland, Dad and Granddad wouldn't have to worry about starving.

Lord help us.

Simon could have won a state fair ribbon for his popcorn. He fussed the kernels around the pan, turned up the heat, turned down the heat, and let the aroma smack us in the nose. When the last muffled pop exploded, he dumped it into a blue granite roaster, threw on just enough salt, and motioned us outside.

"Grab that pitcher of lemonade, Kitten. We'll just have ourselves a party out on the porch."

I brought three bowls out onto the porch along with the pitcher and glasses.

"We don't need bowls, Kitten. You'll just have to wash them later," Simon said and settled into the porch swing. He patted the seat beside him. "You just sit down, Kitten." Ben had already balanced himself on the porch rail, his back against the porch post. I would have rather been where he was, but I couldn't have done it without immodestly hiking up my skirt, so I poured lemonade all around and took up the rhythm of the porch swing with Simon, barely a forearm away from the man and the popcorn bowl.

I'd planned to be wary that week at the Simon Yoder house, but it didn't look like I'd be very good at it at this rate.

We creaked back and forth. The sticky June night air carried the songs of bullfrogs and cicadas. Not much of a breeze poked at the mammoth cottonwoods, rattling their leaves enough. Coyotes yipped at the moon. Kansas was always good with summer nights.

"Nothin' like a good bowl of popcorn on a Sunday evening," Simon said between handfuls.

"Yessir. It surely helps me get my mind off the sermon," Ben said and Simon chuckled.

"So what *was* the message tonight?"

"Shoot if I know. I just told you popcorn helps me get my mind off of it. Must be working, too, 'cause I already forgot," Ben said and Simon chuckled again.

"I'll bet Kitten can tell us what the message was about." He reached over and squeezed my neck playfully.

Now, I have to tell you this. That squeeze felt good and bad at the exact same moment, which was very confusing to me. Once we got out of our early teen years, we Mennonites just didn't touch each other much, even if we were related. Packed into our pews for a good missionary Sunday service or a rafter-shaking singspiration, we left at least a Bible's width between us and the next person. Except for a holy kiss (which was never more than a quick peck on the cheek) after foot washing, we never kissed each other, not even hello or goodbye to Christmas relatives. Even Granddad and

Gramma, who'd been married over fifty years, didn't so much as hold hands in public. Frankly, it was a wonder there were as many of us born every year as there were. So the very thing that made it feel good—a simple touch from another human being—was also what made it feel, well, creepy.

No. Creepy isn't the right word. More like alien. It was the touch stacked on the previous week's kiss that felt creepy, and it carried more layers with it than I could understand.

"It must have been a good one," Ben was saying. "She's meditating so much on what she heard that she can't even respond."

They were both laughing at me now.

"Oh, she's not thinking about the sermon. She's thinking about all the boys that were peeking at her during prayer," Simon said.

"No, sir!" I felt embarrassed and flattered at the same time.

"Yes, sir!" Simon responded, mimicking my indignation. And then he laughed again. It was a big, warm laugh that had arms, the kind that draws a person in and makes a body feel lucky to be in his circle. "I've watched those boys, Kitten. They're not thinking about starving children in China during prayer time."

"Well *I* am!" It was the first thing in my head and out my mouth, and it wasn't even true, but it made both Ben and Simon roar, like I'd told a good joke.

Simon squeezed my neck again. He kept chuckling. "You just keep thinking about those children, Kitten. That's what you're supposed to be doing. Never you mind those Miller boys."

I suppose I could have thought I was the butt of some private joke between Simon and Ben, but I didn't really feel that way. So I let myself be teased along. It was okay. I never got that kind of attention, so I'd be lying if I said I didn't have places inside me that felt happy. Still, that little knot that had started in my stomach wouldn't go away either. Simon didn't squeeze my neck anymore, but he rested his arm along the back of the porch swing, close enough that I knew exactly where it lay in relation to my shoulders. Not quite touching me, but almost. A shadow.

A whisper.

I fell asleep that night not knowing quite what to think and wishing Suzanne were there to talk to.

The week stumbled along, building into the routine of previous weeks. Breakfast, then dishes, gathering eggs, then laundry or ironing or mending, dinner, more dishes, dusting, sweeping, maybe a little gardening, then supper and more dishes. Sometimes it seemed as though those dishes in the sink were breeding like rats when I wasn't looking.

Ben came in occasionally for a snack or something cold to drink. Simon sometimes worked with Ben outside or sometimes left the house clean and smelling good and returned several hours later, still clean and smelling good. He never announced his comings or goings but pretty much showed up in time to wash up for meals and to read one of the papers while I cooked.

He tried lots to make conversation with me even when I didn't give him any reason to think I could. He said simple things like, "Supper surely does smell good." And "Those cookies are a real treat. Where'd you learn to bake like that? Your mama must be real proud of you."

He also said more complicated things: "What do you think you want to be when you grow up?" Or "Isn't it awful what Hitler is doing to those Jews over there in Germany. What do you think is going to happen?"

We didn't ask questions like that at my house. It especially wouldn't have ever occurred to my dad to ask me my thoughts. After all, I was just a girl. I liked it that Simon asked me questions because it was nice to have someone think I'd have an opinion about anything. Also, even if I was clumsy—and sometimes stupid—in my answers, he kept asking me as though he still thought I might have ideas. I hoped I'd get better. If nothing else,

I started to think more about things I'd never thought about. So there was definitely some good in it.

Ethel showed her face about as much as Simon, but she certainly didn't ask me any questions and she certainly didn't go anywhere except for the monthly sewing circle when it finally rolled around. Summertime, I always went along with Mama and Gramma to sewing circle, but Ethel didn't take me. I guess she figured she was paying me to be at her house, so that's where I was supposed to be.

By sewing-circle day, I'd not only stopped being wary, I'd just plain forgotten I was supposed to be.

My mistake.

Ethel had me make a potato salad and shell the last of the peas that she would cook at church for the sewing circle potluck. She also took some cookies along. Around nine, Simon backed the shiny Oldsmobile out of the shed and he and Ethel headed for town. I didn't think Ethel could drive. At least, I'd never seen her behind the wheel.

This was probably the first time I'd been alone in that house, and it felt odd even though every room and corner of it was familiar to me. Next to our house, the Yoder house was Rockefeller-size and filled with fancy furniture, some of it totally useless, so it lent itself to a little pretending. Some days, I was a wealthy young farm wife whose cleaning girl had the day off. Today, with empty hours ahead of me and no chance of Ethel making a surprise entrance, I had a chance to invent a much grander fantasy.

Even when you've only known poverty, you know how to picture wealth. As I swept and dusted in the unused parlor, I was in Paris, in a satin ballgown, smiling mysteriously at an invisible Robert Miller, that boy I'd gone to Sunday school with all my life, who had also miraculously become wealthy and worldly himself. Robert wouldn't recognize me because I no longer looked like the plain little braided girl he'd known. Although Mennonites didn't dance, he would ask me to waltz. And when I delicately floated across the floor, he would be especially fooled because even if I looked vaguely familiar to him, he would push the thought out of his mind since how could a simple Mennonite girl from Sweethome look so exotic or dance so divinely? I was witty and delightful, yet I would choose him over all of the handsome Parisians because he thought to ask me questions about European politics. He would want my opinion and marvel at my clever insights.

Thank goodness I heard Simon's car door slam. It gave me a moment to become me again. Although there were vestiges of that other girl still in the room, I hoped Simon wouldn't be able to detect it.

"Hello, Kitten," Simon called from the kitchen.

I didn't answer right away because I hadn't totally shaken off Paris.

"Hello?" he called again.

I poked my head around the corner. "Oh, hello. I didn't hear you come in." It wasn't exactly true, but not hearing him come down the lane was almost like not hearing him come in the house.

Simon knocked the dust off his hat and hung it on the hook. He showed me his shiny tooth. "Love the smell of the lemon oil," he said. "You do a nice job with the housework, Kitten."

A tiny needle poked me from inside. I realized this was the first time I'd been alone in the house with him. Ever. I could hear my heart.

He brushed past me, whistling "Precious Memories," a couple of letters and a newspaper in his hand. As he passed, he tousled my hair with his free hand. "You done in here? I've got some bookkeeping to do."

Since the room never got dirty from people, only the wind and dust, it wouldn't make any difference whether I was done or not. The house would be in pretty much the same state on Friday. "Sure. I was just headed out to pick some lettuce for dinner."

He was already at the rolltop, sorting neat piles of envelopes and writing in his ledger. His back faced me, so we were done with our conversation.

The lettuce was in a sorry state. I don't know why Kansans think they can grow it in June since it hates heat and June is only hot. I picked a small bowl of wilted leaves and dug some radishes and green onions, which with the heat would have enough bite to bring tears to your eyes. I looked for anything red on the tomato plants, but it was weeks too early and I knew it. When I started checking out the corn that had barely started to tassel to see if we'd have a couple of ears, I realized what I was doing and felt silly. Simon wasn't going to kiss me in broad daylight. That was a goodnight foolishness. I could go back inside and fix dinner. Still, I looked around to see if Ben was within earshot. The cows looked, too, but we didn't see him.

The chorus from "Precious Memories" continued to float from the other room while I fried up some ham. I made some biscuits and gravy and got out the rest of the potato salad. I turned the hopeless lettuce into a miserable salad and salvaged what I could from the radishes and onions. We would eat, but we wouldn't necessarily enjoy it. "Precious Memories" never stopped.

Ben came in a few minutes later and washed up. He sat at the table, looking red and tired and ten years older than he had at breakfast. He still had dirt at his hat line, but the rest of him looked clean, so I didn't say anything. It wasn't my job to anyway. If Ethel had been there, I would have motioned at the line with my hand so he wouldn't embarrass Mama's good name, but I figured Simon wouldn't care.

The whistling finally stopped and Simon sat down to pray.

"Looks like the wheat price is still dropping," Simon said as he helped himself to the biscuits.

I cringed but didn't say anything.

"Where's it at?"

"It dropped below fifty cents yesterday."

If you didn't grow up on a farm, this number probably doesn't mean much to you, but we all lived and died on the price of wheat. In '38, wheat hit a decade high of over ninety cents a bushel, well up from the early '30s where it had been only about thirty-five or thirty-six cents. Of course, price only mattered if you had wheat to sell, which most of those years we didn't. If you had two or three hundred acres in wheat, ninety cents times an average—in a good year—of thirty bushels gave a farmer around eight thousand dollars. Take out the price of seed, fuel, and equipment, and you were left with a living that was tolerable, especially if you didn't have much debt and you liked working with your hands from sunup to sundown. Unfortunately, if you only made five bushels to an acre and the price dropped to fifty cents a bushel, your income was closer to seven hundred and fifty, but your expenses stayed the same, which, if I have to spell it out, meant most farmers spent most of the '30s spending more than they made. If you asked them why they kept doing it, they wouldn't be able to tell you, and they'd be kind of surprised at the question.

I knew for a fact I would *not* marry a farmer, even in a weak moment in Paris.

"I stopped by the feed mill and talked to Hank Burnum for a while. Looks like it could go lower. They had a good wet spring for a change in Oklahoma and Eastern Kansas, so their bumper crop is depressing prices everywhere."

Ben just shook his head and looked like Dad.

Simon kept talking, even though at my house we would have stopped. "Hardly seems fair. Last year when we all had a miserable wheat crop, the price shot up. Now that it looks like we might have a halfway decent crop, the price plummets."

I wasn't really listening to Simon. Instead I kept mentally multiplying the twenty bushels—which seemed a believable average—times three hundred acres times fifty cents. It kept coming out at about two-thirds of what it had last year with an even worse crop, so I finally quit.

Ben didn't say anything either. I'm sure he was doing the same ciphering. When you grow up on a farm, you get pretty good at multiplying numbers like 27 times .48 times 280 in your head, even if it didn't put gas in the tractor.

Simon didn't seem to notice that we both wanted to change the subject. Instead, he rambled on like none of us liked anything better than a good blue funk. "Saw Charlie Hilgendorf at the post office. Hog prices are dropping, too. He just took a half dozen up to Dodge to sell. By the time he paid the commission, filled his tank up, and paid his feed bill at the mill, he had three dollars and forty cents left." Simon sopped up some gravy with his biscuit. "I'd'a thought the troubles in Europe might have given prices a little boost here, but I think everyone's running scared."

Ben still didn't say anything.

"I don't know how folks like the Hilgendorfs manage. They got all those girls—what is it? Six? Seven? All of them too young to hire out. How're they going to eat next winter?"

It was generous on Simon's part to be worried about the Hilgendorfs.

"I have to tell you, I slipped him a five. It was all I had in my wallet at the moment or I would have given him more." Simon smiled at his investment. "You should have seen the look on his face."

Ben's thoughts started to loosen up a bit, and for the first time, he kind of smiled. "Well, Simon. There's a lot of us folks that'd starve without you looking out for us."

It was as close to a compliment as a boy was trained to give. Simon actually blushed and fumbled around for words a minute. "Now that's not why I told you that, so don't go back and tell your daddy what I did. But I have to tell you, it felt a whole lot better to see where that five dollars was going than to put twice that in the offering plate on Sunday."

"Don't doubt it for a minute," Ben said. He got up and gave a half nod of thanks in my direction. "Better go earn my keep." He put on his hat and headed back to the barn. The screen door banged behind him, and a flurry of spooked cat claws scattered across the porch.

I gathered the dishes off the table while Simon pulled out the *Sweethome Tribune* and entertained himself and me with little news bits: Arnold Beechum's cow delivered a five-legged calf, and Mr. Beechum hoped to sell it to the circus. The ladies at the Glad Tidings Baptist Church in Coldwater were holding a bake sale to raise money for Sunday school materials. Sweethome now had its own Mason shoe representative, Mr. Harvey C. Clutter.

I started heating the water for dishes and put on the coffee pot because I knew he liked a little coffee after meals. The small things at Simon Yoder's—like turning on a faucet to get water instead of going outside and pumping it or heating water on a gas stove instead of blazing up the kitchen with the woodburning cookstove—were starting to spoil me.

When the coffee was done perking, Simon got up from the table and reached past me for a cup and the coffee pot. "I'll get it, Kitten. You've got your hands full of soapy water." His hand patted my rear end and then I thought he squeezed it slightly.

I shifted over, more surprised than defensive. He could have put his hand on my shoulder. He'd done that before.

Instead of sitting back down at the table, though, he stood a foot away from me, back against the drainboard, paper in one hand, coffee in the other. Every once in a while he'd put the coffee cup down and turn the newspaper pages and refold it.

"Looks like they found a nest of rattlesnakes under the Kiowa County Courthouse steps," Simon chuckled. "That's only fitting since so many snakes work inside the courthouse." He chuckled some more at his joke. "You got rattlers at your place, Kitten?"

That was like asking, *Does the wind blow at your place, Kitten?*

"We always kill a couple every year. Dad killed one out by the chicken coop a month ago."

"That'd be a good reason to stop eating eggs, I'd think." He smiled but kept on reading the paper.

"Nope. Just a good reason to send someone else out there to gather 'em."

Simon liked my joke. "Yup. If you were my girl, I'd hire someone to go gather those eggs." He still only looked at the paper instead of me. "I wouldn't risk letting a pretty thing like you having to wrestle a rattler. Oh, looky here." He laughed and deftly launched into a news item from Tulsa. "Here's a burglar that got caught because he stopped to have a piece of pie out of the icebox. The lady wasn't surprised at all. She says, 'I won a blue ribbon at the county fair with that recipe.' The burglar said he was sorry he got caught, but it was worth it. 'I *never* get pie like that at home.'" Simon laughed some more.

"Ever have a meal you'd be willing to go to jail for?" He laid the paper on the counter and finally looked at me.

"Just that steak at Betty's Steak House." It was almost true.

Simon liked what I said. "You think that was good? Kitten, one of these days I'm going to take you to Wichita with me. We'll go eat at the Hickory House where they have linen napkins and candles and the waiters wear tuxedos and come around every five minutes to bring you food fit for Mrs. Roosevelt herself. You're the kind of girl who should have nice things and get to go to fancy places."

A girl like me didn't have a chance around a man like Simon.

"That would be fun," I said, but I wasn't sure that was the right word for either of us.

He slid a foot closer and leaned a hip onto the counter top so that he was only a little taller than I was. Then he rested his hand on the small of my back. Every single cell on my shoulders and spine came alive. Sweat prickled my neck even though the dishwater had long ago cooled. I made my hands keep scrubbing on the biscuit baking sheet even though it was clean.

"Kitten," the man said and shifted his broad hand down a couple of inches.

I squirmed, anxious for him to move away, but not quite sure of what was happening.

"Kitten." He said it again. "I'm glad you're here. I just want to make you as happy as I can so that you'll stay." And then he kissed me tenderly on the cheek. I could hardly think about the kiss because his hand was wandering aimlessly from my hip up the side of my body to under my arm. He touched my breast, I was pretty sure. "You won't leave me and go work for someone else, will you now?" he whispered conspiratorially.

I shook my head, too dizzy with his words and his hands to know what to say or think.

"Good. Because you're the best thing that's ever happened to this farm, and I don't want to lose you."

He patted my rear again and slid back off to his rolltop.

My heart pounded for a long time after I finished with the dishes. I couldn't figure out what that conversation had really been about, but I knew enough to know it wasn't about the talking part of it.

The rest of the afternoon, I worked in the garden. I wanted to stay someplace that didn't have any corners to get trapped in. That night after I finished the supper dishes, I went out to the barn to watch Ben shoot baskets. I could tell he liked the audience. He kept telling me all the little tricks he was learning, but he might as well have been talking tires and transmissions for all I understood. Still, I sat with my back to a post and my eye to the door. Simon stopped in for a few minutes and watched, too, but he didn't come over and sit by me. He just stood there, framed by the giant door, his arms crossed and a toothpick in his mouth.

Friday, Simon disappeared for most of the day. I listened all day for the car to crunch the gravel in the lane. A few minutes before supper, he rolled in. He had a couple of small boxes and the mail.

"It surely smells good, Kitten," was all he said. He took off his hat, brushed the dust off and hung it on the hook. He disappeared up the steps, not coming within five feet of me. I could hear the water running upstairs. A few minutes later, he came downstairs, his hair still damp.

At supper, Simon and Ben did all the talking. Most of it was about the heat and the wheat. Some of it was about a new Oldsmobile Simon was looking to get.

"Next week, I ought to take you into town with me, Ben. You can drive it and tell me what you think. Kitten, you can come along for the ride. Maybe help us decide what color to get."

It's easier to bribe a body if you have something to bribe them with.

That night, when I went up to my room, I saw Simon had added an extra little bribe just for me, just in case. A small box of Woolworth's chocolates lay on my dresser. He'd written a note in his neat accounting hand, "Thank you for working so hard. It surely is a blessing to have you here." He'd signed it from both of them, but I didn't really expect Ethel to know she'd given me any chocolates, so I didn't thank her.

I didn't thank Simon, either, since I still wasn't sure who should be doing the thanking.

══ CHAPTER 9 ══

As much as I missed Mama, it was Suzanne I wanted to talk to. Being a working girl like I was now, the sleepovers were gone for the summer since a Saturday night sleepover was as likely as a Monday night sleepover during the school year. We sat together in church, but her family had to rush off as soon as church got out so they could get ready for their Sunday dinner company. The entire Solomon Unruh family, all nine of them including eternally pregnant Gladys, who didn't get out much because she was always busy supplying more children for the Sunday school program, would arrive at their house after Sunday school just in time to eat a Saturday's worth of food preparation. I saw Suzanne again at the Sunday evening service, but she was already in the middle of the Unruh twins, so again the weekend passed without a chance to talk.

I had the jitters on Monday and even Tuesday, but gradually I let my guard down. I don't know what I expected to happen, but whatever it was, it didn't.

On Wednesday morning, Simon made good on his promise and took Ben and me to his Oldsmobile dealership in Sweethome. Ben didn't know what he'd done to deserve this lucky trip, but I had a pretty good idea.

Up to this point in our lives, we'd only stood outside the dealership and stared—Ben more than me—at whatever shiny beasts sat inside. The giant storefront window kept the sounds and the smells on one side and the nose prints on the other. Neither of us had ever smelled a new car before, so how could we be prepared for how intoxicating it could be?

Since Simon owned the dealership, this trip wasn't at all about haggling for the best price. Instead, he was there to pick out his next new car.

I hovered by a midnight-blue touring car, the practical one, while Simon disappeared into the dealership's garage to talk business. Ben tried to hover there, too, but a speedy-looking burgundy coupe kept tugging at him like a magnet. At one point, Brother Bender, who supported his preaching habit by being Simon's lead mechanic, stuck his head into the showroom and gave us a quick greasy hand wave. How he ever got those hands clean enough to turn a Bible page was beyond me.

"That one purrs like a kitten." Brother Bender nodded at the coupe. "Got a mighty powerful six-cylinder engine and a three-speed transmission. She'll pass every Ford on the road. Soup her up and she can hit a hundred." He got a sheepish look on his face. "But don't tell your dad I said that."

"Your secret's safe with me," Ben said and laughed. "She's a beauty, that's for sure. She's real beefed up from those '36s."

Ben had to do all the talking because I didn't know car language. Besides, I was having to concentrate on not actually touching the car—even the running board— while I stood with my head in the open window. I breathed in the leather and the wood. Out of the corner of my eye, I tried to see the price on the window. I think it said $765. Almost thirty acres of wheat in a good year. Make that a record-breaking year.

I whispered to Ben when we were alone again, "If we had a sedan like this, I'd sleep in it."

"Just look at the shine, Cat. And that chrome grill. It'd be a tiger comin' at you." He could have been talking about either car.

I know we'd never felt this reverent at church. Edwin Bender worked in two holy places.

"Hey, Kitten." Simon playfully tugged at my braids. I hadn't heard him come back. I was too intent on not leaving a trace of myself on the car. "Ready for a ride?"

Ben was the one to answer. "You betcha!"

I opened the sedan's back door and prepared myself for a princess moment. The rich leather scent made me weak in my knees. Suzanne would die of envy.

"No, no, Kitten." Simon tilted his head to the burgundy car. "The coupe. We have a sedan. It's time for something a little more fun." He winked and opened the passenger door. I crawled into the jump seat, giggling the whole time. Ben came around to the passenger side to get in, but Simon handed him the key. "Go ahead and try her out." Then he laughed his big, generous laugh that made you want to forgive anything that had ever happened.

Of course, Ben had nothing to forgive, so he loved the laugh more than I did.

Someone opened the giant door to the showroom and we crept out onto Main Street. Simon laughed some more and took hold of Ben's shoulder. "Don't forget to breathe, son."

Ben's ears got red, but he blew out some air and laughed, too.

We tooled along the highway towards Greensburg. Simon kept telling Ben to put his foot into it so he could see what the car would do. I don't know why he thought he needed to encourage a teenage boy to drive faster, but I know Ben loved the excuse. I know, too, that both of us were hoping to beat the band we'd see someone we knew so Ben could honk and wave and make them wonder what in the world we were doing in a fast and fancy car like that Oldsmobile Club Coupe. But we didn't see anyone we knew. When we got to Greensburg, Simon bought us all pie and ice cream. It was the one time in my life I would have rather been in a car, but I politely thanked him and ate it because that should have been the treat in itself.

Simon let Ben drive back to Sweethome, too. When we got back to the car place, Simon finally got behind the wheel of the coupe and had Ben drive his other car back to the farm.

"You're keeping the other sedan, too?" I could hear the confusion in Ben's voice. Why in the world would anyone need two cars *and* a farm truck? Especially since I thought Ethel couldn't even drive.

"Something for church on Sunday." Simon smiled and shrugged a shoulder. "But a man's gotta have a little fun Monday through Saturday."

I wanted to ride back in the coupe, but I wanted to ride back with Ben. I hesitated a moment longer than was safe.

"Come on, Kitten." Simon patted the front seat of the coupe, making my decision for me. "Don't you want to ride in the front seat?"

What could the risk be in broad daylight?

Simon stopped by the bank for a few minutes and then the post office and the mill. I waited in the car each time while he finished his business. Restless adrenaline fingers marched up my back and neck. I kept watching for somebody who'd see me sitting in this rich man's car, but nobody I knew ever came to town on a Wednesday morning.

"What do you think, Kitten?" Simon asked when he climbed in the car for the drive home. "You like the car?"

We were too close. I nodded, sincere but nervous.

"Nothing like that new-car smell." He breathed in deeply.

I smiled and nodded again.

He shifted a couple of times then reached over and squeezed my neck. He left his hand on the seat back while we drove back to the farm. His fingers dangled over my right shoulder and kept brushing the skin just above my bosom. I leaned forward in my seat, like I was eager to see out the window, but that was a mistake, too, because instead of leaving his hand on the seat back, he squeezed my neck again and slowly rubbed my back. Angled forward like I was, it gave him a chance to drop his hand all the way to the seat and my rear end. His fingers spread over my right hip and tightened ever so slightly.

The day might have been a hundred and five degrees, but that wasn't what made me sweat. I couldn't look him in the eye. I watched each telephone pole pass and prayed we would turn into the Yoder lane and not drive past. He could make up an excuse to check the fields or another farm. We could drive for hours, his hand on my body, his fingers getting tighter or finding other places to go where they didn't belong.

The folks in Detroit saved my life, though, because he finally had to take his hand away and shift. I pushed my lower back firmly against the seat but still hunched my shoulders forward. I couldn't keep him from still touching my body parts, but he would have to be more deliberate. He couldn't be so casual about it.

I don't know why I thought this would make a difference.

"Wouldn't it be fun to take a road trip to Colorado in this, Kitten?" His fingers found my neck again. This time he rubbed it gently, like he was distracted and didn't realize he was doing this very intimate thing.

I'd never been to Colorado, even to visit my cousins there. Any other time, to think of going there would be the same as dying and going to heaven, but I couldn't ride for two hundred miles worrying about hands and hips and fingers and bosom. And I would have to be able to breathe so I could think.

I said, "I'd like to go on the train sometime."

I should have said, *Yes, but not with you in the car.* That would have seemed outrageously rude though.

Isn't that bizarre?

My body stayed stiff as a board. If he had looked at my chest, he would have seen my heart thumping. I only had jumbled thoughts. If he didn't turn in his lane, I would have to jump. Four telephone poles to the turn. Three. Two. I fingered the door handle, ready to break a leg if that's what it meant. At the final moment, he took his hand away and downshifted for the turn.

Ethel actually had dinner on the table when we arrived. Simon patted her rear end but she didn't smile or jerk. I wondered if her heart pounded in the same way mine did when his fingers touched her.

I could hardly eat.

Simon and Ben kept talking car talk all during dinner—engines, cylinders, transmissions, bumper guards, driving lights, fenders. You'd think the whole world revolved around that coupe. Ethel and I sat silent. I wondered if my lips were pinched together like hers.

While Simon and Ben were drinking their coffee, the phone rang. Dad wanted Ben to come home with them after prayer meeting. The wheat—spotty as it was—was finally ready to harvest.

"I'll take you home on Friday evening, Kitten. Your mama says she can get the harvest meals around without you till then."

Those adrenaline fingers started marching again. The afternoon dragged miserably long. After supper, I begged off from going to prayer meeting, which was reasonable since I truly had a stomachache by then. I went to bed early, trying my hardest to be asleep when Ethel and Simon got home. The cicada orchestra played for the crickets, and the animals rustled in the barn. The night seemed so ordinary to them. Hours earlier than it should have, Simon's car crunched over the gravel on the lane. Car doors slammed. No voices, but Simon whistled the chorus to "Marvelous Grace."

I lay still, absolutely still as the night and prayed that I was wrong about Simon Yoder. Ethel came upstairs first. I heard the toilet flush and her door close. A while later, I heard Simon on the steps. He'd stopped whistling. My door opened. A sharp slice of hall light cut across my eyes, but I didn't open them.

"Kitten?" Simon whispered softly. When I didn't answer, he crept in and quietly closed the door. My body tingled.

He stayed wordless and soundless, but he came closer until I sensed him standing next to my bed. My bed in his house. I could hear him breathing. I wondered if he could smell my fear. Moments before I felt his lips on my cheek, I felt his fingers stroke my breast. My breast in his bed in his house.

I jolted away, banging his nose in the process. Supper swirled in my stomach.

"What are you doing?" I growled.

"Kitten, Kitten," he said softly. "I just wanted to make sure you were feeling okay."

I didn't say anything, but I tried to get smaller as I shrunk farther back on my bed and held the covers close. I'd had hours and hours to gather up my courage. In a single sentence, I used it all: "I don't think so." We both knew what I meant.

He reached out and brushed the hair from my forehead. His hand flowed down over my cheek and my breast again and stopped a moment. I jerked back again and sucked in a noisy breath. I still didn't say anything.

"I don't want you to misinterpret my concern for you. You feel like a daughter to me. I'm not going to hurt you, Kitten." He leaned into the bed farther and kissed my forehead. "I always kissed my girls goodnight. And I miss that. You understand that, don't you?"

I shook my head. He couldn't see me in the dark, but he could feel the shake.

His giant hand slipped under the covers and fumbled around on my stomach. I could feel him sliding his fingers under the elastic of my panties. "No. Please. Don't." I knocked out the words and tried to push his hand back. His breath left a hot streak on my cheek and his lips covered mine. They were wet and tasted like baking soda and he wouldn't stop.

"Don't!" I choked it out, but his lips muffled the words and his fingers kept fumbling and fumbling.

Out in the hall, a light snapped on and the bathroom door clicked shut.

Simon stopped. He waited until the bathroom door clicked again and the light disappeared. I took his hesitation and dug my fingernails into the back of his hand.

"Don't!" I growled one more time.

And then he left.

I don't know when I finally fell asleep. In the dreams of my aching night, I dreamed of Dess, Dess with wings and shadows. I envied her wings. I knew her shadows.

 CHAPTER 10

ONCE AGAIN, I DIDN'T KNOW how to act around Simon the next morning. I knew now, though, that he wouldn't act any different because he was the same man he'd been yesterday and the day before.

As a good Mennonite girl, I was better steeped in expectations than recourses: I was expected to be respectful and obedient. I was also expected to stand up to wrongdoing, but the wrongdoing we talked about in Sunday school taught me not to throw a punch, cheat in school, or steal a loaf of bread, none of which I was inclined to do in the first place. Very impractical stuff, but very safe. None of our Sunday school lessons prepared me to stand up against wrong if it meant being disrespectful to an adult. At least if we'd covered that lesson, I must have been sick that Sunday.

I certainly felt sick now. For the next two days, I walked around with beady eyes, dreading the night on Thursday and dreading the ride home on Friday. Whenever Simon came in the room, I positioned myself so I couldn't get cornered. But he only winked at me and sat at the table reading.

Ethel pretty much stayed holed up in her room, coming out in the morning only to tell me to pull the shades in the parlor to keep the light out and the heat from coming in. But it was a pointless thing to do since the heat didn't need to see. It just came in anyway.

Thursday night, I wedged the rocking chair under the door handle and slept with my eyes open. The handle didn't move and the house fell into quiet night noises. Friday morning, Simon wasn't around. Ethel said he'd gone into Dodge and not to plan on him for dinner. So then I had to worry all day long that somehow he wouldn't get home in time to take me home and I'd have another nervous night. Ethel was no help at all. She just frowned and lumbered around on her stick ankles. Since I was finally more or less caught up with the housework, I spent the day in the garden, trying to salvage what I could and wondering if Dess had planted the beans.

In the way that gardening makes you do, I started thinking about how if it weren't for Simon and Ethel, this wouldn't be a bad job.

The heat mostly just sat that day. It didn't move because for once there wasn't any wind. Without the wind, it just draped itself over me and the beans and the cows. The cows and I were all a little irritable, pressed in like we were on all sides by the muggy air. The stench from the barnyard sat there too. The cows looked oblivious to the odor, like they were pretending they didn't have a clue it was there, let alone that they'd caused it. I could hardly think of eating anything out of that brown garden since it surely seemed like the vegetables would taste like the air around them smelled. So even this time in the garden was spoiled for me, the one place where I should have felt fifteen minutes of contentment and couldn't.

Simon returned midafternoon with smiles and a present for me from Hartley Brothers Department Store. He tugged at my braids before I could get out of the way and said, "It's nothing. I just saw it in the store window and thought a girl like you ought to have something nice once in a while."

Aside from the little box of chocolates Simon had left for me the previous week, I'd never in my entire life had a store-bought present, but then I'd also never gotten a present when it wasn't Christmas. Even then, Dad and Mama gave me only small things—a handmade doll, an orange, a candy cane, hand-knitted socks.

Simon gave me a blouse, pretty and pink. I'd never owned anything so soft and delicate, so I felt really sad. "I can't take that," I said. I'm still no good at social graces.

"Of course you can take it, Kitten. It's a gift."

"But I can't keep it." If he required the distinction, I'd lay it out for him, plain and blunt.

But Simon insisted, "Of course you can keep it, Kitten."

Forget subtleties when what I really needed was a baseball bat.

"How would I explain to my parents that you bought me a present?" It was my most polite way of asking, *You sick old man, how would I explain to my parents* why *you bought me a present?*

"We'll just tell them the truth. That you've been doing such a good job and I wanted to show my appreciation. It's the same reason I bought the hoop and basketball for Ben and why I've been giving him an extra dollar a week. He's saving it all to go to college. Course, we don't want to tell your folks that. That's just our little secret."

Of course.

Like a crafty spider, Simon spun an intricate web with ephemeral threads so fine that until the strands trapped you in a sticky tangle, you didn't even know you'd been caught.

I packed the blouse with my other things but knew I'd never wear it, the most expensive and prettiest thing I owned.

I stared out the window the whole way home, not even wanting to make small talk. We drove the sedan, which was just fine with me because the front seat was as big as a wheat field. He'd have to stop the car and lean way over to touch me with his poisonous fingers.

"I probably shouldn't have told you about the extra money to Ben, Kitten, but I know you can keep a secret."

Out of the corner of my eye, I could see him looking at me. I didn't acknowledge him, concentrating instead on the burgeoning hedgerows that lined the dusty road. Hundreds of sullen black crows dotted the trees, probably as sorry as we were that the harvest didn't look any better.

As we turned onto our road, we could see the dust pillowing behind Dad's thresher. He and the rest of the harvest crew would be out in the field until the last of dusk settled into dark. They'd be up and working again before the sun set fire to the horizon.

Before the car came to a complete stop, I jumped out, suitcase in hand. I didn't look back. I didn't say thank you for the ride. I didn't even shut the car door. That was as close to a bold statement as I was going to get, but I didn't think Simon would bother to read that one.

Mama appeared at the screen door on the summer porch and watched, her hands wrapped in her bib apron as she cleaned them off from whatever she had been doing. Simon stood out under the big cottonwood, hands on his hips, his hat pushed back to let his forehead breathe. The car purred in neutral, making its own statement in case Simon wasn't being clear enough. Mama stepped out the door about the time I reached the house.

"Everything okay?" she asked me, edgy-like, as I passed her. I appreciated her uncanny vision, but what could I say? So I didn't say anything.

Simon didn't chitchat with Mama. It wouldn't have been appropriate to talk with her long since Dad wasn't around. So he handed her our pay for the week, passed on Ethel's greetings as he climbed back into the car, and left, meeting his own cloud of dust before it could settle.

Mama stood in the yard for a few minutes under the rattling cottonwood. I saw her look at the money, then stuff it into her apron pocket. She turned and waved flies away as she walked back to the house. The barnyard cats ran after her momentarily like she might throw some food scraps their direction. What a strange relationship we had with animals in those days. They never sat on our laps in the house.

"Everything okay?" she asked me again when she came into the kitchen. She had the rotating fan on, but it only pushed the hot air around faster. Nothing got cooler.

I shrugged my shoulders. I wanted to talk to Mama, but I didn't know the place I could begin where she would understand. No one talked about such things back then, so we didn't know the words to use. I didn't know the medical terms, and I certainly didn't know the vulgar ones. If Simon had been a thirteen-year-old boy and had kissed me exactly when and how I wanted, I still wouldn't have been able to say the words *Simon kissed me*. This only added to my agony.

So instead, I picked some roses for the table, then helped Mama finish getting supper on. Tired like she was, she didn't talk much either. She wanted to, though. She kept taking in a breath like a person does just before launching into an important sentence, but then she'd set her jaw and just let out a sigh. I should have helped her out and just blurted something.

Nor did we feel much like talking at supper that night. The men who'd helped harvest all day had washed up and headed home, glum that our wheat crop was turning out so poorly, and theirs, they knew, would be no better. It would be another year of corn-mush breakfasts and wishful thinking.

By this point in the decade, we all knew not to talk about the obvious, but sometimes Mama just couldn't help herself. "Did the wheat look any better this afternoon than what you cut this morning?"

Ben flinched a little.

Dad's lips twitched, but he didn't form any words with them. He just snorted softly. Now that Ben and I were both beyond the age of whipping, no one ever hit anyone in our house, which was a good thing because I think Dad had times, like tonight, when he would have felt better if he could have smacked someone. Instead, he just looked mean at Mama, like somehow it was her fault the rains never came.

What a miserable life this was turning out to be. I wished someone had warned me, and I might have passed this round or at least contracted the whooping cough and died young.

"I almost forgot," Mama said and looked at her plate instead of Dad or Ben. "When Simon dropped Cat off, he told me he'd go ahead and pay Ben for the whole week even though he worked just three days. Gave him a fifty cent raise and a quarter raise for Cat, too." She batted some flies away from the potatoes and laid the money out on the table. "You must be doing good work over at the Yoders'." Now she looked at Ben, but she still wouldn't look at me. Mothers just know things sometimes without really knowing what they know. "He said he surely wouldn't want to lose either of you." One would think a mother would smile while she said things like this, but instead she looked confused.

Dad's lips stopped twitching for a moment. He put his fork down and leaned back in his chair. He shook his head—I'm sure in disbelief—and said, "Simon Yoder is a generous man." His lips twitched some more and he looked as close to crying as a man could back then and still be a man. "That extra money is more important than you could know."

In those years, people were so poor that they easily confused an extra fifty or seventy-five cents a week with a generous spirit. It wasn't a generous spirit that made him do it, though. Simon was buying lots of things, and he got them cheap.

By the time I had finished the supper dishes, Dad had already gone to bed, the victim of harvest exhaustion, and Mama was headed there, too. Ben hadn't turned his light off yet, though.

"Wanna watch the moon come up with me?"

He gave a tired smile, and we crawled through his bedroom window onto the roof of the front porch. When we were younger, we'd spent a hundred or a thousand nights out there, sitting on the sun-warmed shingles, our backs against the house.

We sat for a long time in the hot, descending dark, watching the stars poke their way out of the black fabric sky. I kept trying to figure out how I was going to say what I needed to say. Finally, Ben unknowingly opened the door.

"Nights like this, I wonder where Dess is. I wonder if she's looking at the Milky Way right now."

"I don't know where she is, but I at least know why she left."

Ben stiffened slightly but waited. Most people really don't want to know the truth if they think it'll change what they want to believe.

"Simon kissed me."

He looked at me oddly. "What do you mean?"

Funny how "Simon kissed me" didn't seem to me like a sentence that needed to be interpreted, so I didn't. I just repeated it. "He kissed me, Ben. Three times." I dropped my voice to just above a whisper even though I could hear Dad snoring. "And he touched me."

"Where?" He fumbled with his thoughts. "I mean, why? What are you saying?"

I couldn't bear to repeat what I'd just told him. "I'm not going back on Sunday night."

He didn't hear me, though.

"Are you saying you think he might have kissed Dess?"

I didn't respond because what I was thinking at the moment was that no doubt Simon had done that and much more.

165

"I don't believe it." Which meant, *I don't believe* you.

Tears brimmed my eyes.

"That's not what I meant, Cat. What I meant was even if he did kiss her—and I can't believe he did—why would she run off just because of a kiss?"

"Ben. Simon is older than Dad. What if Dad had kissed her?"

Ben cringed. "I don't believe it."

"He kissed me three times and he . . . he touched me. Are you saying I'm lying?"

"Cat, I just don't think it means what it seems. Simon's a lonely man. Look at who he's had to live with all these years."

"Why are you making excuses for him?"

"I'm not."

He was.

"It's just that, well, where would we be without Simon? We would have lost the farm if it hadn't been for his help. We could still lose it with the money Dad owes the feed mill."

Were we that close? I didn't know.

"Half the farmers in Kiowa County would have lost their farms without Simon's help."

"So what did they lose instead?"

A silken moon finally crested the horizon. Out there in the country, far, far away from any electric town lights, it rose big as a house, casting sharply shadowed light over the endless prairie. Night sounds sang to us.

"So. If Dad didn't need the money, would you believe me?"

The lady or the tiger question grew fatter, bigger in the breezeless heat. When Ben didn't answer, I had my answer. We severed the last thick strand in our relationship, one we could never weave together again.

I lay on top of my sheets that night, unable to sleep. The heat rested like a weight on my skin. Sweat prickled my body, making me feel swollen and slow. I was alone and the sense of it overwhelmed me. I had two days to decide what to do. From now until Sunday evening. I could feign illness, but that would only give me an extra day, two at the most.

Up to that point, I'd lived a small life, made smaller by living it in a Mennonite womb. Nothing could help me. And although I wasn't ready yet to lift my wings in flight like Dess, I understood how the day could come.

But the good Lord works in mysterious ways.

Saturday rose, heated and steamy. Midmorning, a few wispy clouds drifted up from the horizon, milling and collecting with a false promise of a quiet afternoon. By the time we took dinner out to the harvest crew, the cottony clouds had begun to puff higher and higher into thunderheads. A baking wind flew across the fields and roads. Like a giant broom, it swept thick chocolate clouds over the house and pelted dust against our windows and doors.

"You gonna be able to finish before it rains?" Mama asked as she opened up blue granite kettles of fried chicken, slaw, potato salad, and rolls. The wind blew past us so hard that if you weren't standing behind some machinery to stop it, you had to turn your head to talk. It just carried away all of our words.

"Doesn't look that way." Dad shouted downwind as he shoveled in some salad. "If we can just get the binder through the field, I can finish shocking the field by myself next week."

By the time Mama and I had the food loaded back into the truck, the thunderheads filled the western sky, crowding out the sun. They grew darker and darker, first ash gray, then the color of tin, then charcoal, and finally the color of sin itself.

"Think we'll have a tornado?" I asked Mama anxiously.

Mama peered nervously out the truck windows and read the clouds. "We could. It's tornado weather."

"Have you ever seen one?"

"Once. Growing up. Took out an old house about a mile from our home place. But just one tornado in my whole life doesn't seem too bad."

"Unless you're in the house it takes." Clarity and courage were about to intersect for a brief moment. "I'm not going back to Simon Yoder's."

The first fat drops at the front of the storm pinged at our hood.

"What did you say?" She honestly hadn't heard me over the engine noise and the growing wind.

"I said, I'm not going back to Simon Yoder's."

"Why not?" Mama looked at me funny, but she had to have known something like this was coming. "I thought the last couple of weeks had gone better. Simon couldn't rave enough about either of you."

The sky chose that moment to rip open, pouring water so furiously that we could barely see our lane. Mama pulled in and parked under the big cottonwood while we waited for the storm to pass. Lightening strobed over the house and thunder boomed above. But I felt strangely safe.

"Because Simon Yoder isn't what he seems to be. He's all shiny on the outside with his fancy suits and barbershop haircuts. But on the inside, he's sick."

"What are you saying?"

"I'm saying he's creepy. He kissed me. Three times. And he . . . he touched me." I wanted to say where, but I lost my nerve.

We were both shouting by now to hear each other over the vigor of the rushing wind and the pelting rain. The heavy drops gradually turned into frozen pebbles, first pea-size, then marble-size, growing fatter as we watched.

Mama rested her forehead on the steering wheel. "I can't watch. The hail will shred everything."

"Mama," I shouted over the din, "did you hear what I said? Do you understand what I'm saying?"

Like a summer snowstorm, the hail collected on the ground an inch deep, then two. A few egg-size hailstones bounced into the protected circle under the tree. More efficiently than grasshoppers, the hail peeled leaves and petals and produce off of any green thing.

Mama began sobbing. "My roses. My roses." Unlike when the cows died, no one would bring us more roses to tide us over.

Even though clarity remained, courage had traveled beyond the intersection. I couldn't compete with her roses.

I didn't bring up the subject again.

The morning after the storm, the only thing that remained was the thick air, milky white from the humidity and my own stiff resolve that I would never, ever step foot on Simon Yoder's farm again, no matter how I had to do it.

CHAPTER 11

THE SCHMIDTS LIVED IN A time zone that was approximately five minutes behind the rest of the world, so as usual, they slid into their pews just after the first hymn. Suzanne would grow to be an adult and never recognize "Holy, Holy, Holy," our congregation's call-to-worship hymn. That Sunday, she could hardly hold to a whisper, she was so excited.

"We heard from Dess! She's alive!"

"How?"

"She sent us a postcard!"

"Where is she?"

"We don't know. The postcard was postmarked Denver, Colorado, but she wrote she was traveling and by the time we got the postcard, she'd be long gone from there."

Waves of whispered information floated through the pews. Even the amen corner caught the news and shuffled a bit. The rest of the congregation always liked to see them perk up a bit since we could never be sure the row of octogenarians and nonagenarians still had pulses. Brother Paul Shenk, who wanted us to be singing "What a Friend We Have in Jesus," finally stopped and let Henry share the news with everyone firsthand.

I watched Simon and Ethel, actually quite openly. I wanted to see their reaction to this news. But I was disappointed. They appeared as pleased and surprised as their pewmates.

The good news moved Brother Edwin Bender to change his sermon plans and preach on the prodigal son, even though Dess wasn't nearly as prodigal as everyone imagined, and she most certainly hadn't returned. But these details didn't keep Brother Bender from inspiring us all to return to God, even if we didn't think we'd left him.

Details.

The little postcard put color back into Marie's chubby cheeks and a lilt into Henry's step. Even though the lost hadn't actually been found, at least she wasn't dead because dead girls didn't send postcards and Suzanne said it was definitely Dess's writing.

The postcard added another translucent layer to my own situation, although I didn't know if it would work for me or against me.

Dess, naturally, was our dinnertime conversation. The good side to this was that it momentarily took Mama's mind off of her devastated flowers and vegetables and kept Dad from figuring and refiguring how many wheat bushels the hail had destroyed. Granddad and Gramma had come for Sunday dinner like they usually did. Granddad had helped Dad harvest all week and shouldn't have. His leathery skin looked pasty today, almost yellow. Gramma insisted we set a place for Agnes, who once again was nowhere in sight.

"She won't eat much, Rose," Gramma told Mama. "She never does at home at least."

"I was so happy for Henry and Marie! I can only imagine the weight that's been lifted off their shoulders," Mama said when we finally sat down.

"She's not dead, you know," Gramma said.

"No, isn't it wonderful?" Mama talked to Gramma as if she were a child because, of course, that day she was. "Henry and Marie got a postcard from her. She was in Denver, Colorado, of all places!"

"Oh, no," Gramma insisted. "She was fishing over to Beckers'. Agnes and I saw her just last week," she said confidently. Then she turned to the empty plate beside her and asked a true question. "Didn't we, Agnes?" Then turned back to the rest of us. "Agnes thinks maybe it was earlier."

"It was probably earlier, Mutter," Mama said kindly. "I think you fished at Eli Pinkle's pond last week. Remember that big catfish you caught? You told me what a good meal it made for you and Granddad."

"It did indeedy," Gramma said and slipped into German. From the looks on Mama's and Dad's faces, it didn't make any more sense to them than it did to me.

Abruptly, Granddad pushed away from the table, his plate still half full. "I'm going to haf to lie down for a bit." He looked odd, like his body and voice weren't attached to each other. "Don't feel well," he said cryptically.

He made it almost to the sofa before he collapsed, probably crossing over to the land of milk and honey before he hit the floor. Still, we all panicked since it seemed like the most appropriate thing to do.

Dad ran out to start the car while Mama, Ben, and I tried to carry Granddad outside.

Poor Gramma stayed at the table eating and chatting in German to Agnes, who was, as usual when the chips were down, invisible. When we'd finally laid Granddad in the back seat of the car, Mama collected Gramma from the table.

"Clara," Mama said gently, "we think Dietrich has had a heart attack."

"Really?" Gramma said sadly. "He hasn't been feeling well, you know. I told him I thought it was the heat. I told him he'd feel better in October."

"We're going to take him to Doc Sipple's, but we think he's already gone." Mama sounded so calm, so brave. For a moment, I forgave her for not mothering me when I needed her most.

"Will you let me go along?" Gramma asked and started to sob. I think she meant to the Promised Land, not the doctor's house, which was as close as Sweethome came to a hospital. She'd already lived two lifetimes, one in Russia and the other in Kansas. She didn't need a third.

"Of course, Mutter. You'll be a comfort to him."

Ben and I had to stay back because there wasn't room and because they wouldn't have let us beyond the parlor anyway. Even though Ben could drive and sprout periodic chin hairs, the all-knowing medical system still considered him to be a germ-spreading, noise-producing child, just like me.

So the afternoon dragged on and on. I did the dishes while Ben called Uncle Emery's to tell them the sad news. He also called Simon to explain that we probably wouldn't be coming at all this week.

The good Lord does work in mysterious ways. Although, come to think of it, the death of an eighty-year-old man who'd spent his life eating fried chicken, fried bacon, fried beef, fried potatoes, fried onions, and—yes—even fried corn, all ladled with gravy made from fat drippings and pure cream was mysterious only in that Granddad had survived past his wedding night. Back then, cream smothered everything—vegetables, gravies, soups, desserts, cereal, coffee, and eventually hips and bosoms as well. We also tended to cluck about people who died young, young being any age under sixty. We all thought it was from hard work and being poor. Now we know it was because our arteries were as clogged as a ditch of black-eyed Susans and the getting there every bit as pleasurable.

But Granddad couldn't have improved on the timing of his death. As enormously sad as I felt about losing him, this much loved person in my life, it was a mere shadow of the relief I felt at not having to return to Simon's for another week.

Ben and I took rakes, clippers, and bushel baskets and tried to finish cleaning up the hail damage from the day before. Ordinarily, it wasn't a Sunday thing to do to work in the garden like that, but without saying it, we both knew losing her flowers and Granddad, whom Mama loved more than her own father, at the same time would be too much for her to bear. I didn't know when Dad and Mama would return, so I made soup to heat up while Ben did the chores. Then we sat out on the porch swing to watch for them. In final tribute to the good man, the sun set, blazing the horizon and splashing a dozen shades of orange across the sky.

When Mama, Dad, and Gramma finally returned, dusk had settled in, clutching the trees and farm buildings in husky shadows.

"We would have been here sooner, but we had so many people stop by Doc Sipple's." We didn't even need help from the phone-perching Wenger twins. Ben's single phone call would have triggered an avalanche of calls. And whoever didn't get called in the first round would have gotten called in the second round by whomever happened to drive past Doc Sipple's house and see Dad's car there.

I helped Mama put Gramma to bed in Ben's room, where she would live until she died. Ben moved his things into my room, but would sleep on the sofa from now on.

Gramma seemed unusually lucid. "He was such a good man. He wouldn't let me be sad when we got poor. He always said, 'Clara, we may be poor in things, but we're rich in family.' And it was true. Look at how good you've been to us all these years."

Strangely, it was Mama, not I, who was too choked-up to talk. "No, Gramma, we're the lucky ones. Think about Uncle John's and Uncle Jake's families, living way over there in Marion County. They never get to see you like we do."

"I just don't want to be a burden to anyone."

Mama finally found a voice, but it didn't sound like hers. "Nonsense. How could you ever be a burden to us? You're part of us."

"Oh, you'll be good to me, I know," she said and lay back on her pillow. "But Agnes can be such a pill sometimes." She scrunched up her nose and closed her eyes. Her soft snores began before we could turn out the light and close the door.

—≡ CHAPTER 12 ≡—

Since Mennonites didn't drink, we had to dull the edges of our grief some other way. Food wasn't a bad second choice. Whatever we lacked in variety, we made up in quantity and quality. Before we had our breakfast dishes cleared, neighbors and church friends began bringing their sympathy in the guise of pies, cakes, brownies, cookies, dinner rolls, hams, beef and pork roasts, fried chicken, deviled eggs, coleslaw, Jell-O, cuke and onion salad, wilted lettuce salad, garden relishes, pickled everything, and more pies, cakes, brownies, and cookies. There was probably more, but I can't remember. Since the relatives had started arriving, too, the food would all get eaten.

Dad's five sisters and their multi-generations of families started rolling in midmorning: Uncle John's and Uncle Jake's from Marion County, Uncle Hank's and Uncle Abe's from Harper, and Uncle Pete's from Cheraw, Colorado. Of the seven children, only Dad and Uncle Emery had stayed in Sweethome. Dad's five sisters had followed their husbands to the corners of the local Mennonite world and with their wedding vows been magically transformed into no more than an apostrophe-*s* at the end of their husbands' names.

For the more distant cousins, the week would be a party. For Emery's children and Ben and me, it would be a much sadder time since we'd lost a corner of our daily lives.

Midafternoon, the undertaker brought Granddad's body back to our house, where we would hold a vigil for him. The men had cleared a spot in the parlor for the casket, but at the last minute, Gramma insisted Granddad be laid out on the front porch, a not-so-common place for a vigil, but enough cooler that no one argued.

"He loved being outdoors. He should be outdoors now, too."

A wake is an odd custom, really, one that expresses itself in a thousand ways in a thousand cultures. Animals at least understand that when life has left a body, it's dead. It's over. Humans need to hover over the shell longer. All day and all night people sat with the body, and as people are prone to do when they're waiting for a body to get buried, they turned to storytelling.

Though Dad was a man of few words, the rest of his family were all such storytellers that they would begin otherwise purposeless conversation topics just so they could work in "reminds me of a guy I once knew." And of all the family, Uncle Emery told the best stories, even though he began every anecdote with a genealogy. "That's like what Enos Yoder told me just last week," he'd begin. "You know Enos. He married Kermit Yost's oldest girl. Oh, what was her name?"

"Margaret."

"No, Margaret was the second girl. She married Verlin Jantz and moved over to Hutch."

"Oh, that's right. She's the second girl all right. But she didn't marry Verlin. Verlin married that no-good Dodge City girl. Myna something or other. Remember her? Her daddy drank like a racehorse and farmed like a college professor. Inherited everything from his wife's family—those Ewings—then lost it before the ink was dry on the papers."

"Yes, but then Myna passed away from that cancer and Verlin took up with Margaret."

"No!"

"Oh, yes. I thought for sure you knew that. They lived in sin for years before they made it legal. Nearly broke Kermit and Elda's heart." Since Kermit and Elda were the dad and mama, it only made sense that they shared a single heart.

By now, most people would think the original story was buried too deep to ever retrieve. But we're talking about a master of digression. I'd seen him work genealogies through birth orders, ancient deaths, titillating scandals, heathens in Africa, and world war without losing sight of the original kernel. Unfortunately, the original story was rarely as interesting as the gossipy meandering. This was, in part I suppose, because he felt obligated to sanitize his stories for us cousins, but I guess he didn't think we were listening to the conversation offshoots. The other tidbits bloomed with colorful inferences, as well as the occasional outright "Whoa, Nelly!" revelation. So I always listened patiently and quietly, like a lizard waiting for a fly.

That night, out on the porch in the color bath of the sunset, Uncle Emery began his tales.

"Couple of years ago, I sat at the wake of Ruth's cousin Harvey Plett. You know, he come from those Pletts that used to be up by Inman. Fred and Fern's boy."

Heads nodded. No genealogy needed here, apparently.

"Harvey was the kind of kid who wasn't brought up, he was dragged up. He'd lived a hard life, yessir. Way before Prohibition, Fred used to make communion wine with all the grapes they grew. Heavy, syrupy stuff. Course when

Prohibition came along, all us good Mennonites obeyed our government and gave up sin for good." He tilted his head at the row of us cousins lined up on the porch rail. "Or at least we gave up *that* sin. Anyways, Harvey used to sneak hisself into that wine and wouldn't come up for air till Tuesday. He drank like a Lutheran, he did. Always said Fred and Fern must have adopted him."

By now a few coyotes had begun crooning to us. The bullfrogs joined in and croaked along in a deep, arrhythmic song.

"Anyways. Trouble seemed to always find him. He liked to play a good practical joke. He'd drop a chicken in the hole of an outhouse and surprise the ladies. Or he'd grease the doorknob inside the schoolhouse and yell, *Fire!* After a while, when trouble got tired of looking for him, Harvey started goin' out lookin' for trouble.

"He started running with those Benton boys. You know those Benton boys. Their daddy used to pick up—"

One of the aunts, probably Lydia, cleared her throat.

Uncle Emery paused a moment and scratched his head. "Yessir. But those Benton boys are another story." The unfit tale narrowly—and disappointingly—averted, he rolled back into his original story. "Anyways. Harvey began running with those Benton boys. They started smoking cigarettes and drinking beer and pickin' fights and carousing till all hours of a Saturday night. His mama still made him come to church on Sunday, but oh, would he have a nasty attitude. He finally got hisself into enough trouble that he got hauled up in front of the judge. It had something to do with some girl. I don't know what it was, but the judge musta thought it was bad enough that he gave him a choice of either going to jail or joining the Army."

It seemed we were oceans away from the original story Uncle Emery had set out to tell, but he let out a little more line.

"Well, you can imagine how ol' Fred and Fern musta felt. They was just heartsick. Just heartsick. Fern told the family she'd rather see him rot in jail where every murderer at least knew he was a murderer instead of the Army where every murderer thought he was a hero.

"Course, Harvey didn't see it that way. All he wanted out of life anyways was a little adventure, which in Kiowa County was about as easy to find as a New York Rockette."

Aunt eyebrows lifted all over the porch, but Uncle Emery just kept on talking. "Musta been just before the Great War, in '13 or '14. Anyways, Europe was heating up and it looked like we was gonna be joinin' in soon. It was every eighteen-year-old Catholic boy's hope to get hisself into the fray. Some of the Mennonite boys hoped about it, too, just not out loud. Anyways, Harvey worked his way over to Europe and landed in one of those trenches that you read about. You know the ones, where there ain't no atheists."

He stopped talking for a moment, maybe to pick through the story to make sure it was sanitary enough for the youngest cousins. The last trickle of daylight settled on us, giving Uncle Emery paler-than-life skin. No one had bothered to turn on the porch light. The moon would be up soon enough anyway. No point in wasting the Delco batteries.

"When he finally came home, the boy had changed. Every boy that goes over to war and does some killing comes back a little sideways, but Harvey, he was real twisted. You could see it in his eyes and the way he would nervously look over your shoulder when he was talking to you, like he could see something—or someone—you couldn't. I asked him once what he was always looking at."

Uncle Emery took Ben, who was sitting just in front of him, by the arm and pulled him within inches of his face. He softened his voice to just above a whisper, drawing all of his listeners closer, too. Not even the youngest cousin twitched for fear of missing a word. At the moment, I was deeply regretting my perch on the porch rail and my vulnerable back.

"'I'm seeing all those men I killed,' he says. 'They just keep showin' up. Lately, one fella in particular keeps following me. Emery,' he says to me, 'you wouldna believed how awful it was over there. They was just boys like me. They had mamas and girlfriends. Maybe they even lived on farms. But the sergeant would shout, and we'd scramble outta our trenches and dodge our way across the barbed wire and landmines and whizzin' bullets until we either died or fell into the German trenches. I dunno which was worse. And there we'd fight 'em hand to hand. We'd touch 'em and they was real people. Real flesh and blood. And they cried when you stuck your bayonet in their guts or blew them apart.' And then he said it again: 'They was real people we was killing over there. Not just some Krauts.'

"Imagine that. He was a grown man when he told me this and he was cryin' like a child. Then he told me, 'Emery, the one who keeps following me had a little baby boy. I know 'cause I knocked his helmet off when I was tryin' to kill him before he killed me. Inside he had a photograph of a boy, maybe a year old. On the back someone had written *Komm nach Hause, Papa.* Come home, Papa.'"

Uncle Emery loosened his grip on Ben's arm. He took out his bandana and mopped his face even though we sat in the coolest moment of the day. My insides jiggled nervously.

"'*Come home, Papa.* That soldier hadn't done nothing to me,' Harvey says. 'I didn't have no reason on Earth to kill him. None. What'd he ever done to me? And now some little boy don't have no daddy because some German Kaiser got his nose in a snit about something or other and sent off a couple million of his best men to show no one could push him around.'

"I didn't see Harvey much after that. He lived with Fred and Fern on the old home place and just stopped coming into town, even for church. Some of his old buddies would go out now and then. Musta been taking him some hooch when they went because Fred told me once that he didn't think Harvey had a sober day from about '22 or '23 on. I s'pose Fred and Fern must have thought that was a easier way to let go a life. Harvey died, oh, musta been in about '31 or '32."

"September '33," Aunt Ruth said.

"That's right. We was in the middle of an Indian summer, and it was hot enough for the chickens to hard-boil their eggs just by sitting on them. Fred came over about nine o'clock one night and said he needed some help laying Harvey out. The Pletts—none of them didn't have no money and couldn't pay to have the body properly embalmed, so they was gonna try to get the body in the ground the next day, early."

I felt a twinge of sadness as I realized that Uncle Emery had finally found his way back to the kernel of his story.

"I took the truck into town and woke up Buster Toobs, who ran the ice plant back then, and picked up a load of ice to keep the body chilled. By the time I got back to the Pletts, Fred had rounded up a few of the family and a couple of other neighbors. We laid him out in a makeshift casket out on the front porch, just like where we are tonight. Someone had put Fern to bed because she couldn't do nothin' but cry. Fred sat out on the porch with us, sobbin' like a baby about all the things they musta done wrong to that boy. None of us said nothin' because all of us coulda made different choices when Harvey was makin' his, but we didn't, so it was hard to blame Fred and Fern for where Harvey ended up."

Uncle Emery paused again to mop his face. A couple of owls fluttered into the cottonwoods, hooting their presence.

"Anyways. There was maybe a half dozen of us sitting there with the body and with Fred. You could feel a little coolness near the casket because of all the ice blocks around the body. Every now and then, one of us would sop up the melted ice around the body so it wouldn't be covered in water by morning. I sopped it up myself a couple of times and I know the others did, too, because we talked about it later. It woulda been an ugly job with any body, but with Harvey, it was even worse. Fern had tried to clean him up after he died, but he had so many years of grit under his fingernails and on his skin that you coulda soaked him in lye and he still woulda looked and smelled like a wet chicken.

"About four in the morning, Fred finally fell asleep. The other men and I kept sopping water out of the casket and thinking about what we mighta said or done to our own children to sour them. There was no moon that night, but there was swarms of birds, black as midnight that swooped over us and around the yard. Ravens, I think. Couldn't tell for sure in the dark, but you could hear 'em winging wildly. They'd settle then spook, settle then spook for no reason.

"We had a gas lamp since the Pletts didn't have no Delco system back then. Just before dawn, the lamp went out. It was funny because we hadn't paid much attention to it since those things usually burn a long time. So there we was in the pitch black, the ravens spooking and swooping and us soppin' up the water. And then, as God as my witness, we heard a couple of fellas talking German. Their voices were low and faint, so we couldn't make out the words, but they sounded like they was just on the other side of the yard, headed out to the road."

Uncle Emery fell silent, but he lifted his hand to let us know he wasn't done yet. Even the cicadas stopped singing for a moment while we waited for Uncle Emery to continue. I desperately wanted to slip off the porch rail and put my back against something. Anything.

"It was German. There was no question about that. There we sat, six grown men so scared we couldn't breathe. Finally, the barnyard started to stir, so we knew daylight wouldn't be long in coming. Still, we sat there, not moving, waiting for the light. It was my turn to sop up the melted ice, but at that moment I wasn't about to stick my hand in the coffin of a dead man until I could see what I was doing. Finally, the first light shot over the eastern sky, and we could begin to see more than just shadows and shapes.

"I stood up to reach into the coffin, and there on Harvey's chest was a photograph of a little boy, maybe a year or two old. I turned over the photo. On the back someone had written, *Komm nach Hause, Papa.* Come home, Papa."

We didn't stir, not one of us, except to move our eyeballs to peek at Granddad lying so white and powdery in his casket. Finally, Aunt Ruth broke the silence.

"I'll tell you what was strange about Harvey, too. They buried him in the church cemetery even though he hadn't showed his face there in a decade. For years afterward, I dunno, maybe even now, that corner of the cemetery stank. Couldn't get grass to grow on his grave either. Still can't."

"Well, if they didn't embalm him—"

"Oh, but they did then," Aunt Ruth said. "I think Simon Yoder heard they didn't have the money and offered to help out. That's why the stench was such an odd thing."

At the mention of Simon Yoder's name, I tensed. I know I did because my cousin Ruby looked at me funny.

"Now why would Simon Yoder pay for Harvey's embalming?"

"He's a generous man. If it hadn't been for Simon Yoder, half the church would have lost their farms in the last decade. That man's forgiven more debt than all of our worth put together."

"Yeah, but didn't he have some connection to the Pletts? Wasn't he a cousin once-removed to Fern's daddy or something?"

"Naw, I don't think he had any Plett in him."

Another genealogy ensued as the aunts and uncles tried to untangle the complicated noodle bowl of Mennonite bloodlines. If nothing else, Mennonites understood all those begat chapters in the Bible.

Finally, someone remembered a suitable explanation for Simon's generosity. "Didn't one of Fred and Fern's girls use to work for Simon?"

"Now that I think about it, a couple of them did. Bertha and Lorraine."

"No, it was Lorraine and Millie. Bertha worked for the Landises."

"You know, I think Harvey worked for Simon a summer or two as well."

"Well then, Ezra," Uncle Emery concluded and clamped a friendly hand on Dad's shoulder. "Looks like you've got half the family's funeral costs covered. Lucky man." I could see a small smile on Dad's face, but Mama's silhouette twitched in the moonlight.

Not long after this, the second generation shooed the third generation off to bed because as Aunt Irene pointed out, there's nothing worse than a cranky child at a funeral. Even though I could think of at least a hundred things worse, I really didn't mind. The best stories had already been told.

As tired as I was, I wasn't sleepy. Six of my girl cousins spread out on my floor and fell asleep after only a few minutes of whispering about the trustworthiness of Uncle Emery's storytelling. The younger ones believed it emphatically. The older ones wanted to believe it as well.

I could hear the murmurings of the adults but couldn't make out any words. Eventually, only two or three would remain by the body until sunrise. This time tomorrow, both Granddad's shell and his spirit would finally be at rest. My own demons would return then, but for tonight at least, I could sleep.

CHAPTER 13

THE PETERS FAMILY HAD DUTIFULLY been fruitful and multiplied and would easily fill half the church by itself, so people knew to get to the funeral early so they wouldn't have to stand outside in the heat and not hear anything. We gathered in the church basement and listened to the wordless shuffling above us. In the tiny kitchen, church ladies busily organized platters of everything—zwieback and sliced ham, relishes, and sweets—for the funeral lunch that would follow.

Since he was the oldest child, it fell to Uncle Emery to queue us up: first Gramma, who thankfully had left Agnes at home to tidy up, and then Great-Aunt Hulda, Granddad's only living sibling, then the children and spouses by their birth order, and finally the five dozen cousins and their spouses and offspring—still plenty fruitful and multiplying, just not as jackrabbit-fast as their parents' generation.

We filed in row by row pretty flawlessly, except for the awkward shuffling around Velma Mae Amstutz, who had established squatter's rights to her pew somewhere around the Great War when she'd landed on that bench in her sixties. Nothing, not weddings, funerals, special choirs, or visiting dignitaries, budged her from two feet in on the third pew. No one could talk her into taking the leap to the amen corner, to which she was entitled at her age, because she complained the other old ladies snored and she didn't think that was very reverent. Now that she was firmly entrenched in her eighties, she couldn't see, hear, or chew, which meant we could always count on her to bring the soft foods—clear Jell-O or applesauce— to potlucks since she could still at least gum.

The funeral itself went about like these things usually do. Aunt Lydia gave a sweet and tender eulogy. Brother Bender, as always, found the funeral to be the perfect occasion to give an altar call. Mostly, though, we sang hymns about going home.

At the end of the service, the whole congregation filed row by row past Granddad in his coffin and paid their last respects. As sad as the service had been for me, I could hardly watch Gramma. She seemed so small and confused as she peered into the coffin then looked up at Uncle Emery, who held her arm. "He's gone now, isn't he,

Emery?" she said sadly, as though finally understanding the last several days' activity.

Uncle Emery gently patted her and whispered something soft in German.

At the graveside, we all tried to gather under the canopy and out of the mean Kansas sun. Once more, we sang going-home songs, like "Blessed Assurance" and "Shall We Gather at the River," and endured another Brother Bender altar call, this time in his seven-minute prayer. If none of us ended up in the gloryland ourselves, it wasn't because we'd never been invited. Finally, the pallbearers lowered the casket into the grave, and it was over. Well, not really over because we would carry the kind of person he was with us forever.

The adults began drifting back to the church basement for the funeral lunch and to revive themselves with tea so sweet you could nearly substitute it for maple syrup on pancakes. The younger cousins pulled us older cousins out of the funeral flock.

"Where's Harvey Plett's grave?" one of the little Colorado cousins demanded. "We want to smell that awful grave." She giggled uncontrollably until an older sibling shushed her. At least she didn't wet her pants.

"Where is it?"

"Help us find it, Cat."

"We want to see if it's true."

Like little mice, they swarmed and chattered all over the cemetery, checking out each headstone while being careful not to walk on the graves themselves. No one wanted to badger the dead since they could rise up and haunt you for disturbing their peaceful slumber.

Cemeteries are creepy places when you think about it. Each little plot has its own story to tell, of immense sadness or maybe relief or anger.

We wandered for five or ten minutes in the baking June sun looking for the Plett family before Delvin Hedrick— who wasn't even old enough to read—finally spotted it.

"I sniffed until I found it and then I looked for a *P*. Shore enough, there weren't no grass on it neither," he announced proudly.

My back tingled as I smelled the faint sour odor. None of the graves had much grass—after all, this *was* Kansas in June, and it *was* 1937, but Harvey's grave was totally bare of anything green, not even sticker patches or brown sticks of pasture grass, which had survived even the Dust Bowl.

"Oh, my!" one of the older cousins whispered.

Like a flock of startled crows, we turned en masse and fluttered frantically to the church. All through lunch and the rest of the afternoon, we giggled nervously about what we'd seen and smelled until no-nonsense Aunt Irene finally marched into the cemetery and pronounced the smell to be rotting ragweed from a nearby ditch. She never did come up with a good explanation, though, as to why the smell was so much stronger over Harvey's grave than his neighbors'.

When we finally returned to our place, Dad and his siblings decided that, yes, Gramma would live with our family. I hadn't realized there would even be a discussion about it since we seemed like such a logical solution, but Mama told me later that before they could sleep that night, the others had to do some guilty wrangling about why they couldn't keep Gramma. If Gramma sensed that her children, who had truly loved her when she was still with them in body *and* mind, no longer had the spirit to care for her now, she didn't show it. So I think she didn't know, or she would have told everyone what Agnes thought about the situation.

By Thursday, the last of the relatives left. In a few weeks, after harvest ended, the siblings would return to help sort through the decades of living on Granddad and Gramma's farm. But for now, it was just the five of us at the supper table, six with Agnes.

Six and all those demons I faced. For four days, they'd stayed in the shadows, but no more.

Unexpectedly, Mama raised her head and saved me.

"I'm going to need Cat here at home to help with Mutter," she announced matter-of-factly as we helped ourselves to the last of the funeral food at supper.

Ben wouldn't look me in the eye, but he said, "You're going to need some help, Mama."

But Dad just scoffed. "Nonsense."

Gramma brightened a little and said, "Why what a splendid idea. Agnes," Gramma said and turned to the empty plate beside her, "Cat will be able to take us fishing every day. Just think of it!"

Dad couldn't believe he'd been ambushed so quickly, but he couldn't think of a single clever thing to say, so he had to say, "Nonsense!" again.

Mama was done with the subject, though. We rarely saw her stand up to Dad, so even if she hadn't just rescued me, this would be a memory that would stay with me forever. Don't misunderstand me. My mother was not a spineless reed who swayed whatever direction Dad told her. She was a bright, capable woman who had the misfortune of being born into an era where a man would refer to the family farm as "my farm" even though his wife worked along side him from dawn to the moment she collapsed into bed, cooking, cleaning, laundering, choring, planting, and harvesting. Men back then always said, *I* this and *I* that. It wasn't that they didn't love their wives—although they probably defined love differently than we do now—they just had trouble with pronouns.

Dad fumbled around the rest of the week trying to bring up the subject and let it be known that his word was still the final word, maybe the only word in our house. But Mama earned her flamingo feathers that weekend and wouldn't back down. Gramma cooperated and seemed particularly disoriented. Or maybe she'd been this bad and Granddad had managed to protect us from seeing it. But I think the final event that nudged Dad's heels out of their tar came on Sunday morning when I came down ready for church in the pretty pink blouse Simon had given me. Even Dad noticed it was something new and out of the ordinary.

"Where'd that come from?" He asked it pleasantly. Innocently.

"From Simon Yoder," I said as casually as I could, even though my heart galloped.

Dad's face took on a strange look. "Well, that surely was nice of Ethel to buy that for you."

"Ethel didn't buy it for me. Ethel probably doesn't even know or care that I have it." I looked Dad in the eye and said it again. "Simon gave it to me."

The strange look on Dad's face grew stranger. He told me to go change my clothes and get in the car or we'd be late for church. All in one breath.

Mennonites truly hate violence. A natural outcome of this is that we also tend to hate conflict and sometimes confuse them as the same thing. This is especially true because sometimes it seems that the only solution to conflict is violence, but violence is really just the result of a stunted imagination. So it should come as no surprise we all felt agitated along with the rest of the world as we watched the rooster Hitler scratch and preen for more *lebensraum*. Living space. In spite of his anxiety-producing tactics, the nasty little dictator continued to have an aura about him though.

"It's not that I like how he's treated the Jews, but you have to admit he's performed miracles in Germany," I overheard Roy Friesen say to a small gathering of men after church that Sunday. Roy had been poor for so many years that you could hardly blame him for overlooking a little aggression in the formula for improving the national economy.

"Seems like he could have improved the economy without going into the Rhineland, though, doesn't it? Or Austria?" I overheard my dad say. He usually listened more than he talked.

Simon chuckled, maybe a touch patronizingly. But he didn't know he'd made a mistake. "Have to take the good with the bad sometimes."

The other men nodded cautiously, even if they didn't agree. Most people liked being on Simon's side of the fence. Funny how dollar signs hook people in like that.

"No," Dad said firmly. "You have choices. You always have choices, even when you think you don't."

"Well, Ezra," Simon said kindly, "I wish the world were that simple."

"It is," Dad said and walked off to the car.

Everyone probably passed it off as after-funeral blues. Even in the '30s a man had the right to feel grumpy after he'd lost a good Christian father as honest and goodhearted as Granddad. But I knew it was more, and so did Simon. Or at least he figured it out that night after church when Dad told him I wouldn't be going home with him and Ethel.

"He didn't like it one bit," Dad reported as we drove home, "but he finally understood that we needed extra help at home because of Mutter."

It didn't surprise me Dad hadn't confronted Simon. For European leaders and Mennonite farmers alike, righteous indignation can seem perilously close to conflict, and no one wanted to teeter on the edge of that precipice. I have to admit it's more in retrospect that I see the wrongness in not confronting Simon. At the time, though, I felt like I'd climbed into the rifted rock, taking shelter from a storm. I was safe, and I couldn't see beyond my hiding place what—or who else—might be swept away.

═══ CHAPTER 14 ═══

EVEN THOUGH I DIDN'T HAVE to carry that knot around in my stomach anymore, taking care of Gramma, and, by extension, Agnes, was no Sunday-school picnic either. On good days and bad days she wanted to fish. In other summers, she and I would climb into her car and head for anyone's pasture. But since Gramma never could get the hang of driving—even though she'd been driving for decades—the trip always cleared my sinuses. Back when Granddad still had money, he had bought the first Model T in Kiowa County. But just because you could afford a car didn't mean you knew how to drive one. And if you had the first car in the county, there certainly wasn't anyone to teach you. Of course, the older you are, the harder it is to learn something like driving an automobile. It was made all the harder because Gramma'd probably seen no more than a dozen cars in her lifetime when

Granddad got the goofy idea of buying one. It would have been a little like trying to learn Latin in her fifties, without having ever heard or seen the language and doing it without a teacher. Actually, maybe it's not like learning Latin since mangling verb conjugations doesn't carry the same danger as forgetting which pedal is the brake and which one is the accelerator.

Poor Gramma. She was one of those women who just shrank with age. I didn't know sometimes whether she'd die first or just eventually disappear. She'd get behind the steering wheel and, because she was so short, had to look through it instead of over it. Cars were bigger back then and seats were deeper, I guess. Anyway, people could always tell when she was driving because it looked like no one was behind the steering wheel and the car was just gliding along by itself.

They might have been safer if no one *had* been driving it. She never quite figured out the sensitivity of the steering wheel. First she'd drift way over on the right hand side of the road, then jerk it way over to the left. It didn't matter if anyone was coming down the road or not. Anyone we knew had the good sense to just get out of her way. Total strangers learned fast, too, but they usually looked pretty mad about it. They shouldn't have, though; she didn't mean anything by it. Sometimes she'd drive right through the ditches without intending to. Most of the time she'd just drive right back out with nothing more than a little surprised huff: "Ach!" It was a good thing we lived where it didn't rain much.

Even though none of us could see any difference Granddad's departure made on Gramma's driving skills, Dad still wouldn't let her drive anymore. Instead, he thought it was safer for me to have control over the steering wheel. Gramma, Agnes, and I all had a good laugh about that since no one had taught me to drive either. I did have the distinct advantage, though, of being able to see *over* the steering wheel. Of course, I was sitting on a Sears catalog and pillow.

Gramma liked to fish some place different every day. Sometimes we'd fish Willow Creek, but more often than not we'd try a new spot. We'd go to the Bontragers' pasture or the Selzers' or the Weavers', but we usually had the best luck at the Beckers'. We'd leave in the cool of the morning when it was still in the nineties and spend the working part of the day sitting in the steamy shade of a giant cottonwood, perched on three-legged campstools and eating butter-and-onion sandwiches. Gramma never had a fancy rod, only a bamboo pole that cracked under the weight of a dinner-size catfish. Even as old as I was, I sometimes felt restless sitting quietly like that all day. Gramma didn't cotton to any movement though.

"If you're goin' fishin' with me, girly, you got to sit still."

I couldn't ever sit still enough. Sometimes I'd walk along the bank of the creek, swishing the tall grasses. The grasshoppers would arc up and away from me in furious fear. Once in a while, a confused hopper would leap towards me instead of away, its dry, stick-firm body thudding against me. They rattled off the grass, startled by my giant motions. When they landed in the water, they rippled the water across to the other bank. As stupid as the catfish were, they knew the water wasn't supposed to move and wouldn't bite Gramma's worm. That's what she thought anyway. I thought the catfish were so busy scooping up dirt and crawdads off the muddy bottom in self-protection against future frying pans that they weren't going to come topside anyway.

Some days, I'd take a book and just read or nap in the car if I could find a good shade tree to park under. If I parked just right, the open car doors acted like a scoop for the warm breezes and felt like a giant fan. Of course, that would be a giant fan for a blow furnace.

Holy Samolies, were those ever hot and stinky days.

At the end of the day, Gramma would carry her line home and toss the fish in the tub we bathed in to keep them as alive and fresh as she could. It didn't make much difference since an old catfish tasted only marginally worse than a fresh one.

"You'll never guess who stopped by Weavers' pond today," Gramma said at supper one evening. I'd been there the whole day and hadn't seen anyone.

"Tell us who you saw, Mutter."

"Calvin Coolidge," she said emphatically.

"The President?" Mama said. Her mind must have been elsewhere because she actually sounded surprised, like she believed Gramma.

"Yes," said Gramma. "He'd stopped by Edna Weaver's to get a quart of buttermilk, but Mr. Coolidge told me that Edna was fresh out. Agnes asked him what that nonsense was about a chicken in every pot and a car in every garage."

"Mutter, I think that was Herbert Hoover who campaigned on that promise."

"That's what I told Agnes," Gramma said, clearly pleased with herself and surprised to have been right. "I told her Mr. Coolidge's slogan was 'The business of America is business.'"

Sometimes the clarity of Gramma's confusion could almost make you think you could see Agnes. And then there were days that made you want to cry for what we'd lost.

One Friday over supper we were in the middle of yet another conversation about Dess Schmidt when Gramma interrupted us. "Did I tell you I saw Marie Schmidt this week?"

I looked at Mama and shrugged my shoulders.

"Girly, I think you were napping in the car. It was when we were over to Beckers'. She sat down and fished all afternoon with me. Caught the prettiest catfish in the pond. Big she was." Gramma held one hand out from her body, oddly illustrating the length of a giant fish.

"Now what would Marie Schmidt have been doing way over at Beckers' fishing?" Dad asked her politely. We tried not to correct Gramma in her confusion because it only agitated her. But sometimes we tried to help untangle the momentary yarn knot in her memory.

"Well that's what I asked her. And she said she was living with them."

"Marie Schmidt is living with the Beckers?"

"That heathen bunch of monkeys? Lands no!" Gramma scoffed and then giggled.

"Mutter, I think Marie Schmidt lives with her family."

"Yes, that's what I think, too. She lives with them."

We seemed to be confusing her confused state even more, so Dad tried to steer the conversation away from the Schmidts and onto how good Mama's potato crop was that summer, even with all the hail.

"I told her she looked all happy even though she was pleasantly plump," Gramma said to the potatoes, then looked at me. "I didn't want her to feel bad that she'd got herself all fat like that."

"Who's that, Gramma?"

"Marie. Marie Schmidt. Weren't we talking about Marie Schmidt?" she said, sounding like a confused but persistent six-year old. "Agnes just told her right out, 'You look fat, girly. You shouldn't put so much cream in your coffee.'" Gramma was saying this as she poured a half cup of cream into her coffee.

We at least could unravel that knot.

"Poor thing just burst into tears. I felt so bad I told Agnes I wasn't going to talk to her the rest of the afternoon. And I haven't, have I, Kittycat?"

Funny thing was, I didn't think she had. Usually, Agnes was so much a part of our days that she could be real.

"But I'd like to start talking to her again." Gramma said, tearing up a little.

"Of course, Mutter," Mama encouraged gently. "I'm sure Agnes would like that too."

Gramma abruptly got up and left the table, but instead of heading upstairs to her room, she fumbled her way out of the kitchen door and onto the summer porch.

"Mutter," Dad called after her. "Where are you going?"

"Home," she called back. "Agnes and I have visited long enough. We have to get supper on for Dietrich."

She was halfway across the yard before I caught up with her and gently turned her back to the house. "Granddad asked if you could stay with us tonight. He won't be back till late, so you don't need to fix him supper."

It was getting harder and harder to dissuade her when her confusion took a wrong turn. As much work, though, as she was on bad days, I still preferred those to her good days. She missed Granddad so much, which made it harder for all of us to leave him behind.

Summer drifted on towards fall. The elaborate patchwork of field colors shifted from dull green to copper to mahogany as the milo ripened. Ben continued to come home on weekends. If he felt awkward about continuing to work for Simon, or if Simon resented Ben because I didn't come anymore, we never heard or saw it. He no longer played "Simon Says" with us, but he still clearly came home with ideas that weren't any of ours. Questions too.

"What do you think Europe's going to do about Hitler?"

We were sitting at the supper table where I know Dad would have preferred concentrating on his potato soup and not the trouble in Europe, which he claimed was none of our business.

"I don't know, son. They created him, so I guess they'll just have to figure out how to deal with him."

"Do you think he'll go after the Sudetenland next? He keeps badgering the Czechs about all those Germans living there."

"I don't know, son."

"Well, what do you think we *ought* to do if Hitler invades Czechoslovakia?"

"Try to grow some wheat and mind our own business. That's what I think we ought to do."

"So you're an isolationist?" Ben asked a touch triumphantly. What a good-sized word to boot.

Dad thought about it for a while and finally nodded his head. "I might be. What's the alternative?"

Now it was Ben's turn to pause and think—something that doesn't come naturally to most teenage boys. "Well," he said slowly or, more probably, carefully, "when Hitler tried to invade Austria the first time in '34, all it took was for Italy to start mobilizing troops and Hitler backed down."

"So you think the US ought to start mobilizing troops?"

"Maybe." Ben cautiously avoided a full commitment to a heretical opinion.

"I guess I don't understand what's been solved if some dumb Kansas farmer picks up a gun and shoots some dumb German farmer except that there are two less dumb farmers in the world. Maybe you can explain how this would help those folks in the Sudetenland."

"You make it sound so simple, Dad." Ben's subtle condescension positioned him on some slippery mud. "Like it or not, wars have solved a lot of disputes over the centuries—"

"And in the solving, created even more. How do you think Germany ended up with a fella like Hitler in the first place? After the Great War, the war, they said, to end all wars because everyone saw how purposeless it was, England and France wanted to do to Germany like Hannibal did to Alexandra. Remember that story in your history book?"

Ben looked irritated. "He burned the city down then spread salt on the ground so nothing would grow there for ten thousand years."

"That's what Germany's enemies wanted. But they couldn't burn down an entire country and pour salt on the soil, so they did the modern thing and destroyed her economy so she could never rise again. They wanted to humiliate and impoverish her. And they did, which made the country go looking for a man like Hitler."

I think that was more than I'd ever heard him say without taking a nap in the middle.

"Okay, so France and Britain should have been more forgiving of the country that caused the death of millions—what? Almost one and a half million in France alone? They should also have been more willing to overlook the millions of dollars of destruction Germany caused." Ben should have been careful here. His voice had such a sneer. "But they didn't and so here we are now. Since you can't turn back the clock, what are you going to do about Hitler?"

Dad took a long time to answer, making it look like Ben had won this round of the Great Hitler Debate, as it became known between Mama and me. Finally, he stacked his dishes together and pushed them away. He pulled his coffee closer and leaned into his words. " I don't have the answers, Ben, which is one reason I don't go around picking fights. I'm not so sure where war fits into the greater scheme of things, and so it's good I don't have the power to start or stop them. But I suppose if I were Chamberlain or Roosevelt or that Frenchie, Daladier, I'd start with a little more righteous indignation before I'd send my son out to be cannon fodder." In a very rare gesture of fatherly affection, Dad reached over and squeezed Ben's shoulder.

Dad: one; Ben: zero.

The following Saturday night, after a week of Simon talk, Ben began Round Two.

"You know, Dad, I think Europe tried a little righteous indignation when Hitler took over the Rhineland."

"Maybe. But if you ask Britain and France, I think they called it 'appeasement.' Has a different sound to it, doesn't it? Appeasement. Sounds like you're throwing a lamb to a wolf so he'll be happy and leave and never come back."

Ben looked grim. He hated losing, especially when it happened so fast.

"Do you think a wolf would be happy with just one lamb and not ever come back for more?"

Ben didn't answer. The answer was obvious.

"I think that wolf is going to feel pleased as a sweet pickle he's found such a stupid sheepherder. He'll be back for more."

Dad: two; Ben: zero.

"So what does righteous indignation look like?" Ben asked in Round Three. It sounded like a question, but it also sounded like Ben had a pocketful of comebacks prepared.

"Sometimes it looks like embarrassment because you call a spade a spade and the polite thing to do would be to call a spade a rake."

I wondered if that included old men who kissed young girls.

"Sometimes it looks like a sacrifice. Gandhi in India, for instance. You're not old enough to remember the fuss in India when the British started taxing the salt. Must have been around 1930. The poor were so poor that they could hardly afford salt. The tax was just an added insult. Gandhi and his followers marched two hundred miles to the sea to make their own salt. 'From Ahmadabad to the sea.' Doesn't that have a mystical sound to it? 'Ahmadabad to the sea.'"

"I know, I know," Ben said, but he sounded grumpy. "They made their own salt from the sea and eventually the British had to back down. We studied it in school. But the part you're leaving out is that before it was all said and done, the British arrested thousands of Gandhi's followers, so in spite of their best attempts at nonviolence, they still resorted to violence."

"What violence was that?"

I could smell the trap because I knew the story, too. Ben, though, was too intent on winning to pick up the scent.

"The British and the Indians."

Dad shook his head. "That's part of the sacrifice. I'm sure for some of those families, violence would have seemed quicker and easier, but they didn't fight back. It was really fairly clever of them because they used the Brit's own system. They clogged the jails and made a mess of the justice system. But they didn't hurt anyone."

"What about when the Indians marched on the salt mines? The Brits just kept clubbing them. They killed and hurt thousands. If that's not violent, I don't know what is." Ben looked smug but shouldn't have.

"I didn't say nonviolence means no pain or violence. It just means you don't have to be party to it. Since you brought up the salt mine, let's talk about it. Who had the clubs?"

"The Brits," Ben said warily.

"That's right. Who got hurt?"

"The Indians."

"Right again. Did the Indians fight back?"

Ben paused but refused to concede.

"What happened?" Dad asked, having made his point.

"They just lined up and passively marched forward and the British clubbed them away. It was like marching into a meat grinder. How does that kind of sacrifice help anyone?"

"Did the Indians fight back?"

"No," Ben responded, annoyed.

"That's right. They didn't. They marched forward. Every one of them knew that within a few minutes they would be beaten down, maybe even killed. They didn't fight. They didn't struggle. They simply marched forward."

"But the British still control India, so it didn't do them any good. Conflict after conflict followed. The British kept using guns and clubs."

"Oh, but it did make a difference, son. But it's taken a lot of years. The British have given more control over to the Indians. Some day, the Indians will have self-rule. We'll both live to see it. And they'll have done it with great personal sacrifice, but they won't have done it by killing. Nonviolence can change history just as surely as an army tank and rifle."

And so the debate raged, weekend after weekend. I often wondered if it wasn't Dad and Simon who were doing the actual debating since I had the feeling Ben was trying Simon's side of the argument out on Dad and Dad's side on Simon. I suspected that Ben was losing at both supper tables, but I never asked him.

I also never entered the fray. Instead, I listened from the edges, mostly agreeing with Ben. Dad's ideas were noble but unrealistic for our modern world. Besides, what good were those ideas if they were only for countries an ocean or two away?

Bifocals. That's what the world really needed. You should always start with the wolf in your own backyard.

CHAPTER 15

MILO HARVEST EVENTUALLY ARRIVED AND the Schmidts received another postcard from Dess—this time from Kansas City. Meanwhile, the European sheepherders tossed the Sudetenland lamb to the German wolf. Satiated for the moment, the wolf politely thanked the other countries and promised to behave. So that month, Ben and Dad finally agreed on something.

"He won't be satisfied, that's for sure," Ben said.

"He'll be back for more, that's for sure," Dad responded.

Ben was once again spending the school year living with the Yoders. It annoyed me that, one, he could live there glibly ignoring what I'd confronted him with, and two, that Dad's reaction was pretty much the same. It might have meant a little awkwardness or inconvenience, but if all those Indians died from the British club, shouldn't we have been at least willing to take a stand against the man when he was nominated for church treasurer?

We all have compartments in our minds, though. I guess my Simon compartment at least had doors to every compartment I suspected he touched. Dad's and Ben's, and sometimes even Mama's, tended not to have doors or windows.

The Yoders had finally found someone to keep house again for them. Ethel's niece, Selma Lichti, from Goshen, Indiana, came on temporary loan. There are at least a dozen ways you can spell Lichti. Selma spelled it with a *ch* and two *i*'s, but no *g* or extra *t* or superfluous *e*'s. If you were an astute Mennonite, you knew this meant she was an Indiana Mennonite, not a Nebraska or Iowa Mennonite. To some people this was an important distinction.

Selma was older than I was by a few years, plain but pretty, topped by the dot of a perfect hair bun. I watched her carefully Sunday after Sunday to see when the first crazing in her veneer would appear. Simon had wasted no time dabbling with my innocence. The first kiss had come within the first two weeks, but as I thought about it—which I did as often as the sun came up—I realized he'd started making his moves the first time he called me Kitten.

Unfortunately, Selma flirted aggressively. This annoyed the girls her age at church, so that after the first few Sundays they fairly successfully ignored her. Ben didn't think much of her either.

"She giggles too much" was all he said. It hadn't occurred to me girls could giggle too much for boys, so that fall I practiced not giggling whenever the opportunity came up. Instead, I tried to learn to smile mysteriously, like pictures of Bette Davis I'd sneaked a peek at while walking past the Chief Movie Theater in Sweethome.

Gramma recognized the smile for what it was worth. "You got gas, Kittycat?" she asked me one morning after church. "You didn't look so good standing there talking to the Miller boys this morning. I've got some castor oil in my pocketbook if you want some."

So that afternoon, Suzanne and I rearranged my mysterious smile into more of a Schmidt-girl lazy smile, but I knew how much potential trouble that could get me into, so I figured I'd probably just fall back on mindless giggling.

"Promise you won't tell?" Suzanne asked me as we were staring into her dresser mirror.

"Of course I won't tell. I never tell."

"Inez is going to get a baby."

"You mean she's going to *have* a baby," I said, missing her point entirely. Suzanne's parents were both almost first-generation Americans, their parents having arrived on one of the last boats in the Russian Mennonite immigration tsunami. And although they both spoke English fluently, they also retained that clipped German tongue that added some sharp edges to their words and tone. Suzanne had traces of the clip that surfaced whenever she was really angry about someone or something. She also had an occasional German word or grammatical structure sprinkled in. For instance, she referred to "hair" in the plural, as in "my hairs just won't braid today." I tried to get her to understand she had hair, not hairs, unless she was looking up her nose, which we do talk about in the plural in English. But she just scoffed at me like I was trying to trick her. "You only have one hair? I have many hairs."

Did I warn you that sometimes I digress?

"No. She's going to *get* a baby. Anna Joy came down from Wichita"—she never mentioned Anna Joy without mentioning Wichita, in case I might think she'd up and married a pig farmer from Buhler without my knowing it—"for Mama's birthday and told us about a family she knows whose daughter is in a family way and shouldn't be." Her story took on added drama because she told me all of this with her face reversed in the mirror. I'd never

221

noticed that her face wasn't quite symmetrical. Right now, her nose was pointing ever so slightly towards Oklahoma.

"You mean she's not married?" How horrible it would be for the poor girl, whose life would be ruined in every direction.

"Exactly. Inez and Tim felt so bad for the girl they said they'd be happy to adopt the baby." I would have crossed into that well-defined no-man's land of mind-my-own-business topics to ask why Inez and Tim didn't already have two or three children of their own. So I didn't.

"So you're going to be an aunt!"

"I'm already an aunt to Betsy's children," Suzanne reminded me. "Now I'll be an aunt to Inez's child."

"That's wonderful! When will they get the baby?"

"Soon. October."

Every day as we rode our horses to and from school, Suzanne and Emily would chatter excitedly about the new addition to the family.

"Anna Joy says the girl is very pretty but the mother is so heartbroken she won't even speak to the daughter."

"Mama is so upset with the girl's mama. She wants to just sit her down on a chair and say, 'Just be glad you know where your daughter is! Forgive her!' And then she starts crying all over again."

"If the baby is a girl, Dad wants Inez to name her Dessie, but Mama says no because that would be like plunging a knife into her heart every time she said the baby's name."

"Mama hopes the baby isn't one of those part-Negro babies you hear about. Inez says she'll love that baby even if it's all Negro." This wasn't altogether surprising to me since Inez herself had married a brown-skinned man.

"But what would the people in Sweethome think?" Since there were no boys around, the three of us could giggle about this picture. Even though we truly meant it when we sang, "Red, brown, yellow, black, and white, they are precious in God's sight" on missionary Sunday, we preferred to imagine an ocean —even if it was just an ocean of wheat—between us and most of those colors.

"Dad hopes it's a little boy. He says six girls are enough for any man. Now he wants a boy. Tim says he doesn't care as long as it's one or the other."

If we'd had church buses back then, Marie, Henry, various aunts, uncles, cousins, and half the Sweethome Mennonite Church would have gone with Tim and Inez to pick up the baby in Wichita. But since this was decades before churches had buses and even more decades before a Mennonite church had one, the congregation ended up gathering a love offering for Tim and Inez to drive to Wichita and pick up the baby by themselves.

Almost the entire church had been very, very poor all through the Depression, but things were starting to look up and now we were only very poor, so people gave generously. Someone even put in a crisp twenty-dollar bill, which was a man's weekly wage back then. While everyone was thrilled for Tim and Inez that they would finally have a baby, people also secretly felt a little relieved for themselves because it was always a touch awkward to talk about being fruitful and multiplying when people in our midst didn't.

They named him Moses, a grandfather's name, because he was a found baby.

"He's just on loan to us," Inez said through her tears at Moses' dedication. The rest of us nodded through our tears, too. We thought we understood since God only loans any of us out.

Marie needn't have worried about a Negro baby. Moses came with a sweet little cleft chin and looked like every other German descendant baby in the church— bald and blue-eyed and could have been Tim and Inez's own, if their last name had been Unruh or Miller instead of Smallbrook.

For the way the church ladies fussed over Moses, you wouldn't think he was a gift from the bullrushes so much as the lost lamb that was found, the one out of a hundred. They quilted baby blankets and sewed baby clothes enough for an orphanage. They brought in meals for weeks even though Inez felt as spry the day after they picked up Moses as the day before, just a little sleepier.

I liked to watch baby Moses and Tim and Inez in church. For the first few months, Tim usually sat on the women's side with Inez, which was socially acceptable for a new father to do for some reason. Neither of them paid much attention to the services. They stayed more intent on whether Moses had the same number of toes from Sunday to Sunday and where his fingers traveled and how perfectly his little mouth rounded into an *O*. Suzanne and I took to sitting behind them on the very last row, which was two rows further back than tradition put us and, unfortunately, out of sideways-glance range of the boys across the aisle. So we were making a sacrifice of sorts to baby watch.

This spot, though, also gave me a less obvious vantage point from which to stare at Selma. I didn't like to do it, but I was drawn to wondering what it would be like to be a two-day train trip from home, be ignored by everyone my age, and get kissed by an uncle. I didn't think I'd have any trouble spotting the crazing when it started, and I didn't. I watched Simon, too, but I didn't expect to see any changes in him since Simon was Simon.

Familial courtesy being what it was in those days, he left her alone longer than he had me. But by November, the first signs crept into her mannerisms. For the first Sunday since she'd arrived, I didn't see her bat her eyes once in the direction of the men's side. And when Brother Bender ended in his usual flourish, inviting us all to surrender yet again to Jesus, Selma unexpectedly raised her hand.

Over the centuries, we Mennonites have honed our sense of guilt, no doubt because we were German and liked to be the best at everything, and also because we'd long ago given up cards, drinking, dancing, smoking, swearing, picture shows (which was easier than the rest since we'd never gone in the first place), and every other source of fun and so had lost our perspective on what a good time actually was. Ultimately, though, since we wouldn't think of beating up anyone else, we indulged in the joys of beating up ourselves.

Poor Selma. Even I knew now she could get washed in the blood of the lamb a hundred times or even give up giggling for Lent (if Mennonites had observed Lent), and it wouldn't change a thing on the Simon Yoder farm.

"How's Selma doing?" I asked Ben late one Sunday afternoon. He was doing the evening milking before we left for church and so was conveniently trapped.

He shrugged his shoulders. His fingers rhythmically squeezed and squirted.

"Think she's happy?" I asked him.

I think he tensed a little, but it's hard to tell with milking.

"Dunno. She does her work and I do mine. I hardly ever see her except at meal times."

I nodded and waited. I had time. Two more cow's worth.

After a while, I asked, "So when you see her at mealtimes, do you think she's happy?" I wanted to know, but I also wanted to know how many doors I had to open in Ben's mind before he'd be able to see into his Simon compartment.

"I don't know," he said. He sounded annoyed. "I think she's homesick. I sure was the first few weeks I was there."

"Uh huh."

"You were, too, Cat," he said, but he was foolish for saying that.

"I surely was. From the first night. How long has she been at the Yoders?"

"I dunno. Since late August? Early September?"

"Isn't it odd that she didn't get homesick until just now? Wouldn't you think she would have been homesick the first month and that now she'd be getting used to it?"

He shrugged but wouldn't open his mouth. If he pulled the cow's teats any harder the cow was going to kick us. I moved my stool out of hoof range.

Janelle Diller

"Think Simon's kissed her yet?" I just felt a little mean and I didn't know what to do with it.

Ben didn't answer.

"'Course, that's probably okay since he's her uncle and everything. Let's see, if Uncle Emery would kiss me, wouldn't I feel special?" I don't know why I felt so spiteful. It just welled up in me and spilled out faster than I could stop it. It really wasn't the conversation I'd meant to start, but here it was now, all over the floor of the stall.

He wouldn't look at me, but the cow shifted uncomfortably. "I guess it would depend on what you did to provoke him," he finally said.

If he'd swung a fist at me, I couldn't have felt more pain. The smells in the barn—the hay and the cows and the manure—closed in around us. I felt dizzy, claustrophobic.

"Is that what you think?" I finally sputtered. "That I provoked Simon so he kissed me?"

Ben still wouldn't look at me. He couldn't risk looking at me or he'd have to admit the truth. He also wouldn't answer me. He just kept on milking.

"How did I do this provoking?" I demanded. "I need to know so that I don't stupidly provoke someone else. Who knows? Maybe I'm provoking Brother Bender just

228

by showing up in church on Sundays." I was flying high and loose.

"Stop it," Ben whispered. "You sound like a lunatic."

"There's only one of us who's a lunatic here." I stood up to leave but couldn't. "Do you really think I provoked him?" I asked deliberately, but he still refused to acknowledge the question. "Benjamin Dietrich Peters. Look at me."

He stopped milking and turned his head, locking his eyes on mine.

"You really think I provoked him." I couldn't believe it.

"He said you did," he said. His eyes didn't waiver. "Simon wouldn't lie to me."

"Then you're a fool because that man's life is a lie." I stumbled out of the barn, anger more than tears blinding my steps. Instead of going back to the house, I turned left and headed into the chilly early evening for the pasture. I walked without direction but with a purpose: I never wanted to see Ben again. He had been my brother, but he'd chosen Simon Yoder over me. Even the best mirror distorts, but Ben had chosen the carnival house of mirrors.

The sunset threw colors all over the sky. At some invisible signal, crows rushed out of the hedgerow and swarmed overhead. They gathered themselves into a giant ring and rose and dove as a single body, sweeping low over the grass before soaring up again and disappearing over the hedgerow.

I waited as long as I could to go back to the house to join the rest for a quick supper before we headed off to the evening service. I couldn't wait for Ben to climb into Simon's car after church and disappear down the road because that's where he belonged.

CHAPTER 16

"HOW'S THE JOB GOING, SELMA?"

It was the first time I'd ever talked to her one-on-one. We were standing with all the other young people outside after evening church, so no one took much notice of our conversation. The Miller boys were putting on quite a show with a Sunday bulletin, making it talk in a heavy German accent about how glad they were Velma Mae Amstutz always brought Jell-O to potlucks. It really was funny, but I'm guessing you had to be there to catch the humor. Anyway, it passed for some clever flirting, which gave all the girls something to giggle about, at least those of them who hadn't heard you could overdo it with the giggling. The other boys ignored us, too, since they were concentrating on how to steal the show back from the Miller boys. You'd think it wouldn't be that hard, but they were stumped. Ben was in the midst of the other boys. Just being within ten feet of him made the knot in my stomach swell.

"Oh, good. Good. I really like it. It's going good." Selma giggled, but her eyes looked a little dazed. I'm sure she had no idea how many times she'd said "good." "I miss my family, though. I'm a long way from Goshen!" She giggled some more even though she'd only said something inane and not something funny.

"Have you been here before? To Kansas, I mean."

"Once. One Christmas. It was sunny so I liked it even though it wasn't pretty. You know, like Indiana."

I didn't know because I'd never been to Indiana. But I nodded. Even though I'd only been to Oklahoma, which certainly was not prettier than Kansas, it wouldn't be hard to believe that someplace else could be more beautiful.

"Will you be going home for Christmas?" I asked politely.

"I don't think so. I mean, I don't know. I hope so. It's a long time to be away from my family." She kept winding a knot in her hankie. "Have you ever been away from your family?"

This was my moment.

"Just when I worked for Simon and Ethel last summer."

"You worked for Uncle Simon and Aunt Ethel?" Her eyes widened. They darted nervously over my face. She giggled and tugged her coat a little tighter around her waist. She actually didn't even need her coat since we were having a freakish warm spell that November.

I just nodded.

That was the extent of our first conversation, but that was all it took. Selma sought me out the next Sunday, even though I was a good four or five years younger. Unless you're related, at that age, a year is the same as a decade.

"How long did you say you'd worked for Aunt Ethel and Uncle Simon?" She'd slipped into the pew beside me but didn't whisper anything to me until we started singing "Holy, Holy, Holy." Mennonites are nothing if not creatures of habit.

"A month."

"That was short. Why did you quit?"

Selma had a lot to learn if she thought I could explain anything in four short verses, no matter how slowly Paul Shenk dragged the congregation through the notes.

"My granddad died."

"What?"

"My granddad died. My mom needed help with my gramma."

"Your gramma couldn't take care of herself?"

I shook my head. "She's an onion-and-butter sandwich—without the onions. Or the butter. She's losing the bread, too."

"Huh?"

No one appreciates my humor. I tapped my head. "She's senile. Hardening of the arteries." I shrugged like it was no big thing even though it was and getting bigger.

"Oh." She stopped whispering a moment. I wondered if she was thinking hopefully about people who might conveniently die in Goshen that week. Then she leaned over and asked, "Were you glad to quit?" Not *Were you disappointed?* but *Were you glad?* You can learn a lot just by listening to what people don't say.

The hymn finished and the congregation rustled into their seats.

"Of course. Wouldn't you be?"

I thought Selma was going to burst into tears. She looked so lost, so very lost. "Yes," she whispered and bobbed her head up and down. Then she whispered it again. "Yes." And again, "Yes." She didn't giggle at all, but her head kept bobbing.

On the way home from church, Gramma wanted to know who that girl was that kept following me.

"Selma Lichti."

"Have I seen her before?"

"She's been coming with Simon and Ethel Yoder the last few months."

"Do I know her?"

"No, you probably haven't met her yet, Gramma."

"Who does she belong to?"

So Dad began the begats. "Oh, she's Ethel Yoder's niece, Roy and Anna Lichti's daughter." He traced her lineage back on both sides a couple of branches to the generation before Gramma's in the slender hope she might recognize a name.

"Well, have I seen her before?" Gramma had entered a stage where she'd take us in a circle of a half-dozen questions, never remembering the answer to the last one before asking the next one.

"She's been coming most Sundays and Wednesdays with Simon and Ethel, but she probably sits behind you, Gramma."

"Now why is she living with Simon and Ethel? Don't they have their own children?"

"All of Simon and Ethel's children are grown and gone. Selma is working for them, Mutter. Like Cat did."

"And Dess Schmidt," Gramma said. She sounded so pleased she'd suddenly made a filament of a connection to the conversation.

"Yes, Gramma, that's right."

"Well then. Maybe she'll take me fishing sometime."

That bizarre conclusion seemed to be all she needed on the subject of Selma Lichti.

That night, Selma sat with Ethel instead of with us girls on our pew behind baby Moses. From my angle,

Selma looked jittery. She bobbed her head as she looked up and down the rows in front of her.

Baby Moses continued to dazzle all of us, even Tim and Inez.

"He smiled today," Tim turned around and whispered proudly to Suzanne and me when we sat down. "It wasn't even gas. I think we can get him to do it again."

Throughout the service, Tim and Inez kept their heads bent, all the while making big faces at their son.

Good thing winter was coming on and Tim's fieldwork was done or they were looking to starve.

After church, we all headed down the church steps and to our cars. This Sunday was a true November Sunday, nothing that invited lingering conversations and games of steal-sticks between the old hitching posts.

All of a sudden, I dropped my Bible. Or more accurately, someone poked my Bible out of my hand and sent every bulletin and Sunday school paper inside it flying. Suzanne and I and the Unruh twins scrambled awkwardly after them as they went with the wind.

I know this sounds little, but that poke stayed with me on the ride home. After I helped Mama put Gramma to bed, I sorted through the re-collected papers in my Bible. Most of them were the junk papers that just keep gathering if you don't open your Bible a few times during the week. But one was a folded bulletin from church that morning. When I opened it, I wasn't surprised to see an unfamiliar scrawl.

Uncle Simon wants me to sit with Aunt Ethel and the ladies instead of the teenage girls. Please be my friend.

Yours truly,
Selma Lichti

I turned out the light and crawled under my covers, very sorry that we didn't have indoor plumbing with the knife-sharp wind whistling outside.

I didn't know what it meant to be Selma Lichti's friend.

Thanksgiving folded into Christmas with several family get-togethers and too many gigantic turkey dinners, homemade cookies, and candy that added more inches than joy. Baby Moses now knew how to smile without any rubber faces from Tim or Inez, and he practiced it exuberantly. Henry and Marie received a postcard from Dess, postmarked Knoxville, Kentucky. And Selma Lichti went home to be with Jesus. She just sliced her wrist with her Uncle Simon's straightedge razor one dry and cold Wednesday evening instead of going to prayer meeting where she belonged. With gracious consideration for the next cleaning girl, she sat fully clothed in the empty bathtub and tried to catch the blood on a bath towel. Ben said that even repeated bleach rinses couldn't take care of the stains the blood rivers made. They turned yellow instead of white. Simon had the tub replaced by the weekend.

Ben moved back home for the rest of the week while Simon and Ethel packed up Selma's things and accompanied her body back to the land of Goshen. It wasn't a good arrangement, and we knew it after just those four days together. Ben commuted into Sweethome High School, continuing to keep up the chores at the Yoders' farm and attending basketball practice. It wasn't just that or that he had to sleep on the couch at home or that he and Dad escalated the volume of every discussion, whether it was over the wolf in Europe, wheat prices, or even the weather.

Tell me, how can people argue about the weather? The weather just is.

No, we knew it wasn't good for him to be there because, well, Ben just didn't want to be with us anymore.

Poor Gramma. She was so confused by it all. At Saturday supper, in the midst of a high-pitched and pointless discussion about whether or not Dad should get into hogs, Gramma turned to me. "Agnes wants to know if that man is your husband," she asked me and tilted her head at Ben. If we all hadn't been so crisp around the edges with each other, we might have been able to laugh. But even Mama and I were disgusted with Ben that he'd pick a fight over what color the salt was and mad at Dad that he would jump into any fray so joyfully.

"No," I said.

"Good" was all she said, and she went back to her job of eating.

For a moment, that broke the tension and now we all did laugh, even Ben. A few minutes more, though, and they went back to table-thumping about hogs.

At church the next day, the whole congregation seemed unsettled. None of the religions in my world knew what to do with suicide. Mennonites maybe had more tension about it because on one hand, taking any life—even your own—equaled the worst of the many, many, many sins we could commit. On the other hand, no one wanted to speak ill of the dead, let along judge them, even if we thought they'd just committed the most egregious sin.

You would have thought this to be the perfect opportunity for the congregation to slap its collective forehead and say, *Wait a minute. What in Sam Hill is going on at Simon Yoder's? First Dess Schmidt disappears and now Selma Lichti takes her own life? And weren't*

there some fishy things that happened even before that?
But most people's long-term memories didn't take
them back any further than how the last wheat crop had
done. (Poorly, by the way.)

So even though we had a sermon about judgment
day and the requisite altar call, mostly people just stood
around and whispered about what had happened and
what they thought had happened, and how awful it must
have been for Simon and Ethel. A niece. In their own
house. And all the blood.

Don't get me wrong. The congregation felt plenty
of guilt, too. It was, after all, a delicious opportunity
for it since Selma hadn't left a note that we knew of to
absolve us. Everyone thought about the kind things we
hadn't said to her and the subtle slights poor Selma had
endured. Her suicide might have made us better people in
the end if we'd resolved not to repeat our sins, but
mostly we just tried to justify our mistakes and say we
certainly wouldn't have ever done what we might have
done if we'd only known. It's not the same.

I carried the most guilt of anyone since I really
hadn't been Selma's friend, even after she'd asked me. I
could have been the one person to stand up, shake the
congregation's collective shoulder, and shout: *Can't you
see what's happening? Save her!* But I was only twelve at
the time and wasn't predisposed toward heroics.

Ben moved back to Simon's on Monday, and I was glad because I didn't like him anymore, and his presence was a more prickly reminder of my own failings.

Probably the only thing that saved us as a family that winter was Ben's basketball obsession. Suzanne came to most games, too, as did a growing portion of the church. We all sat together in a frumpy-looking clump, proud that one of our own could be so good.

Ben's compulsive practicing over the months in between seasons knocked us dead. It seemed he couldn't miss. Game after game he walked away with more baskets than anyone on either team, partly because the Sweethome boys wisely fed him the ball. Even the seniors.

The *Sweethome Tribune* called Ben the next Paul Arizin, whoever that was. Even though we didn't have a clue, we bought multiple copies of the paper and cut out every article to send to relatives.

At the games, Dad would puff a little and Mama preened, both quite self-consciously, though, since they weren't used to having something to feel so proud about and it went against their natures to be boastful. Simon puffed a whole lot since he knew who'd blessed Ben with this opportunity. His favorite stories seemed to center on how he and Ben had tricked everyone, including Dad, first with Ben going out for the team and then by getting so good. Selma Lichti never even came up.

For a little time, basketball sutured over our family wounds and we could all have civil conversations. But once the season ended, the stitching came undone, and we went back to who we really were. Ben continued to come home every weekend. I'm not sure why. So where weekends had been the time to look forward to—no school, times with church friends and Sunday company—now they were the times of misery.

I'm sure Hitler never intended it as a byproduct, but his invasion of Czechoslovakia only added to the tension in the Peters household.

"We should declare war on Germany," Ben said. He'd shifted from *Simon says* to good questions to bold, declarative statements. The source remained the same.

"Why?" Dad asked.

"Because they have to be stopped. They think they can just grab any country."

"How would the US declaring war stop them?"

"Sometimes you just have to stand up to a bully."

"By being a bigger bully?"

"If that's what it takes."

"Who do you think is behind Germany's land-grab?"

"Well, Hitler. Of course. And the rest of those Germans."

"You mean like us?"

"You know what I mean. I'm not German. I'm an American! Mennonites haven't lived in Germany for a hundred and fifty years."

"I don't mean Germans like us. I mean people like us, with families and farms and vegetable gardens and soup and bread on the table."

"Sure. Just because you're common folk doesn't mean you can't be greedy about land or blindly patriotic and follow a bad leader."

"I guess I still don't understand what declaring war is going to do."

"Stop Hitler, of course."

"How?"

They sparred, round after round, neither of them edging out in decisive victory. It was to their credit, at least, that they warred with words and never resorted to fists, but some of their words bordered it.

To be fair, in the late '30s, it wasn't just Dad and our handful of Mennonites who thought we should stay out of Europe's fight. There was a grab bag of thoughts on the subject.

Zeke Turple, down at the Standard Oil gas station, had fought in France during the Great War and had no use for the Frenchies, as he called them. "Why should we risk our necks for those snail-eaters? Do ya think for a minute they'd come rushin' to help us out if the tables was flopped? Heck, no. They'd just keep swillin' their wine and smokin' those funny-smelling cigarettes." He said this while puffing on his own potent-smelling cigarette.

"Did Hitler invade France?" I had asked Dad on the way home from that soapbox speech. I didn't know how I'd missed *that* news.

"No. But some people hate in the same way a skunk sprays. When they get scared, they just lift their tails and let go. To him, the French are the same as the Czechs because they're all over there."

Bob Mest at the post office had a different spin. "We got our own problems to take care of here. Think we're out of this Depression yet? Only by a nose hair. We can't afford to get ourselves into a war." Roosevelt, of course, had the exact opposite idea, and since he was president, he eventually got his way over Bob Mest.

But Ben had like-thinkers, too. Mac Halburt, the owner of the *Sweethome Tribune*, occasionally moved his editorial to the front page so he could shout at us without our having to lift a finger. He loved to rage about Hitler's idiocy, eerily predicting the fall of the entire European continent unless the United States of America brought "our broad shoulders into the fray."

But all through the spring and summer of '38 and even well into '39, among the few people who knew

much about the goings on in Europe, more people than
not thought we should mind our own *p*'s and *q*'s and
stay at home. There was probably plenty of ignorance
in that since most people would have had as much
luck throwing a dart, blindfolded, at a world map and
hitting Czechoslovakia as finding it the usual way. So
there certainly was plenty of "who are those folks to us?"
sentiment, although it wasn't meant to be mean.

Hitler's invasion of Poland on September 1, 1939,
changed all that, particularly since Britain and France
declared war on Germany two days later.

"We should declare war, too!" Ben insisted. "Or
Hitler'll run over the rest of Europe in a month. Look at
how fast he beat Poland."

"For goodness sake, Ben, the Poles were on horseback.
I'd surrender, too, if the Germans came rolling down our
lane in a tank and we thought we were going to defend
the farm with Sparky and Little Willy."

"You think the Maginot Line is going to stop
Germany for any longer?" He pronounced it "Ma-ji-no"
like they'd taught him in school instead of "Mag-i-not,"
like Zeke Turple had said, which only made Ben sound
uppity instead of smart. "That's thinking out of the Dark
Ages. How's a two-hundred-mile trench going to stop an
airplane?" He snorted at the stupidity that the rest of us
in the world suffered under.

"Probably not. But I'll ask you again, Ben. Who's going to be killing who? You think Hitler and Chamberlin and Daladier are going to meet at dawn and duel it out with pistols? Boys like you are going to be killing boys like you. Why would you do that?"

"To save my country from Hitler."

"Sometimes it's worse to be saved than be left alone. Would Europe truly have been any worse off with Kaiser Wilhelm? Eight and a half million people died in the Great War to find out."

"I don't know and I don't care. We're here now."

"That's what I'm trying to get across to you though. Nothing happens in a vacuum. How did we get here? Maybe it'll keep us from ending up some place worse. You realize, don't you, that the Great War could have taken a very different path. The US was probably more sympathetic to the Brits because we shared a common language. But there were plenty of folks who sympathized with the Germans. In fact, if the Germans hadn't foolishly sent that telegram to the Mexicans promising them New Mexico, Texas, and Arizona as a reward for joining Germany in the war, we might have stayed neutral or eventually found some reason even to fall in with Germany." For a man who spent most of his days smelling like dirt and manure, he had an amazing grasp of history. Blame it on listening to the radio while he milked.

"And maybe a Hitler would have risen out of the ashes of France or Britain."

"Maybe."

"Maybe, maybe, maybe!" Ben shouted. "Don't you care at all that Germany is like a big wicked machine, grinding its way across Europe? Don't you care about how Hitler is treating the Jews—taking away their right to be citizens, taking away their businesses, not letting them even go to school?"

"Yes, but if I thought war was the solution, then we'd have to declare war on Britain and France and the Dutch. You think what they do in those African countries is any nobler than what Germany is doing to its Jews? Or why didn't we declare war on Japan in '37 when they invaded China? They were savages. For that matter," Dad rambled on, "Russia. Why don't we declare war on them? Those communists." Dad snorted since he was leery of communism even then. That was before any of us realized that a communist wasn't born, he was created. If you bump up against enough poverty and chaos for long enough, you'll make all kinds of choices just to get a little bread on the table. We could have landed there ourselves if we'd had four more years of Herbert Hoover. "Look at the stories coming out of Russia. You think

Stalin's any kind of saint? Why is Hitler worse than any of them?"

"Hitler's taking land. He won't be happy until he controls all of Europe and Africa. If ever there was a just war, this is it."

"A just war," Dad repeated slowly, like maybe there would be such a thing. "Now you explain to me what a just war is."

Ben should have shifted in his seat a bit, but he swaggered on instead. "It's a war where your goal is to reestablish peace."

"A war to make peace." Dad nodded like he understood, but he sighed then and shook his head. "You don't see any contradiction in that?"

"You're twisting things up." Whether Ben realized it or not, he'd made one hand into a fist and was rhythmically hitting the fist into the palm of his other hand. "It's a just war if the peace established after the war is better than the peace you would have had if the war hadn't been fought."

"Isn't that a little tough to decide before you start the war?"

Ben locked his teeth. He took several deep breaths but didn't say anything. I don't know why he always started these arguments. They never made him happy.

"And who's supposed to decide that the peace after a war is better than the peace before a war? The man who sends my son to die? Or the man who sends his own son to die?" Dad tapped the table in front of Ben. "You find that man who sends his *own* son to die in a war first, and I'll show you a man who's finally fighting for principals and not just real estate."

The two of them didn't talk for a minute, but their chests heaved up and down.

"And even then," Dad finally said, his voice barely above a whisper, "I'm not sure in the end we'd call it a just war."

As if Hitler's invasion of Poland wasn't catastrophic enough, that was the weekend Dad chose to tell Ben he would need to quit his job at Simon's and live at home. There were two of us, now, who needed to drive into Sweethome for high school. Besides, I think Dad hoped he could slow some of the Simon poisoning.

Simon, of course, offered to let me stay free of charge with them so Ben and I could commute from their place. Since Selma's death, he and Ethel had only had a series of older women come for the day to clean, cook, and do the laundry.

"Ethel would like to have live-in help if she could," Simon confided to Dad.

"No" was all Dad said, and he walked away. No explanations, no apologies, no accusations. I suppose it was as close to righteous indignation as he could get given the year he was born.

As for Ben, well, to put it simply, he was furious. If the Brits could have bottled him and dropped him, bomblike, on Berlin, World War II, as it came to be known, would never have been.

Dad tried to make it better. He even cemented a patch outside the barn and bought a basketball hoop and ball for Ben to keep practicing. He couldn't afford it, but it was still cheaper than losing a son. Ben didn't even thank him for the sacrifice. Nevertheless, until school started again, he pounded the ball every waking moment when he wasn't helping with the fieldwork or choring.

Unfortunately, for all of us, even the most generous peace offerings can come back to haunt you.

CHAPTER 17

In Europe, the non-war war—or "phony war," as the American press began to call it—dragged on. We'd all expected to see some quick tumbling of countries after Germany's blitzkrieg against Poland, but instead they just sat, letting the real war grow slightly staler with each passing month. Mothers began to relax slightly, and sons grew disappointed since it looked like the fight Europe had been spoiling for would fizzle instead of ignite. Funny, the things that teenage boys can wish for.

At home, school began. Those first few weeks of school would have been much easier for me if Ben and I had been good friends. He knew the system and knew everyone—not just because of basketball, but because he was Ben. I felt shy and lost, even with Suzanne as my shadow. It would have helped if he'd just told us not to worry about our two-room-school education, that we'd be able to hold our own. But we were hardly speaking those days, so he let me stew in my own anxiety. As it is, every fourteen-year old has a barn full of insecurities. Imagine adding to that a lifetime of being poor, plain, and unsophisticated in the ways of anything so simple as walking the streets of a town of a thousand. To top it off, I had being Mennonite to contend with. For this sojourn we may have adopted the local language, but we still thought, talked, worshipped, and married like those Mennonite ancestors on the Russian Steppes. From my uncut braided hair to my dresses made from cotton feedsacks, I was different and I knew it.

Our little country school might—or might not—have actually done a pretty decent job of preparing us in math, English, and social studies, but we were at a distinct disadvantage because we'd missed the navigating-the-halls class all the town kids seemed to have had. Like a river that knew its banks, they flowed from classroom to classroom, upstairs and back down again, so confident in where they were going that they could casually walk *and* talk to each other instead of clutching each other like Suzanne and I did and spooking like jackrabbits at each bell.

In the early weeks, I just wanted to go to the gym, lie down on a bleacher, and not throw up. Our many Friday night basketball games had made me at least feel at home there. Besides, the gym was the only place I was pretty sure I could find without leaving a breadcrumb trail.

Gradually, though, the halls and the faces in them became familiar, so the school year drifted on, almost pleasantly at points. The seasons took their turns, first Thanksgiving, then Christmas. Basketball nipped at their heels and, in some ways, was the best season of all because it lasted so deliciously long.

Dess Schmidt continued to send postcards sporadically from scattered cities that had no pattern. In fact, if I'd stood in front of a US map and thrown darts at it, one by one, I would have had as much of a path. She'd be west, then south, then west again, only to send a card from the east. If she ever landed in one of the Mennonite wombs in Kansas, Iowa, Indiana, Pennsylvania, or Virginia, she didn't reveal it. No one asked the question, but I certainly wondered how she could move from place to place like that unless she hitchhiked or rode the rails like a hobo, which was precisely what made the question too scary to ask.

As a rule of thumb, it's always better not to ask a question in the first place if you're not going to like the answer.

Her postcards all sounded the same:

Dearest Loved Ones,

I'm doing just fine. Please don't worry about me because I'm safe and not in any danger. I hope to see you soon.

Love, Dess

Even though her postcards came from exotic places like Colorado Springs, Colorado, or San Francisco, California, she never once wrote about how the mountains or the ocean looked. You'd think something in her traveling would have struck her fancy enough to mention it, but it didn't.

Marie sank into an indigo funk around the holidays and again in March around Dess's birthday.

"Mama thought for sure she'd come back for her birthday," Suzanne whispered to me one Sunday morning in church. "But Inez told her not to get her hopes up. She doesn't think Dess'll come back until she's old enough to make her own decisions. On Thursday, it will be three whole years to the day that she left. I don't want to even be home this week!" Suzanne just stood there during "Rock of Ages," wrapping her arms tightly around herself and not singing. She studied the top of the pew like she was praying, but her eyes weren't closed. By the third verse, she started whispering again. "Dad and Mama are worse than ever. They're hardly speaking to each other. Mama blames Dad for Dess running away and Dad tells Mama to deal with it. What he means, of course, is 'Deal with it like I do instead of crying and sulking.'" Suzanne gritted her teeth and whispered loudly through the hymn's final words. "But then that would mean two short-tempered tyrants in the barn instead of just one. No, thank you."

Mama must have talked with Marie Schmidt at church, too, because at dinner she said, "Anyone can see how miserable Marie and Henry are. They're just invisible to each other."

Even at my age, I knew that unchecked misery streams flow into raging agony rivers and begin to carve away at their banks. The misery erodes away trees and houses, eventually taking away the dirt walls that contain it. How long would their house stand?

"If it hadn't been for Tim and Inez's little fella, I think Henry would be completely off the deep end. As it is, he's hard to have much of a conversation with anymore," Dad said. "Whatever made Dess run away couldn't have been so awful as to do that to her family."

"She should just go home then," Gramma stated matter-of-factly. "Yessir. Agnes and I are going to tell her to go home the next time we see her."

"That would be good of you, Mutter," Mama said in all sincerity. "I know Marie and Henry would really appreciate that."

The dinner conversation must have trickled into a crevice in Gramma's brain and started fermenting because she stayed agitated all week about Dess Schmidt. By Wednesday evening, Mama looked weary, which she rarely did, even after all her long days with Gramma.

"Mutter's been shadowing me around like a housecat all week. She insists I have to take her fishing. In *this* weather!" It was March, so the wind blew hard and wet. "Ezra, can't you take her? I need a little break." Mama actually sounded exasperated and not just tired.

If Mennonites had had saints, my mother would have been the patron saint for daughters-in-law. She didn't just tolerate Gramma's chaotic behavior, she fussed over her and pampered her more than Gramma's own daughters would ever be capable of, which is why she ended up at our house rather than Aunt Lydia's or Aunt Irene's. Mama always pointed out that it doesn't take much to be nice to someone who's nice to you. Real character comes from being nice to someone who wakes up unhappy every day and is mad at you because of it. I told Mama once that I already had enough character and didn't need anymore. But Mama pointed out that I *was* a character, which is not at all the same as *having* character. "Besides," she told me repeatedly, "Gramma's life started out easy, with wealth and comfort and status on the Russian Steppes, and ended up hard, with tired hands and little in her pocket, which is the hard way to grow old."

"Well maybe we should have Aunt Hulda come over more days to help," Dad suggested. He was standing at the kitchen sink and was watching the rain soften the edges of the world, but mostly, I think he was watching it touch the roots of his young wheat crop a pasture away. It's hard now to describe how powerful an elixir just a little rain on a spring wheat crop could be to lighten our household.

Mama's face and shoulders sagged. "Some days, that's twice rather than half the work. At least Mutter has stayed sweet in her confusion. Aunt Hulda gets so cranky that she complains about which side of the bread the butter's on—and she was the one who buttered it." Mama rubbed her face and then propped her cheeks up with both hands. "Besides, Mutter's not going to give up until she goes fishing. I've been able to talk her out of it the last few months because of the weather, but her teeth have locked onto the idea now and won't let go."

"Let Aunt Hulda drive her out. Then they won't be underfoot for you," Dad said and smiled.

"Ezra!" was all Mama said. It was, after all, a foolish thing to suggest since the last time the two of them went fishing, they ended up a hundred miles away in Great Bend. They would have landed in Nebraska if they hadn't stopped the car to look at a roadkill muskrat. Some kind soul stopped to ask what they were doing and courteously pointed their car in the opposite direction for them.

Dad just kind of laughed sheepishly. "Well, at least you wouldn't have her underfoot for a couple of days, maybe a week if we gave 'em enough gas money."

"Ezra!" Mama said again, but this time she laughed, too.

"Maybe Ben or Cat could take off a day of school and haul her around."

"Can't," Ben said immediately. "I've got a big chemistry test on Friday. Tomorrow is the review day." He never would have done it anyway because this had the indefinable markings of women's work.

"I can," I said and shrugged my shoulders. School and I were getting along well enough these days, but it would never hurt to take a little break from each other.

Thursday ended up being one of those weather days that keep people living in Kansas in spite of the other three hundred fifty-two or fifty-three days. Blue skies stretched from hedgerow to hedgerow without a whisper of white in between. The ever-present wind—if it had been a color—would have been a honey yellow, so kind and fresh it was. Yesterday's rain had draped a gauzy green over the world and left a sweet dirt smell that promised that life could still be good. No doubt even Ben regretted he couldn't skip school to do women's work.

Gramma and Agnes and I packed a picnic basket of butter sandwiches, pickles, canned pears, and little cherry bars that Mama made in celebration of her day alone. I put in my schoolbooks and a novel while Gramma gathered her fishing equipment and campstools and we set off.

I thought we'd go someplace close, but Gramma insisted we drive to Walt Becker's pasture, which lay on the other side of the world, five miles south of Sweethome.

"Maybe we should just fish over at Fred Mosier's place," I suggested to her a couple of times. "I hear one of the Unruh boys caught a two-foot catfish there last fall."

But Gramma was persistent. "Nossir. We're going to fish at the Beckers'."

So I drove and drove, not minding the drive. The spark of yesterday's rain had ignited leaf buds and grass blades, and a gossamer haze of green hung on everything we saw. Less than a mile before Beckers' lane we passed Tim and Inez's farm. The house and barn had simple, tidy lines. Both had been painted in the past year, so it looked like a place where you could live. Inez's forsythia gushed color already. I'd have to remember to tell Mama.

Even though I didn't see anyone, I honked the horn. If they were around, they'd hear it and maybe catch a glimpse of our dust trail. It was the sort of thing you did back then because a honk was almost the same as a stop and visit. It said, *I was here, I thought of you, but—by goodness—I just didn't have time to stop.*

Walt and Middie Becker and their six stair-step unschooled boys had put their farm at the end of the earth, and then built a long, long lane. Nothing lay between them and Oklahoma except coyotes, rattlesnakes, and some graying pastureland. Suzanne had told me that Inez had said Walt was "different." She never explained what was different about him, but a giggle always accompanied the description. The Beckers, of course, could see me coming long before I ever turned in their lane, so by the time we reached the house, Walt was outside waiting for us, thumbs tucked neatly behind his faded but freshly washed overall straps. Middie Becker knew how to cook, she did.

"Morning, Mr. Becker," I said.

"Mornin'." He pushed his hat back a bit and nodded to both Gramma and me.

"Mind if we fish your pond a little?" I asked. It would take an unusually rude person not to ask permission, but it would take an equally rude person to turn us down, so I already knew the answer.

"Surely. Just leave a few for us'ens." He said, making the plural pronoun an art form. He smiled and waved us on to the lane to the pasture. "This time of year the fishin's best on the nor' side over by the knoll with the cottonwoods. Don't worry about veerin' off the road. Nothing to trample out there but thistles. Watch out for the vipers, though."

We followed the dust ruts over a dried-up creek and out onto the dead grass. This early in the spring, the pond didn't smell stagnant yet and even looked greener than brown. I parked the car under a grandfather cottonwood and settled on the pond's bank in the sun. I conjugated Latin verbs and hunted for absolute value inequalities while Gramma fished and snoozed and fished some more. Gramma caught a couple of small ones quickly and then nothing again for several hours, but she didn't seem to mind.

We didn't talk much, but sometime around midmorning she said, "I hope I die when I'm fishing. That way I'll never know when I've passed over to the Promised Land. I'll just be there." I think it was a prayer.

Early noonish, I pulled out our picnic lunch and we nibbled, happy in the sun. I could have been diagramming sentences about then if I'd been in school.

Janelle Diller

I lay back on the blanket to doze then, thinking I could pass over to the land of milk and honey myself and never know. I didn't really dream, so when Gramma started talking again, I only noticed I'd come back from the edge of sleep.

"Well, there's that girly. I knew she'd come."

I opened an eye and it looked like she was waving to a bird by the hedgerow.

The bird, fishing pole in hand, fluttered down the slope to the pond's edge before realizing I wasn't Great-Aunt Hulda napping on the blanket.

"Cat!"

"Dess!" we said simultaneously.

Dess turned to scramble back up the bank but stopped a few steps later, paused, and then dropped her shoulders and trooped back to our blanket. She flopped down and said simply, "Now you know."

But I didn't know. Questions rushed past me at a dizzying speed.

"What are you doing here? I thought you were in—" the last geographic dart forgotten.

"My, no!" Gramma said. "Dessie-girl's been fishing here the whole time. She just lives in that hedgerow and brings me butter sandwiches."

Dess smiled at me, but lightly kissed Gramma on the cheek. "I missed you the last few months."

"Well, girly, they wouldn't let Hulda drive anymore, which was just fine by Agnes and me since she took us to Nebraska instead of Bontragers' that one time."

"So I heard. How's Agnes doing?"

"Oh, she's doing poorly. I don't think she's long for this world. But thank you for asking." Lately Gramma had taken to worrying about Agnes' health.

Dess patted Gramma's arm tenderly and said something polite about hoping she'd be better soon. "So what are you doing here, Cat?" she asked me in a funny reversal.

"Hooky," Gramma said.

I supposed so, even if I had an excuse.

"Mama needed help with Gramma. Gramma insisted she needed to tell you to come home and wouldn't stop pestering Mama about it."

"I did?" Gramma asked, genuinely surprised. She skinnied up her nose. "I thought I'd kept a good secret."

"You did, Gramma. I surely was surprised to see Dess here, wasn't I?" The murkiness was beginning to clear a bit. "You're living with Tim and Inez, aren't you?"

Dess nodded.

"You've never gone anywhere, have you?"

Her eyes darted slightly. "Just to Anna Joy's a couple of times. When the family comes to Inez and Tim's, I go stay with Tim's sister Hannah."

"But the postcards?" I didn't have much imagination for how that sort of thing could happen.

Dess laughed. "That worked, didn't it? Anna Joy knows . . . well, she knows lots of military boys who are stationed in Wichita." She whispered this awful hint of a sin, one more nail in her mother's coffin had she discovered it. "I wrote a bunch of postcards, and Anna Joy's friends take them with them when they get transferred or go on leave." She looked at me so innocently. "I really didn't want Mama to worry." Funny how running away might do that to a family.

"So no one in your family knows you're here?"

"Just Anna Joy. We couldn't tell Betsy because she can't keep even her monthly visits secret after she's had a few." Dess tilted her hand a couple of times and pantomimed drinking from her thumb. Then she looked at me, emotionless. "It's bad enough I've come to this. I certainly wasn't going to end up like that."

"Simon," I said.

"The man with the shiny tooth," Gramma told me. "I see him in church every Sunday and Wednesday prayer meetin'. He always shows me that shiny tooth, but I don't show him mine back."

Dess shook her head. "You can't begin to understand."

"I can. I was there for a month."

"No, you can't," Dess said firmly. Angrily. "A month is nothing. He probably did nothing to you. Maybe kissed you or touched you a few times. Nothing. Nothing!"

Gramma gripped my forearm and looked oh so troubled. "He steals the souls of little girls. And once he has them, he never gives them back!"

"He's more evil than Lucifer himself," Dess spat, "because he pretends to be so holy."

My stomach felt icy, burdened by what I knew to be true. "What are you going to do?"

"What do you mean?" Dess asked. "I've already done it. I left." She began to cry. "I haven't seen Mama in three years. Or Suzanne or Emily." Henry was noticeably absent from the list.

"You can't stay hidden forever."

"I can till it's safe for me."

"Surely you can go home now. They miss you so much. Your parents are heartbroken. They wouldn't make you go back to Yoders."

Dess huffed, furious. "You think? Look at Inez. Look at Betsy and Anna Joy. Why would they believe me when they didn't believe them? I begged not to go back after I ran away the first time. I cried and begged and begged. But Dad wouldn't believe me. He said I was too awful for words that I would say such evil things about a good man like Simon Yoder." She stopped to catch her breath.

"There's really no such thing as truth in the world. People believe what they want to believe, and that becomes the truth."

Gramma wrapped her arm around Dess and tried to comfort her, but she had drifted far beyond what a single frail arm could do.

"Tell me, Cat, who's the worse person? Simon or my dad. The one commits the awful act and the other refuses to do the one thing God put him on earth to do: protect his children."

I shook my head. "Why bother to choose?" They were both evil incarnate, but I wouldn't say that out loud.

"You're right. They can burn in Hell together." She gritted her teeth. "You have to promise on the Bible that you won't tell anyone I'm here. Not even Suzanne. It would be too hard for her to keep a secret like this living at home still."

When I didn't respond immediately, she repeated her demand. "Promise?"

"I promise," I said but felt a little weak since I didn't know how I would ever keep such an oath.

Dess finally put a worm on her hook and tossed her line in the water. She didn't say much for a while, and I tried to imagine what it must be like to go into hiding right in front of everyone you knew.

"It must be nice to at least be around little Moses," I finally said, thinking about all the things she'd missed out on and how lonely she must feel some days.

Dess only nodded and wiped a couple of tears.

"So when do you think you can come out of hiding?"

She shrugged her shoulders. "Maybe a year from now when I'm eighteen. I'll go get a job in Wichita. I just don't want to go away too young and end up like Anna Joy."

I nodded, thinking I understood.

"People misunderstand what's happened to her. They think it's city life that gave her a wrong turn."

We had more silence for a while since that's really the whole point to fishing. I wanted to ask her a bushel of questions, but I worried that the more I knew the harder it would be to stay silent.

Gramma sat upright between us and snoozed softly, her chin drooping just above her drooping bosom.

"Inez is the lucky one," she said, bringing her inner monologue to the surface. "Everyone thought she'd gone bad when she married Tim, but he was the one who saved her." And then her thoughts retreated just below the surface again.

The sun crept across the sky. Gramma woke up and then napped again. Dess and I chatted loosely about people and things Inez hadn't been able to fill her in on because they ran in different circles—Ben's basketball career, who flirted with whom at church, which schoolmates still asked Suzanne about Dess. While she seemed curious, the three years apart had left her detached, and it was hard to get much emotion out of her.

Around three o'clock, she wrapped her line back on the pole and stood up. "Mose is probably up from his nap, so I need to get back and help Inez. Bring your gramma back fishing again. It was nicer than you could possibly know to see you."

She gave me a quick hug and pecked Gramma awake with a quick one on the cheek. "You and Agnes take care now," she said.

Gramma nodded and squeezed Dess's hand.

We packed up our things then and headed for home, too. Middie and a couple of the little boys were out on the porch when we drove out the lane. The boys waved and hopped after the car a ways, but Middie didn't wave. She just watched a small string of her catfish head off for someone else's supper table.

CHAPTER 18

THAT SAME MONTH, THE RUSSIANS finally swallowed Finland whole. In a knee-jerk reaction, Britain mined Norway's waters, nervous that she might trade with Germany. The plan backfired and Hitler used the event to support his claim that the power-hungry Allies hovered on the edge of invading Scandinavia. Germany delivered an ultimatum to Norway and Denmark, demanding they accept the "protection of the Reich." Denmark, that thumb of land on the German hand, acquiesced. The Norwegians didn't.

The protest didn't make much difference since in less than a month, Norway raised a German flag in defeat. From there, the dominoes tumbled. Just over a month later, on May tenth, Germany invaded the Netherlands, Belgium, and Luxembourg—the Low Countries—the very same day that Britain's King George VI said enough is enough. He asked Neville Chamberlain to step down and Winston Churchill to take command.

In spite of Britain's commitment to giving their blood, sweat, and tears, they watched while the Low Countries and then France fell into the German war machine. By June fourteenth, it looked like it was all over but Great Britain for dessert.

And then the Germans started bombing London.

"Surely. *Now* you agree we should declare war on Germany," Ben demanded.

"I'd rather go to my grave than harm a hair on the head of someone who's done me no wrong," Dad responded. He refused to let Ben goad him into a fighting corner. I imagine he thought consistency to be a virtue unto itself, but had that been his parents or children hiding in the subways at night, he might have been willing to waffle a little. After all, maybe what the Germans really needed was a good smack.

"But pacifism will never work now. What's your solution?"

"It's hardly fair to throw up your hands and say, 'See, I told you nonresistance won't work.' If you keep posturing for a fight, you shouldn't be surprised to end up in one. And you definitely shouldn't wonder how you can get out of it without giving someone a bloody nose."

True.

And that was that. Dad finally refused to get drawn onto Ben's turf and fight.

A little over a week later, nearly three hundred forty thousand British troops were almost trapped behind German lines. Britain evacuated the troops from Dunkirk by way of a heroic flotilla of small boats. Little people who had everything to lose—including their lives—decided they had to help those who were trapped and would be certain to lose their lives. Sadly, the Herculean episode didn't matter much to us since that was also the same week the biggest hailstorm of the decade leveled the best local wheat crop in a decade a half-dozen days before harvest began.

Dad sat at the table, his hands holding up his head. "I thought we were out of the woods."

"I'll go back to work for Simon Yoder," Ben said a little too enthusiastically.

"No" was all Dad would say, but he said it so firmly that there was no arguing with him. The irony was that Dad wasn't standing up to the evil Simon Yoder did to little girls as much as preventing more contamination of Ben's mind. But I suppose multiple paths can take you to the right end.

Suzanne wasn't so lucky.

Within hours of the end of the storm, before the last of the hail had even melted, Simon Yoder purred down the Schmidt lane in his shiny and unbattered Oldsmobile Club Coupe to offer unsolicited help to Henry and Marie.

I'd ridden Little Willy over to the Schmidts' farm to see what had been destroyed there. Sometimes the only pleasure you can get out of a disaster like that is seeing how much misery you share with everyone else. We were up in Suzanne and Emily's room when we saw his car crest the last knoll before the Schmidt lane.

"No!" She sounded like someone was strangling her. "No! I can't believe he would come here. After everything that's happened. I won't go. I tell you, I won't go!"

We watched Simon climb out of his car. From this angle, he looked little. One soft white hand sympathetically clasped Henry on the shoulder, the other shook Henry's sun-worn hand. A moment later, Simon unpacked his wallet and pushed some folded money into Henry's hand. Lily-white hand and Kansas-baked hand.

"I've just been sold and bought," Suzanne said. She began to pace. The caged animal inside her readied to slash out. "What do you think I sold for? Two hundred dollars? A hundred? I'm not worth much. Maybe fifty or twenty-five." She sneered softly. "I won't go, though. They can't make me go. I'll kill myself first."

Even though she meant it, she didn't. Instead, the following Sunday night she arrived at church so agitated

I thought she might start pacing the center aisle. To her credit, Marie looked as close to catatonic as one can be and still be walking. Victorious Henry looked grim, too.

We were sitting back on the row of teenage girls since tonight Moses slept in Tim's arms across the aisle. Robert Miller sat in my line of sight just past Moses' head, which was convenient.

"He says I only have to go until school starts," Suzanne softly sneered to me as she slid into the pew during a painfully slow "Are You Washed in the Blood of the Lamb?" Mennonites were such zealots about a cappella four-part harmony. I wished I'd been born colored since those folks knew how to sing, and they weren't afraid of a piano.

"Only." She snorted.

It looked like Henry had set up his own little lend-lease program with Simon before Roosevelt thought to arrange one for Britain. Henry would lend Simon the goods but would look the other way even if they didn't come back in the same condition.

"If he touches me, I'll scratch his eyes out."

Nonresistance is not one of the natural instincts.

Suzanne pumped her funeral fan furiously in front of her face. Her Schmidt trademark curl wisps flew and dropped, flew and dropped.

Blame it on the rescue at Dunkirk, but I just couldn't believe that if the Brits would risk everything to save so many lives that I couldn't risk something to save my best friend. It wouldn't even require a boat on the storm-tossed sea. The Unruh twins sat next to me, and Emily sat on the other side of Suzanne, so I had to be careful.

"You could always run away," I whispered as soundlessly as I could.

"What?" It was a *What? I can't hear you*, not a *What could you possibly mean?* So I whispered it again, paranoid about who sat in front and beside us. We both stopped fanning a moment and tilted our heads in.

"You could always run away."

"What?" She'd heard me this time because I could see the panic in her eyes. She shook her head more vigorously than the fan. "I'm not courageous like Dess."

"Dess might have been smarter than she was courageous," I said, sounding smarter and more courageous than I'd be in a century. Then I dropped a rock into my own stomach. "I'll help you."

Suzanne looked at me, her fan frozen so that the twelve disciples and Jesus ate the last supper while tilted. She didn't say anything, but the fan swept into action again.

The second hymn finished and the pews creaked under the weight of too many desserts. Brother Bender launched into a prayer in which I think he named every

274

family in the congregation. I worried he might try to name everyone in the world. Someone in the amen corner, probably Earl Diener, rhythmically rattled his own list of prayer requests, but they sounded suspiciously like snores.

Church ended a decade later and we slipped outside where a breeze brought in some heat from Oklahoma and carried a tiny bit of it away from us toward Nebraska. The cicadas sang and sang their sunset hymns to us while the circle of teenage boys and the circle of teenage girls milled slightly, shuffling closer and closer to each other like two giant magnets.

"I have to use the privy," Suzanne whispered loudly enough so a couple of girls heard her but not so loud that the circle of boys would hear her. No one admitted to bodily functions back then.

"I'll go with you," I immediately jumped in. We turned and strolled off before the power of suggestion could trigger another girl to join us.

"Don't step on any rattlers," one of the boys called out.

"Don't sit on any black widders," another teased loudly.

The others laughed at the old jokes, mostly because people tend to laugh at what they have a tiny fear of.

"How could I possibly run away? I don't have any money. I couldn't even get bus fare together and where would I go? And how would I live?" She rattled off her questions while tears flooded her voice.

"Maybe you won't need bus fare." I kept glancing around to see who might be near enough to hear.

"What do you mean?" Instead of going to the privy, we crossed into the shadow of the church. Instinctively, people never stand in the dark when they can stand in the lamplight, so we had lots of space and a little privacy. Just to make sure, we strolled in the direction of the cemetery. Ahead of us, oval-topped moon shadows lined up like soldiers.

"I mean, maybe you could run away to my house. You could live with me."

"That's ludicrous," she scoffed too loudly.

"Shhhh!" I hushed her. "It's not ludicrous. If not with me, then I'll help you find a place." I truly didn't know if my parents would ever stand for the thought, but I knew in my heart someone would. We shrank further into the shadows.

"Simon goes up to Dodge City to the stockyards almost every week. On one of those days, you could call me. I could take Gramma fishing and head over in that direction, maybe Alvin Bontrager's pasture. You could walk that far from the Yoders."

"Edith would hear me ring you. She'd connect everything to you."

"Then we figure out a code. Maybe you call home and ask your Mama for her sponge cake recipe or something. I'll pick up the phone whenever I hear your ring."

The pieces shuffled into place, but not fast enough. The clusters of people in the churchyard were thinning. If anyone came looking for us, they'd be suspicious, standing in the dark like we were.

"This week you think about how to make it work. I will, too. I'll find a place for you. Next Saturday, we'll plan out the details." I squeezed her hand. "Don't give up hope yet."

"But what will happen this week?" she asked weakly.

"Nothing. It's the first week. You told me that a long time ago yourself."

She shook her head. "I don't know, Cat. He's been without a girl there for too long. I have a bad feeling about this."

I did too, but we didn't have much choice.

"Cat?" Ben's voice called out of the light and into the shadow. "Cat? We're waiting for you."

Suzanne looked at me, worried. I shook my head. He couldn't possibly have heard us," I whispered.

We separated ways in the lamplight, me to our car and Suzanne to Simon Yoder's. Simon and Ethel were just sitting in the car, like two ravens on a telephone wire, waiting. I looked him in the eye as we passed, the exact opposite of what he expected. He looked back at me, which I didn't expect either.

On the way home, I was sure Ben hadn't heard Suzanne and me. He was spilling over with a conversation he'd had with Ed Jantz. "Ed thinks he can get me a job down at the mill. Wiggy Dunder quit last week to go join up the army." None of us had the syntax quite right yet since not too many folks had joined up yet. We'd figure it out all too soon, though. "Ed says Hank Burnum said to ask around at church to see if anyone wants the job. Says he likes the way Mennonite boys work." He slapped the car seat in excitement. "Says they pay twenty-five cents an hour! Can you imagine?"

Dad let go a nervous laugh in relief. "That'd surely help out."

"So it's okay if I go down and apply tomorrow?"

"If Mama can find some clean overalls for you. Wouldn't want you showing up looking shabby."

The next morning, Ben was off in the pickup at six thirty. Since the mill opened at seven, he thought he'd make a better impression if he were waiting by the door when Hank Burnum arrived. It was a smart move on his part since he already had the job in his pocket by seven fifteen when one of the Unruh boys showed up. He called Mama to tell her he wouldn't be home until suppertime.

While I would have been foolish not to be happy about Ben's new job, the twist in our daily lives created a dilemma for me. There was no guarantee I'd have a car to go pick Suzanne up unless I took Ben in to work every day, which I knew Dad wouldn't let me do since it would be such a wasteful—and pointless—extravagance in both time and gas money.

Even though I thought I'd figured out a feasible way to get Suzanne away from Yoders, the more I stood in front of the reality, the more dismal it looked. I didn't know how I was going to approach Dad and Mama or what Ben might do when Suzanne showed up. To whom would he be loyal? I didn't know how Suzanne and I could communicate clearly enough. We wouldn't have two chances at this like Dess did. I didn't even know if I could count on Gramma to be lucid enough to go fishing. The loose ends in her brain seemed to be fraying faster. Agnes disappeared for days at a time, leaving Gramma to asking for her and Granddad. She often woke up so confused that she'd taken to calling Mama Mrs. Roosevelt. Having a car to get me to the other side of Sweethome looked like the easiest part.

That night, though, as Ben relayed in the finest detail every moment of his new job, Gramma interrupted. "Take us fishing tomorrow, Lydia," she said to me, taking us both back thirty-five years. "There just might be a big catfish in it for you." She nodded and smacked her lips.

"Why, that's a fine idea, Mutter," Mama said. "We can spare Cat tomorrow, can't we, Ezra." She didn't say it like a question. "Maybe you can take Ben to work in the morning and pick him up at the end of the day if Dad needs a vehicle."

I know Mama was as worried as I that Gramma would forget about the fishing, but she'd hooked her elbow around that idea and the next morning was still insisting we go.

"That Mrs. Roosevelt surely is a nice helper," Gramma said as we pulled out onto the country road. "Agnes even likes her, and Agnes don't like many people any more. Says they make her itch."

We were going to have a good time that day, just Gramma and me. And Agnes, of course.

"I like your idea of fishing at Becker's, Gramma," I said, hoping to plant the notion.

"Yessir," she said, "We'll have ourselves some worm sandwiches." She had fishing on her mind.

Gramma was catnapping when we pulled into Tim and Inez's. I parked under the cottonwoods and rolled down the windows. Cars were like farmhouses back then and didn't have locks, but I didn't think Gramma would be able to figure out how to get the door open if she woke up. Just in case, Inez and Dess and I stayed in the warm shadows of the back porch. Little Moses busied himself on the steps with a couple of small, simply carved wooden trucks. His curl wisps ringed his face in a sweaty halo. Fine strings of drool drizzled down the cleft in his chin and left teeny mud splotches on the dusty porch.

"Do you know how she's doing?" I asked them.

"Tim stopped by their place early this morning. He seemed real agitated but said Suzanne said she was okay, just homesick. He said Ethel stayed in the kitchen the whole time they talked so he had to read between the lines." Inez laughed nervously. "He's a Kiowa, so he's still none too good about reading between the lines with us German girls."

"It's just the first week," I said.

"It's just the first week," Inez repeated.

Dess didn't say anything. We'd already said the most hopeful thing we could think of. Moses dropped down to the dirt patch in front of the steps. He tried to blow truck noises with his lips and make dust clouds puff behind his trucks. At his age he wouldn't have seen many moving trucks without a dust trail billowing behind them.

"It'll be simple," Inez said. "If you can pick her up the day she calls, do it. If you don't have a way over here, call me and tell me that your mama says she's got extra green beans to pick. We'll know to go fishing at Alvin

Bontrager's pasture and look for her. The Wenger sisters won't suspect a thing."

"I'm worried Bontragers will make the connection that you go fishing the day Suzanne disappears," I said. None of us wanted to get Suzanne back only to lose Dess and Suzanne both. "They'd be less likely to think of me, but it'd be possible."

"Is there a big enough hedgerow on the road over there that she can hide in till a certain time?" Dess asked.

"Tim will check it out this week. We'll figure out how to save her."

"Lord willing and the creek don't rise."

Moses crawled up the steps and puckered his truck-weary lips up to Dess. "Mama," he said and she kissed him. He toddled over to Inez. "Baba," he said and puckered again. Inez kissed him. He came to me and puckered a third time. I gladly kissed him, gooey residue and all.

"Time for a diaper change for you, Moses boy," Dess said and scooped him up. She blew a raspberry on his tummy and made him giggle.

"One more thing," I said. "If I have to, can I tell my parents about you, Dess?"

The two sisters exchanged looks, but Inez wouldn't tell Dess what to do. Finally, she nodded. "Yes." She stood a moment, unconsciously rocking like mothers do to soothe their children and themselves. Her silence seemed longer in the heat, but she finally added, "And if you need to, you can tell them about Moses, too."

Gramma and I drove over to Beckers' pond and fished for a while. Gramma mostly slept, but she had a smile on her face, so I think she knew she was in her own Beulah land. I landed a beauty of a catfish, big enough to make me think I could learn to like it so I'd have an excuse to catch some more. We drove home by way of Bontragers' farm even though it was way out of the path home. It had been a few years since I'd been in their pasture. I wanted to help Tim scout out some hiding places.

By the time I rolled to a stop, Hester Bontrager couldn't wait till we came to the door to say hello but had stepped out onto her back porch to see who her visitor was.

"Land sakes, girl, what are you doing all the way over here?" She came down off her porch and out to the car, wiping her hands on her apron and giving a teeth-filled Miller smile as she came. She was from the Fred Miller bunch, and they all had toothy smiles. Even if you hadn't known who they were, you could pick out every one of Fred Miller's grandchildren and great-grandchildren in the Christmas program. "And you've got your gramma along, too." She waved at Gramma and hollered into the car. "Clara, how're you doing? I haven't seen you out fishing this way for a while."

"I ain't deaf. I'm senile," was all Gramma would say. She huffed and tucked her arms around herself and stared straight ahead.

"Guess she's not feeling sociable at the moment," Hester said and smiled to let me know she didn't take it personally, and she rattled on. She had trapped visitors and she intended to chew some fat. "Girl, why don't you get out of the heat? I'll make some mint tea, and we'll sit out under the shade where we can catch a little air." She fanned herself with her apron as she talked. Her lips moved as fast as her apron skirt. Hester Bontrager was a woman with powerful lungs and so could talk circles around any audience without pausing for air. When she finally had to fill her lungs again, she took deep, noisy breaths to let me know it wasn't my turn to talk yet. She raced on about the heat, the hail storm, the Germans, German chocolate cake, her fat granddaughters who lived over in Coldwater, the south forty, the grasshoppers, and the heat again. "Are you sure you don't want some of that mint tea?" She drew in a breath as loud as a question, and I thought I'd wilt if I had to travel her conversation circle again.

Fortunately, Gramma had lost the ability to detect this conversational signal and finally interrupted Hester. "Nossir. We just want to go fishing."

Hester laughed her big teeth laugh and said oh of course, of course, we could visit lots more when we were done fishing, which I could have told her at that moment wouldn't happen either. She continued to talk and wave to us long after we could possibly hear her.

What the solitude of farm life does to a body.

Gramma and I drove on out to the pasture and around the edges of it to get a feel for where Suzanne could hide if she needed to. As we drove, I waffled between thinking the Bontrager farm was the perfect place to run to or the worst. From the south side of the pasture I could see the Yoders' grove of trees around their farmyard and the roof of their house—all of it too close if we missed connections, but a perfect distance to disappear fast if we didn't. And then there was conversationally starved Hester.

None of it could be helped. I guess this is where faith comes in.

Gramma and I stopped and fished for a short bit, but it was late enough in the afternoon that the thunderheads had begun building. So after about a half hour, we had to dash for the car. Gramma wasn't much of a dasher, though, so we both got a little wet, which made us comfortably cool for the ride home.

"I surely do like the rain," Gramma said.

"I do, too, Gramma."

"That is rain, isn't it?"

"That's rain, Gramma."

I just honked and waved as we rolled back past the Bontrager house. Hester stepped out onto the back steps and called something to us, probably on the order of *Stop and I'll bake us a turkey and we can visit.* But we couldn't hear her for the clatter of drops on our roof.

CHAPTER 19

Suzanne arrived at Wednesday evening prayer meeting with the Yoders. She looked like one of those mornings where the sun rises in a milky haze and doesn't leave any colors. She sat next to me but wouldn't talk until the first hymn.

"He touched me, Cat. All over." Her eyes looked glassy, and when she squeezed my hand, it felt clammy. She breathed in a funny pattern. "All over. Places I didn't know people ever touched." She shook slightly.

"You have to go home with me tonight." Panic slipped around us. We were too late.

Suzanne shook her head and whispered under the music. "He said no one would believe me, but if I told anyone, then he would ask Dad for Emily to come work for him, too."

The room spun slightly, the moment too surreal to comprehend. All around us the congregation just kept on singing verse after verse after verse of "Leaning on the Everlasting Arms" while the funeral fans fluttered in triple time.

"He said he likes it that she's getting such full breasts so young. He says he's been watching her."

"You can't go home with him. You can't! We'll call the sheriff."

"Why would the sheriff believe me if my own dad won't after all these years?" Her trembling wouldn't stop. "Anna Joy says you just have to go inside your head where his fingers—where his—where nothing can touch you. I just have to go there. I just have to find that place."

She wiped her hands on her skirt. "I'm going to be sick. I'm going to go lie down in the car." She looked me dead in the eye. "You can't tell anyone. If you do, Emily will be your fault, too." And she slipped out of the pew before I could stop her.

I couldn't save Emily, too. I didn't know if I could even save Suzanne. So now my knees shook a little and my palms sweated. I wanted to go find a car of my own to lie down in, but I stayed since I didn't think it would help much if we were both sick.

Prayer meeting lingered on forever that night. Usually, Wednesdays were singing and praying time.

Someone would read a little scripture and we'd sing and pray some more. We certainly had enough to pray for, what with all the killing going on in Europe and the miserable harvest. Myself, I was praying fervently for some kind of a miracle for Suzanne. Unfortunately, lacking in creativity like I was back then, I was short of ways for the good Lord to work unless someone died.

You should always be careful what you pray for, though, because you might just get it.

This Wednesday, instead of the usual pattern, the fresh-from-the-African-mission-fields Myron Remple family had the service. Myron and Dorothy Remple stood at the pulpit, he with a Bible-waving arm. She didn't wave her arms. Instead, she tightly hung onto one hand with the other. They seemed to want to get away from each other, though, because they kept twisting and knotting around. I got the impression Myron had survived his purpose out on the mission field better than Dorothy. She didn't smile much. Matter of fact, the whole evening she didn't have much of any kind of expression on her face, which only made all of us in the pews a little anxious. Eventually, Myron's story began to explain why.

While out on the mission field, their youngest daughter had taken quite ill one night, but they had to wait until morning before they could set out through the jungle for the three-day walk to the nearest village with a nurse. They started out the next morning, taking turns carrying their limp child, who had a raging fever. They walked all day under the jungle's fragrance, praying for a miracle, singing their missionary songs, and eventually attracting a small parade of ebony-skinned jungle people who, although they didn't know the love of Jesus, knew the sadness of a sick child, and so they helped carry the ailing little girl. Long about the second day, the child took her last breath and went home to be with Jesus. They stopped where they were and dug a shallow grave with their hands and buried her, lining up a cross of rocks to mark the spot. The folks whose skin was "darker than midnight" helped dig the grave and cried along with them. And then they all walked back to their village, knowing that by nightfall, the lions would have scratched the grave open and had themselves dinner.

But Myron knew that the Lord could work even in the midst of tragedy, and he saved some souls of those very folks who had helped carry their daughter. They in turn saved others, who in turn saved even more. Imagine how the Lord works in the midst of tragedy, he told us.

Imagine.

I'm sure Dorothy was still imagining, too.

I wondered if Dorothy was sorry she'd ever prayed to save souls out on the mission field.

My short list of life vocations dropped by a third that night since I now had no intentions of becoming a missionary. I was down to nursing and teaching.

By the time church ended, it was nearly nine thirty, well past a farmer's bedtime, so the parking lot cleared out quickly. I caught a glimpse of Suzanne's face in the back seat of Simon's car. She still looked very sick. And no miracle had happened.

I still hadn't managed to figure out how to raise the question with Dad and Mama, but with each day, I lost finessing time and gained panic. The closer it got to Saturday, the more I worked myself into a corner. It wouldn't do any good for Suzanne to run if she didn't have a place to hide.

But what would happen to Emily.

We rushed headlong to Saturday noon. By then, my stomach muscles actually physically ached from the tension. I had to believe that if we could help Suzanne, we could find a way to help Emily, too.

Unfortunately, the Germans were still bombing the love of Jesus out of London every night, which kept giving Dad and Ben something old to argue about. To Dad's great disappointment, it turned out that either the Simon talk had been so firmly planted in Ben's head that a year later he couldn't be swayed, or Ben was bent in that direction anyway. Either way, the discussions hadn't changed one iota.

"The Germans are dropping tons of bombs on London every night! Once Britain falls, Hitler will own the continent."

I couldn't help but do the math on that. How many bushels in a ton of wheat? Fifty? A Hundred? Night after night like that, they could have buried the city. No one would have died and no one would have starved. It seemed like a better kind of war to me.

"And I suppose you propose we drop bombs on Berlin to stop Hitler."

"Yes. We should give them a taste of their own medicine."

"Hate's a powerful medicine. Are you sure you want everyone to have a taste of it?"

Ben glared at Dad in their momentary stalemate.

"So." I cleared my throat. I hadn't thrown into these arguments in the past, so they both gave me a wary eye to see where I might land. "So if you could take a stand against violence without using violence, would you?"

It sounded like a trick question and I didn't want it to, even though it was. I'd practiced twenty—no, fifty—different questions in my head all week long. This one had sounded subtler when it was just me and that girl in my mirror doing the talking.

"Yes," Dad finally said hesitantly. This should have been an obvious answer for him, but he was sniffing the air.

"Yes," Ben eventually said, echoing the word and the tone. They were father and son.

"Then," I took a long breath and looked at Mama. Mama, the flamingo, who would surely understand. "Then you'll be willing to help hide Suzanne when she runs away."

No one said a word. No one breathed either. I think the clock stopped ticking, too.

Finally, Ben asked, "What stories has she been filling your head with?"

Since I had the advantage of having practiced this discussion for a week, I was ready for this question in one form or another. "I guess a different version than the ones Simon filled your head with."

"Well then. It's a question of who's more believable."

Wrong comeback, Ben.

"Well, you choose." I let my statement hang for a minute. "You can choose to believe Hitler or the Jews, the Russians or the Finns, the Germans or the Brits. Simon or your sister. Keep in mind which side has the most to lose with the truth. That's where you'll find the biggest lies."

I could hear the air slide through Ben's nose. It had a certain tone to it that didn't leave any doubt about his position on the subject.

Dad swallowed and said, "Cat, I know you're worried about Suzanne, but this is really something between Simon Yoder and Henry and Marie. Henry's a good man and he wouldn't put his daughter in danger. I think you're overreacting a bit."

"Am I?" I looked at Mama, who didn't look down at her plate.

She didn't say anything, but shook her head slightly and silently mouthed, "No."

Dad just stared at her.

The clock started ticking again, louder than it had ever ticked before.

"I think Henry has his hands a little too deep into Simon's pockets. So far in that he can't see out of it and what's happened to his girls," Mama said softly. "Or what happened to Selma Lichti."

"I don't believe you," Ben snapped.

"Why?" Mama asked. "Because someone can only be good or bad, but not both?"

"Simon would never hurt a fly."

"You mean hurt the way you leave a black and blue mark?" I asked.

"I mean hurt." Ben was shouting now. "Prove it. Prove it! If he's done these awful things, prove it!"

"Ben," Mama said quietly; then she seemed to think better and stopped. We all looked at her until she started again. "Ben. Don't you think it's remarkable how much little Moses looks like the Schmidt girls, except, of course, for that cleft in his chin?"

Like Simon's.

You could see the truth spread through Ben's body. He went limp and finally pushed his palms hard against his eyes.

I wanted to be Mama when I grew up.

"If you want to stop Hitler so badly, let's start at the neighboring farm," she said simply.

"You realize," Dad said, "if we follow through with helping Suzanne, it'll cost us the friendship of a lot of folks at church. Doesn't matter if we're right or wrong. People will choose sides." He'd clenched up his jaw, so you could tell what he thought.

"Just as they'd choose up sides if we did nothing when we could have helped," Mama said. "I know which way I'd want to err."

"Rose, this *will* cost us. I just don't want to go into it blindly without thinking about the repercussions." Tiny little twitches crept around his mouth and eyes.

"That's why they call it sacrifice, Ezra. If it were easy, everyone would do the right thing all the time."

"I don't think you understand, Rose," Dad said slightly through his teeth. He clearly didn't want to be having this conversation at this moment. He certainly didn't want to be having it in front of Ben or me. "Simon Yoder has his hand in just about every wallet in town." His mouth twitched a little more, which was his body's way of shouting. "The feed mill included."

Ben jerked slightly but didn't take his hands from his face.

We were teetering once again in the weight of choice.

"That's why he can be such a fox in the hen house," Mama said firmly. "I'd rather live in a ditch than see that man take one more child." She hovered on tears. "What if Marie and Henry were having this discussion about Cat?"

No one said anything at all.

"Tell Suzanne," Mama said and paused. She clearly didn't want to cry in front of us. "Tell Suzanne it would be our privilege to help her." She got up and left the table. For the first time in our lives, I was left to do the dishes by myself without so much as a would-you-please.

Nobody talked to each other. We were strangers. Ben finally left the table, gray and sullen.

In spite of Mama's boldness, it wasn't a good decision. Only Dad, Mama, and I believed it was the right thing to do. Only Mama and I were willing, and only she had the courage. Yet it would take all four of us—five on Gramma's lucid days. It was a mistake. I should have never suggested it. Not only could Ben give away our secret, he could actually sabotage the plan. Worse, it wouldn't take much and he would figure out that Dess stood only a breath away. And then Simon would take Emily, too.

I'd destroyed them—us—all trying to save Suzanne. And I couldn't put the apples back on the tree.

Near tears, I did the dishes and helped Gramma into the rocking chair on the east porch to snooze in the shaded afternoon breeze. Then I saddled Little Willy and cut across the pasture, off to the Schmidts' farm. Ben hadn't reappeared.

I couldn't imagine how the day could get any worse. But then that just shows you what a limited imagination I had.

With the wheat down and broken, the land was dry, lifeless. Crows picked at the downed grain—feathery black dots on yellow—and cawed to each other for more. In the hedgerows at the edge of the field, buzzard shadows watched and waited. What would the rest of the summer bring?

Little Willy kicked up small dust pillows, leaving a smoky trail behind us and coating my mouth and throat in dust. I ached for water, but I wasn't paying much attention to anything but Suzanne and the rock of panic I'd carried with me since Wednesday night.

Sunflowers on shriveled stems waved from the ditches. The land felt as empty as my heart.

I longed for the days when the grass was lush and thick and the wheat as tall as my father's waist. Maybe all of that was only a dream, a fairy tale. But those fairy-tale days were gone in every way.

I crested the last hill to Suz's.

In front of me, the grove of cottonwoods around the Schmidt house poked above the ground. Then the spine of the barn's roof lined the horizon. Gradually, the barn grew larger and the house appeared, dusty white like every other farmhouse in my world. The barn doors gaped open, as well as the haymow doors another five feet above it. The barn looked like a giant with a yawning mouth and a Cyclops eye. Summer colors swirled out of the eye and back in.

Heat waves will do that.

Greens and blues emerged; mirages wavered. The mind plays lots of tricks to get you to think Kansas in July isn't so bad. I might have even been fooled except I heard a shout and the dogs began yapping frantically and then a man's body flew backwards out of the barn's eye and into the thick summer air. It landed with a sickening *oomph*. Small pillows of dust rose and settled around him. Men don't do much that's interesting in Kansas. And they certainly never fly out of barns. I was sorry I hadn't stopped to pick some sunflowers and missed the moment.

Some secrets are just better not known.

CHAPTER 20

LITTLE WILLY AND I WATCHED the changed world from our crow's eye view. The flies found us soon enough, but I hardly noticed. In the small distance ahead, I watched people scurry in and out of the house and barn. They didn't turn to look at me on the horizon, but I wouldn't have cared if they had since you can't give back what you know.

The man continued to lie there. His head and arms and legs seemed to point in odd directions, but they probably didn't. It was more that they didn't move at all that gave him such a scarecrow look. The Schmidts kept bending over the body and fussing with it without changing it. At one point, one of the girls came out of the house with a quilt. But instead of laying it across the body, they held it sun-side of the body to give a little shade. Maybe it was still sweating.

I saw the dust cloud from my dad's truck before I heard the rhythmic *pa-pa-pa* of his engine. He pulled into the Schmidt lane and stopped a few feet from the body. He and Ben got out of the truck and stood with the others over the body. When Dad pushed his hat back, I could see the white of his forehead where his tan line ended.

Ten or fifteen minutes later, a blue sedan floated down the road in front of its own dust cloud. It, too, turned into the Schmidt lane, and the driver and his helper got out. They took some pictures and measured all kinds of distances and body angles. The men disappeared into the barn. Lights flashed in the haymow, and every few minutes a head would poke out and stare at the body on the ground, which lay just beyond the concrete apron to the barn.

Finally, they moved the man's body parts, but all they really did was straighten them before all the men picked up the body and tucked it on the back seat of the sedan. The blue sedan left with the body. Dad and Ben stood a few minutes more and talked with the Schmidts. Then Dad climbed back into the truck and Ben started up Simon's shiny Oldsmobile Club Coupe. They pulled out of the lane but headed towards Sweethome instead of our farm, probably to pick up Brother Bender and take the car back to Ethel. With party lines being what they were, it was hard to imagine she didn't already know she was a widow, but it still only seemed right to tell her in person Simon was dead.

Dad's dust cloud still hung in the air when I got back on Little Willy and rode on down into the farmyard. Suzanne met me at the mulberry tree behind the chicken shed. She didn't say anything but reached her hand and foot up to get up behind me on the horse. We trotted out to the Schmidt pasture not saying a word, but I could feel Suzanne's forehead on my shoulder and the sobs that shuddered through her.

I stopped in the cool of a weeping willow, and we settled ourselves on the edge of the walnut-colored pond. Suzanne sat with her knees scrunched up to her chest and her head and arms resting on her knees. She couldn't stop crying.

"It's over. It's really over," she kept saying. Though it was really just starting.

Little Willy nibbled easily in the dusty emerald grass tufts around the water. Afternoon thunderheads congregated on the horizon, looking for a bold one to lead them across the sky.

Finally, when Suz's sobs slowed, I asked her what happened.

"He brought me home and invited himself for lunch. I think he wanted to know what I would say and do

301

after—after this week. I also think he wanted to prove to me just how untouchable he is. As if I didn't already know." Her voice sounded tinny and small. She had to stop again to let a few more sobs escape. "He winked at me. Can you believe it? He winked at me and told Dad I was such good help, he'd be glad to have both Emily and me next week. And since he knew that might inconvenience Mama, he was willing to up our wages." Suzanne closed her eyes and took in a ragged breath. "Dad just grinned like the fool farmer he is and said he was sure we could work something out."

"Suz—" I began but no logical word would follow.

"I snapped, Cat. I hovered up by the ceiling and watched myself scream at them. I don't even know what I screamed except, 'Never, never, never.' I jumped up and ran outside to the barn. I don't know what I was going to do or what good it would do me to run there, but I did. I climbed up into the haymow to hide up in the rafters. He followed me and he—" She stopped a moment to gather the details to her story. "He stepped wrong and tripped. He fell out of the haymow. He just fell out and broke his neck." She repeated it again and started crying again.

I put my arm around her and held her tight. Outside the willow tree, the sky gave up a few fat drops. Little Willy whinnied softly and plodded closer to the tree.

"At least Dess can come home now," I said.

"But how will she ever find out?"

It wasn't my secret to tell so I didn't say anything. Besides, now Suzanne and I had other secrets we kept from each other.

They waited until Wednesday to bury him. It took that long to find and retrieve the four grown Yoder children, who had scattered like tumbleweeds.

Ben insisted we get to church early enough to sit inside upstairs since Mennonites from six states and half the population from the adjoining counties would show up. Mama needed to get her dozen pies there early, too. So spurred on by pew space and pies, we arrived forty-five minutes early and just barely got our seats.

The Schmidt family, including an unexpected Anna Joy, sat a few rows ahead of us. In some cultures, they could have claimed to be shirttail relatives, what with all the commingling. But since no one was inclined to make that public, they sat on the friends side of the church, although that too required a stretch of definitions. The Schmidts had spread out on two pews in order to save space for Tim and Inez and Moses when they arrived. Betsy and Pete and their three raggy-looking children sat just behind Henry and Marie. The whole family looked like they'd slept in the car.

By the time the Yoder family filed in, people covered every inch of pew and folding chair space in the sanctuary and the anterooms and outside under a makeshift canvas awning. You could tell by all the tieless men and covering-ed women that the crowd consisted mostly of Mennonites. But lots of fancy folks were there, too, even some Presbyterians. Their wives wore gloves and matching hats with veils.

After the family had finally settled into their pews, the pallbearers carried in the casket and centered it under the pulpit so as we all thought our last thoughts about the earthly body of Simon Yoder, we could stare at him and see if he twitched.

Gramma leaned over to me and in her very practiced church whisper asked, "Is that the man with the shiny smile?"

I nodded and she patted my arm. "Good."

The Unruh twins giggled behind us.

Brother Bender began with an invocation and then invited us to sing. The song leader had only known the generous side of Simon, so he had us sing only those bound for gloryland funeral songs. I didn't sing but paged through the hymnbook to find something more appropriate. Apparently, the hymn choosers didn't think to include songs like that because I couldn't find any.

Brother Bender gave a brief sermon from Matthew 25 about the story of the man who leaves his money with his servants for safekeeping. Simon was the servant who had the most, so he got more because he'd made his money grow. Brother Bender should have read all the way to Verse 40: "Whatever ye have done for the least of these my brethren, ye have done it unto me." He might have had a lightning bolt of inspiration. Or even better, he could have preached about that awful story in Genesis where Lot offered his two daughters to the men of Sodom so they wouldn't hurt Lot's two guests.

But I guess that would have been more a sermon at Henry's funeral.

Then the eulogies began, followed by the spontaneous testimonies about Simon's generosity. In respect for the time and heat, no one talked long, but dozens of people got up to share how Simon had started or saved their farm or business and what a pillar he was in the church and community. Tears accompanied many of the stories.

Gramma fidgeted beside me and I fidgeted beside Mama who fidgeted beside Dad who tried not to fidget beside Ben. They both had the good sense not to get up and give tribute to the man, but Henry Schmidt didn't.

Sometimes, there's just no accounting for how foolish humans can be.

Henry stood and began to tell a life of repeated woe and rescue. While he talked, his family rustled uncomfortably around him. He prattled on, not quite realizing his tribute to Simon was really more of an indictment of his own many failings. When he sat down, Inez stood up. But she just stood, too full of emotion to choke out her thoughts. The mourners who could see her waited respectfully while she tucked her feelings back inside with a wilted white hankie. You could hear the people outside shuffling and whispering because they couldn't see why no one was talking. Henry kept throwing father looks at her, trying to get her to sit down, but she wasn't catching any of them. Finally, she just stepped out into the aisle, walked to the front of the church, and stood in front of the casket.

A couple of people cleared their throats. Mennonites are never comfortable drawing attention to themselves. They're even less comfortable watching one of their own do anything out of the ordinary. Uneasiness bubbled through the congregation. Most people clearly wanted her to sit down.

But she didn't. Instead, she stared at the chiseled face and the cleft chin. When she turned back to the congregation, she dabbed at her eyes. You could see her shaking. This wasn't funeral behavior. People weren't supposed to look in the casket until the end when we all paraded past the body to pay our last respects. Finally, in a quivering voice she announced to an entire church full of people who'd stopped breathing, "I hope he burns in Hell." And then she walked out of the church.

The mourners froze, not even knowing what to whisper to each other about. Only Ethel Yoder gasped. Simon's three daughters jerked their heads around and watched Inez leave. I watched them do it and wondered what they were thinking. Harold, the slouching son who had grown into a slouching man, just stared at the picture of Jesus in the Garden of Gethsemane behind the pulpit.

Before anyone could unfreeze, Anna Joy stood up and threaded her way past her family's knees out to the aisle. She, too, walked up and paused in front of the casket. One would have thought someone would have stopped her, but the congregation was still trying to figure out if they'd really heard sweet, gentle Inez Schmidt Smallbrook say what they thought they'd just heard her say. No one's muscles and brains worked together.

That, or they just didn't want to draw attention to themselves.

Anna Joy's generous bosom swelled a bit as she took a deep breath. Then she blessed the moment with a shout: "Hallelujah! He's dead!"

Some doddering man in the amen corner—probably Earl Diener—rolled out his own, "Amen, Sister."

Ethel gasped again. Apparently, she hadn't realized her husband wasn't a saint. The daughters didn't twist around again, but they also didn't dab their eyes.

Other necks twisted around, though, to see if Betsy or Suzanne would be next, but they sat motionless, almost catatonic. Henry's neck and ears provided a show, though. They matched the crimson velvet casket skirt, except that Henry's neck pulsed.

Brother Bender finally woke up his feet. He stumbled to the pulpit, fumbling for something to say, but there'd never been an occasion quite like this, so nothing came to mind—not a hymn or verse or prayer. He almost seemed relieved when one of the Presbyterian women stood up since a Presbyterian would never speak poorly of a dead Mennonite in the dead Mennonite's church. But she surprised everyone. She stepped into the aisle, took off her hat and veil, and shook her ash-colored curls loose. She worked her way forward through the center aisle and stopped at Tim Smallbrook's pew to pick up her son.

"Dessie!" Marie Schmidt blurted, unbelieving, and then Marie began to cry fiercely as she stood to go after her daughter. Henry yanked her back into the pew, unwilling maybe to draw even more attention to the mess his family was making at the funeral of the man who'd saved him so many times. Marie obediently stayed put but continued to wail. Like a song, she cried Dess's name over and over, a descant to the girl's walk up the aisle.

When Dess and Moses reached the casket, Dess lifted Moses up so he could see his father one final time.

She paused only a few seconds. Then she spat into Simon Yoder's face. She kissed her son and carried him down the center aisle as she walked out of the church for the last time. Her eyes shifted to Marie as she passed, but she couldn't stop.

The congregation finally stirred awake, unsure about what to do and frozen by the very cocoon of social propriety that had surrounded and protected Simon Yoder. Brother Bender *finally* cleared his throat and called on Paul Shenk to lead the final hymn. But everyone was confused because it wasn't really time for the final hymn. A quartet was supposed to sing and directions given about going to the graveside and an invitation given to join the family for the funeral luncheon. Then Brother Bender was supposed to pray. And the quartet was supposed to sing one more time while all the mourners filed slowly past the open casket to pay their last respects, although that seemed dangerously provocative at the moment. Still, no one in our denomination knew how to leave a funeral without going past the open casket. So there

Brother Bender was, trying to figure out how to put the thread through the needle's eye again.

Paul Shenk finally stood up, pitch pipe in hand, and asked the congregation to turn to page 127, "For All the Saints." It was a good funeral song, just not this funeral. Heavens to Betsy. What was that man thinking?

People gratefully thumbed through the hymnals and cleared their throats, ready to catch the pitch pipe's lead. Unfortunately, in his befuddlement Brother Shenk made a tiny error. He should have had the congregation stand and truly gained their attention. Instead, we all sat and watched Suzanne unloosen herself and rise. A couple of people glanced her way and reflexively started to stand, as though they'd missed the instruction. Most everyone else, though, realized that Suzanne was one more Schmidt girl, and they weren't done.

The hymn started robustly enough but began to lose voices almost immediately as one singer after another let themselves get distracted about what they now knew would come.

Brother Shenk kept trying to coax the congregation along. The voices outside sang longer. They didn't even help much, though, because they were all craning their necks to see what for the love of Jesus they were missing. Rumors flew faster outside because that's all they had.

By the time Suzanne reached the front of the church, only a few voices carried on, incredibly enough still in four-part harmony. Even those died, though, as Suzanne, in sisterly fashion, paid her respects to the man she'd just spent the last week with. She spat into the casket. Then she turned, collected the rest of her courage and walked back to her pew. She didn't go in, though. Instead, she stopped in front of her father and spat in his face.

And then she left.

For years afterward, people talked about how no one had ever seen anything so violent inside those church walls. But what they didn't understand was that it wasn't violence. It was righteous indignation that finally welled up from the scary and unanswered pits of rage.

With the rage spent, I wish I could tell you we all lived happily after. That's the way it's supposed to work in the books we read, but it's not true. Every seed grows into something. Fair or not, the seeds planted here were never designed to flower and give a sweet fragrance.

But that's another story, for another time.

COMING SOON:

NEVER ENOUGH SISTERS

CHAPTER 1

As much courage as it takes to cross an abyss, it takes even more to return.

This is particularly true when a body is dealing with the likes of a Henry Schmidt. Although Henry wasn't a card-playing man, he had a lot in common with the Queen of Hearts, who practiced half an hour a day believing impossible things. And like the Queen of Hearts, sometimes Henry himself had believed as many as six impossible things before breakfast. Even though every one of his five daughters who'd worked for Simon Yoder had told him the very same thing, he still believed the impossible: that for some unfathomable reason, each of his own daughters was lying to him, and that Simon Yoder could do no such thing. He also believed another impossible thing: that somehow there was no connection between the confused lives his offspring led and anything that had happened in the prior ten years or so.

And then there was Ethel, the poor, suffering widow of the wealthiest man in three counties, who had survived the heartache of horrible funeral behavior and still attended church Sunday morning, Sunday evening, and Wednesday prayer meeting. She'd spent nearly all of her adult life believing wildly impossible things and so was awfully surprised the rest of the congregation wasn't willing to join her in keeping up the pretense that her Simon—as she now began to refer to him—had been a saint.

Our fellow churchgoers were less practiced at believing the impossible, but they also weren't very practiced at knowing what to do when they could no longer believe what they wanted. So it fell to a lot of discussion about what it was they *should* believe. Unfortunately, between Ethel, the last three Schmidts who still attended church, and the dozens of shirttail relatives they all had, the congregation had a hard time knowing whom it was safe to whisper to or about. This didn't necessarily stop anyone from gossiping—the phone-perching Wenger twins especially—but they ran the risk of tromping on some toes. Still, opportunities of this proportion didn't come along very often, so most people thought it to be a tolerable tradeoff. The gossip raced while everyone sorted out what they thought had happened and what they thought it meant. The really industrious ones even offered projections about what might happen next, although they were all completely wrong since the only ones with a bird's eye view on past events certainly weren't going to offer their ideas.

It's still a little amazing to me to think how Henry the Patriarch managed to stifle Marie and Emily into submission. They clearly didn't believe the impossible, but they weren't allowed—I'm pretty sure that's the right word—to talk about what had happened with anyone. Suzanne probably had some responsibility in all of this since maybe if she hadn't committed the final insult against Henry as she left the funeral, he would have been allowed to save the tiniest amount of face and thus wouldn't have had to start believing one more impossible thing: that he didn't have a daughter named Suzanne anymore.

It also says something sad about what we all—that's humans in general, not just Mennonites—believe about forgiveness. It's a redeeming habit in theory. Most of us even highly recommend it, especially when we're standing in personal need of it. But when we're confronted with a first-rate opportunity to actually practice it, it's easier to take a coffee break from our beliefs. We think maybe by the time we're done with the coffee, the opportunity will have passed, and we can pretend that we *meant* to practice what we preach, but we were gone at the moment. Too bad we stayed for the second cup. And the doughnut.

Suzanne, for her part, wasn't in a forgiving mood either, and she certainly had more to forgive than a little humiliation. Walking out of the Sweethome Mennonite Church that cranky July day wasn't something she'd planned on doing ahead of time. It just seemed like the logical conclusion to a miserable culmination of events over which she'd had no control. Her statement had dealt drama, that's for sure, but it didn't bode well for solutions, or even options for that matter.

Initially, Suzanne moved in with Tim and Inez, but Tim already had a houseful to feed, none of whom was handy with a tractor. Although I never heard any of the Schmidts talk about it, Dess probably could have moved back home, now that she no longer had a reason to hide. I can't imagine she would have been willing to, though. Being the older one, she also should have been the one to move out and leave Suzanne in the Smallbrook sanctuary. But no one was clear about where Moses should go. Dess certainly couldn't support Moses and herself, yet she didn't want to leave him with Tim and Inez since that might be a turning point she didn't want. The adoption, after all, had only been a pretense to explain the presence of Baby Moses. And Suzanne, at fifteen, certainly couldn't support herself; she had many years yet during which she would depend on the mercies of others.

So here were the fragments of the Schmidt family. Everyone knew the family was broken and the parts couldn't take care of themselves, let alone fix the brokenness, but to offer help to one remnant was to alienate another. So the first week after the funeral passed with a lot of telephones ringing but no cars driving up a lane to offer a little help. It wasn't even that people were frozen because they didn't expect any of the five older Schmidt girls, even Betsy, to darken the church door again. Under the circumstances, most people wouldn't have held a grudge against them for leaving the church. It was more that the congregation just didn't have much practice with this kind of pain. Even stranger, in the past, it had always been Simon Yoder who was first on the scene to offer cash and some ideas, most of which, in retrospect, were kind and generous ideas. Of course, the few evil proposals he had were cosmically dark. Still, isn't it ironic that the man who'd always played the savior role in the past was at the center of all of the present Schmidt anguish? Only more so now because he was dead.

Finally, though, my mother the flamingo raised her head above the flock of turkeys.

"I think we should have Suzanne come live with us," she said at supper one night.

"Really?" I said hopefully. I'd been a little nervous about praying for a solution like this since my last significant prayer request had been, unfortunately, answered. Too, I didn't quite know what to hope for since I now knew more about Suzanne than what a friend would want to know.

Dad and Ben didn't say anything. They just rearranged the ham gravy, potatoes, and pickled beets on their plates.

"We'll be crowded, but no more crowded than Tim and Inez are."

"Seems like everyone in the family ought to have their own bed before we start bringing more people to live with us," Ben finally said, but he said it a little too firmly. It was going on three years now that Gramma had been sleeping in his bedroom, but this was the first time I'd ever heard him complain.

Mama's voice sounded a little thin, but she said, "Is that how we should make the decision? If someone's sleeping on the couch then we don't have enough extra room in our hearts to take someone in?"

Dad cleared his throat. "Have you talked this over with Marie?"

What he meant was, *What will I say to Henry at church?*

"No. Marie isn't talking to anyone, probably not even Henry. I hardly think she'd be angry with me."

"And if she is?"

"Why should that be the deciding factor?" Mama sounded edgier than I'd ever heard her sound. I wondered if she and Dad had already had some words about this.

"It won't be just Marie. It'll be lots of people." Dad cleared his throat again. It was a nervous sound. He unconsciously rattled his fingers against the tabletop. His ears grew pink. "It would be especially awkward now that the church has asked me to fill out Simon's term as treasurer." It had been a proud day for him when they asked him to help shepherd the Sweethome Mennonite flock, but in this first opportunity it didn't look like he was going to venture very far outside the sheep pen. "I think we'd be better off staying out of this. Suzanne isn't in danger anymore." A surprising nod to what he wouldn't openly admit to only a little over a week before. "There's nothing we can do to help the situation except mind our own business."

Ever the isolationist, even when no guns were involved.

"If you don't have the courage to do this for Suzanne, then we can at least make the sacrifice of helping out Tim and Inez with a little money."

Dad still didn't say anything, but Ben snorted softly. "With what money? The money *I'm* earning at the mill?"

I couldn't believe he'd said that, even though it was painfully true. Dad's body drooped. All of us, even Ben,

319

had truly preferred pretending Dad was the one providing for the family, and now we couldn't anymore. Ben would earn even more in the coming year since he planned to work part time and go to school part time so he could stretch his final semester of classes a whole year and play one last season of basketball.

Mama's breathing moved her shoulders up and down several times before she answered. Her fork shook slightly. "Yes."

Mama's shoulders kept moving. Up and down. Up and down. Her elbows rested on the table, and her hands rubbed her cheeks and forehead and covered her eyes. I couldn't tell if she was crying or not.

The rest of us didn't move except for Gramma, who just kept soundlessly chewing and chewing. She seemed more shrunken than ever beside Dad. A couple of flies buzzed over the apple butter, but no one shooed them away.

Finally Mama whispered through her hands, "I can't believe we've come to this." Then she got up and started cleaning up the kitchen, even though we weren't really done with supper. She kept her back to us while she worked.

"Maybe," Ben began, his voice sounding thick and a little hoarse. He cleared it, taking it almost back to his own voice, and began again. "Maybe then, you can give Tim and Inez whatever you have to give them.

And maybe," his voice thickened again, "maybe I'll take the money I'm earning and find a place in town." He squeaked his chair over the floor and away from the table. Gramma stopped chewing long enough to look at him. He stood, but he looked awkward there, like he didn't have a place to go, which he didn't.

Mama froze in her cleaning up and rubbed her cheeks again. Her shoulders moved up and down some more.

Dad didn't say anything.

I put my fingers to the corner of my eyes to hold back the tears.

Gramma looked at the tension in the room and fidgeted with her fork and spoon. "Is Dietrich here? I think I should go find Dietrich. Agnes, it's time we pack up and go find that man. Someone told me he took the train to Chicago last week. It's time to get our tickets punched."

I wrapped my arm around her. "It's okay, Gramma. Granddad will come and get you when it's time." I tried to soothe her, but with the tears in my voice, it wasn't working at all. She kept tapping the fork and spoon together like she was getting everyone's attention. "Where's Dietrich? We have to go to Chicago. We have to go to Chicago." She'd never been to Chicago in her life. I don't know where she got that.

Ben just stood, defiant. Challenging.

"No, Ben," Mama said. She sighed with the weight of an entire decade on her shoulders. "No." She said it again and finally turned around. Her red, wet cheeks said more than her words. "You win, Ben. I won't lose our family to save another family." She slipped into her other world and helped Gramma out of her chair and into the rocker, all the while saying soft things to her.

I knew what Mama meant, but I also knew there wasn't much we could do to save the Schmidt family.

Of course, nobody really won that day. Ben certainly wasn't happier. I don't think he meant to up the ante, but he also didn't like being forced to support—literally—something he didn't agree with. In his heart, he still couldn't believe that generous, brilliant, sophisticated Simon Yoder could have done the things that we all accused him of. I guess he had a little more of the Queen of Hearts in him than any of us wanted to admit. Sadly, the whole conversation cut another of the cords that bound us together as a family. We were becoming hopelessly unraveled in ways that would never mend.

Mama, I think, tucked the whole thing into the folds of her heart. Ben she could understand because he was her son and you forgive your children for not being as wise at seventeen as you are when you're scratching the underside of forty. But I don't think she ever quite forgave Dad for not standing up for Suzanne. I know for me, all his talk about not fighting the Germans took on a whole new tilt. I just knew whatever I ended up believing the world should do, I wanted to be able to live it, not merely say it.

I only wished I'd had another ten years or so to have to bump into that reality. But the mess with Suzanne was here and now. I would have been a fool to think it wouldn't get worse.

BOOK CLUB QUESTIONS

1. The book begins with this statement: *How you get to where you don't know you're going determines where you end up.* How have you gotten to where you are? Given how you've gotten to this point, where will you most likely end up?

2. What is the effect of the author's use of first person narrative? What's the impact on how it engages you as a reader?

3. Secrets are a major theme of the book. Which secrets caused more problems because they were kept? Reflect on your own secrets. Why do you keep them or share them? What's the impact on your life?

4. How does the story parallel events in Europe during the same period in history?

5. The Peterses were poor and the Yoders were wealthy. Both families were raised in the same culture yet had very different values. Is wealth a catalyst for changing values and beliefs?

6. Several times throughout the book, characters question what the truth is:

   Chapter 5: Life was simpler in those days. If Dad said something, it was the truth, whether it was true or not.

   Chapter 10: Most people really don't want to know the truth if they think it'll change what they want to believe.

   Chapter 17: There's really no such thing as truth in the world. People believe what they want to believe, and that becomes the truth.

   Do you agree or disagree with the statements? Why?

7. At the macro level, countries sacrificed an enormous amount to fight Hitler. Cat gives the example of the rescue at Dunkirk, where a heroic flotilla of small boats crossed the English Channel and saved three hundred forty thousand British troops that were almost trapped behind German lines. What are we called to sacrifice—in war or at

the societal level? What are you willing to sacrifice for your country, your faith, or your loved ones?

8. Suzanne took action because she believed she had no other choices. If we think of morality on a scale of one to ten, with ten being completely right morally and one being completely wrong morally, where is Suzanne on that scale in the final chapters? Why?

9. A familiar idiom in America is that the end justifies the means. Do you agree with this? If it's situational for you, what are the situations where you would agree with this? Where do you disagree? Is this idiom truer for you on a macro (or country) level or micro (or personal) level? Why?

10. How would various characters answer the previous question? Ezra? Ben? Cat? Simon? Suzanne? Henry? Dess? Rose?

11. On a macro (or country) level, many people would say that going to war is morally right even though on a personal level, they would never intentionally hurt someone. Is your value system the same at the macro level as it is at the micro level? If not, where are there differences? Why are there differences?

ACKNOWLEDGMENTS

ANY WORK OF FICTION DEPENDS on so many people and events. *Never enough Flamingos* is absolutely a work of fiction. However, I couldn't have written it without the decades of stories I heard from my grandparents; parents, Milford and Rosie Roupp; and in-laws, Ivan and Doris Diller, about life in Kansas during the Depression and World War II. My mother-in-law, who is the only surviving parent of the four, will recognize details from her life that are woven into the story. Rest assured, though, that while the details are very real, the story of Simon Yoder is entirely fiction.

I especially appreciate the people who read this manuscript in many forms. My flamingo sister Patrice Dunbar and my flamingo friend Lisa Travis have been with me forever on this journey, and I'm incredibly grateful to them both.

A heartfelt thank you goes to Elizabeth Cameron, the editor who made the manuscript sing. I'm also grateful to Susan Bartel, who provided intriguing cover concepts, and Adam Turner, who turned the concept into a captivating cover.

Thanks, also, to John Willems, who deserves special appreciation for all of his real-life feedback on the historical accuracy. Thanks, too, to John Sharp for his insightful historical eye on everything Mennonite. Forgive me for simplifying our very complex history. I take full responsibility for any errors.

In addition, thank you to the following people for their willingness to read, give feedback, and encourage me: Teresa Barnes, Dena Charlton, Sarah Conrad Yoder, Diana De Pry, Marjorie Ehrhardt, Sandy Elvington, Christie Gilbert, Nan Graber, Mardell Hochstetler, Becky Holsinger Rand, Denise Pruett, Ingrid Weisse, Anouk Kooijmans, Kristi Lawrence, Scott Morin, Cameron Smoak, Gary Van Voorst, and Faye Yoder.

And, of course, thank you to my most important critic and supporter, Steve. You're a flamingo of the very best kind.

ABOUT THE AUTHOR

JANELLE DILLER WAS BORN AND raised in Kansas. She'll forever have a soft spot in her heart for golden wheatfields, sunflower-filled ditches, and sunsets that explode colors on the horizon. Her Mennonite linage dates back to when the Anabaptist movement first grew out of the Swiss Reformation in the sixteenth century. Janelle is a true mongrel Mennonite, with Swiss, Dutch, German, and Russian Mennonite roots. She remains a member of the Mennonite church today and will forever love a cappella four-part harmony (with an occasional rousing piano accompaniment) and potlucks.

Currently, she and her husband divide their time between sailing the Mexican coast in the winter and spending summers in Colorado. In addition, she writes political thrillers for conspiracy lovers and early chapter book mysteries for the award winning Pack-n-Go Girls Adventure series. Someone forgot to tell her to stick with a single genre.

Janelle loves to connect with her readers in person when possible and on Skype with book clubs and classrooms. Contact her through her website at www.janellediller.com.